AUTHOR'S NOTE

I grew up in central Tennessee. As a child we frequented the gulf coast of Florida on vacation. This was my introduction to the sea. Later I was shown a larger stretch of sea by the music of a well known troubadour. It sparked my interest and taught me to look beyond my backyard. I first visited Key West on a sailing trip from the middle keys out to the Dry Tortugas. I fell in love with the islands and my next trip to the keys was a search for a place to live and to enroll in college. During my studies I learned about the slow decline of Florida's ecosystem. Much of this is visited in The Lost Republic. Most visitors only get a glimpse what the state has to offer, rarely looking outside their vacation. I hope that my work gives a snapshot of the reality of the southernmost state of the union, the shadows and the light. Enjoy the read and I hope you pick up the next one.

For my family, who I live everyday for.

Nobody knows, from sea to shining sea, why we are having all this trouble with our republic....

-Thomas McGuane

The future lies ahead.

-Unknown

CHAPTER ONE

I pulled up to the County offices and sat there. The Development Review meeting didn't start for another twenty minutes. I scanned my notes and focused on the chief points. Once I had made my statement on record, everything would be ready to leave with the review board.

The sweltering heat was taking hold, but the perspiration on my back had nothing to do with the rising temperature. Out on the main road, cars thundered by as if on a racetrack, heavy bass thumped in the distance, and people pushed shopping carts down the sidewalk. A black SUV with tinted windows pulled up as I exited my truck. Liona, the head developer for the Emerald Oasis Towers project, glared at me from the back seat.

"Hello Mr. Gonzalez," she said with a slight nod.

Inside the car, there were three occupants: Liona's security team. The conditioned air hit me in the face from where I stood.

"What are you doing here?" I clenched the papers in my hand, knuckles burning.

"We're scheduled to address the Development Review Board in a little while. I assume you're here for the same thing?" she asked.

"That's right."

"Mr. Gonzalez, I respect what you are trying to do here, but you have to understand progress is just that. This land is going to be developed one way or another." She lifted a rolled-up set of plans. "Progress is here, now."

I glared back at her and the others, soaking in the cool air. "You know why I'm doing this."

Her lips, resembling inflated earthworms, turned up into a smile. "Yes, you made your stance clear when you crashed my fundraiser last week."

I glared at the men in her car. "Yes, and your hired help here made it clear I wasn't welcome." My hand instinctively rubbed my jaw, still sore from their persuasion tactics a week later. Even now, my cracked ribs kept me from taking a full breath without wincing. I got a smile from the one in the front seat as he put his hand on the door and the other muttered something in Spanish as he reached into his jacket.

This was enough to bring me back to the task at hand. I focused on Liona once more. "I'm not here to talk to you. I have an appointment with the board."

"Mr. Gonzalez, I'm sure you mean well, but I don't think you want to go down this road. I've done some homework on you. I'm familiar with some trouble you got into when you were living in the Keys. Did you ever get that matter resolved with the Monroe County Sheriff's Department? Murder is tough to beat."

I was frozen. My legs felt like they would give out any second, and the humidity had turned into a cold sweat. "That's all over and done with. I've got nothing left to say to you."

"Very well. Until next time," she called out. Both windows rolled up in tandem, the group disappearing behind tinted glass.

Once inside the office building, I took a moment to soak in the AC and calm my nerves.

The secretary at the front desk was a young woman in her twenties. Her name tag read Ashley.

"I'm here for the DRC meeting," I said.

In a deep southern drawl she replied, "Yes, you're Ace, right?"

"Um, yes. But how did you know?"

She responded, "Hey, we all know you around here and what you do. But don't worry, most of us are right there with you. We don't enjoy watching the place we grew up destroyed. We also know you're the best bartender at The Lost Republic."

I laughed. "So it all comes out. Well, next time you come by, be sure to say hello."

She bit her pen. "I sure will. They're meeting at the end of this hallway, the last room on the left. The door should be open."

Still trying to shake off the confrontation with Liona and her goons, I took the path Ashley had indicated. Approaching, I caught snippets of conversation in the room, and then Marc, the Environmental Staff Scientist for the County, met me at the door.

The Planning and Zoning director led the discussion, and I had a few minutes to speak. I focused on the environmental resources, local traffic, height of the proposed towers, and how close they are to the flight path of the Navy base. I ran through what I had put together in a few minutes, and then it was over. They didn't ask questions, only thanked me for coming in. It was apparent this was strictly an exercise to show they had formally "heard" the public, and the concerns on the record for the meeting.

Marc stood and motioned to the door. He shut the door behind him as we walked out.

"Ace, thanks for coming. I want you to know I'm doing what I can, but from where I sit, it's a done deal. They hired Hurst and Associates to handle all their permitting. You know their background, half of their staff are attorneys in environmental law." He paused until we reached the end of the hallway. "I can't speak for the rest of the board, but the decision will be in the meeting minutes. They should be posted on the website later this week. Of course, then it goes to the County Commission for approval."

"Ok, thanks man," I replied. We shook hands and I waved to Ashley on the way out.

As I neared my truck, two men closed in on either side of me. Liona's minions.

They had shed their jackets and wore dress slacks with flat colored purple and maroon button-down shirts. They had their sleeves rolled up, with blue tattoos reaching out on their arms. As I opened the door, one turned and lifted his shirt to show me the pistol he had stuck in the front of his pants.

Behind a thick accent, the larger one said, "Hey, how did your meeting go?" followed by a guttural, high-pitched hyena laugh.

I glanced at him but didn't reply.

"Hey, I'm talking to you. How did that meeting go? Huh?"

"Back off!" was all I could come up with. As convincing as I could be, knowing there was a pistol within his reach and mine was under the seat.

They exchanged looks and laughed. One moved around behind my truck as the smaller one with the gun stepped off the curb toward me. He had one hand on the pistol and the other on the door of my truck.

"What do you want?" I positioned myself so that I could see both of them, my back to the truck with the plan to duck in if I needed to.

The larger one reached into his pocket and pulled some pistachios out. "Take it easy, man." Resting on my truck, he crushed a handful of nuts and let the shells fall to the ground. "That little knock around we gave you the other night was nothing compared to what's coming."

My ribs throbbed. "Look, you bastards, I'm not backing off so you can beat me down right here or whatever you have to do." I faced the one closest to me and yelled louder, "You're dumb enough to try it right here in broad daylight, too."

With impeccable timing, two deputies pulled in a few spots down.

My aggressors took a step back. The smaller one had taken his hand off the pistol and leaned in to hiss, "You know this isn't over, right? We'll see you again soon."

They disappeared between the cars in the parking lot.

I scrambled into my truck and pulled my carry gun, a Glock 43 from underneath the seat, did a press check confirming I had one in the chamber, tucked it on my hip, and finally exhaled, all the while questioning my decision to leave it in the truck. The security at these government buildings is laughable, but I didn't see a reason to take a firearm through the metal detector.

I stopped by my house in East Hill and picked up my dog, Trigger, then headed toward Mile Marker 171 Marina, where I keep my boat. The drive down Old Gulf Beach Highway beneath the live oaks, pines, and jets approaching the landing strip at the Navy base was uneventful. I passed the compound I knew to be Liona's home, on the water. I saw her SUV parked behind the gate, and I counted three guards within view of the road, with her massive yacht tied to the dock on the lagoon beyond.

A short ride later, I was sitting on my aging motor yacht, the Origin, with Trigger at my feet. Clouds obscured the horizon, but the tide was coming in, which meant the bite would be on. I loaded the skiff and cast off, easing through the no-wake zone toward the seashore. Trigger took his perch on the bow while I stayed focused on the bay to the east as the clouds gathered on the western horizon. I killed the motor, trimmed it up, and we drifted across the grass beds. Lazy waves lapped against the boat as I searched for tailing fish on the surface. I spotted movement about twenty yards out. I cast out as a web of lightning scattered across the southern sky, followed by a roll of thunder. The fish hit the first cast in tandem with another clap of thunder. Trigger let out a loud bark as if to say, time to go.

With the quick temperature drop on the lagoon, a curtain of water moved past the bridge in my direction. The wind shifted and mixed with the smell of rain and electricity, a foul smell floated in.

Along the edge of the marsh island, not more than a few yards away, the body of a man was floating face down, the waves pushing him into the needle rush.

CHAPTER TWO

I pushed the skiff up the small strip of beach on the island, donned my foul weather gear, and went to investigate. The wind sliced the rain sideways, lashing my face. I nearly lost my lunch from the smell and switched to mouth breathing.

After calling 911, they asked me to wait at the scene and not touch anything. I hunkered down in the skiff with Trigger under my jacket. Between the pops of lightning, the seashore came into view through the columns of rain. Developers who cared little for sentimentalities had targeted the island, where I had spent much of my childhood. It was a depressing thought; even more depressing that I was the only real opposition to the project. Now, after the fruitless meeting and the confrontation with Liona's thugs, I was sitting here with a corpse.

In the distance, two deputy cruisers came to a stop at the east end of the marina. An hour later, the rumbling of an outboard motor caught my attention. I emerged from my cocoon and gave a wave of my hand. The boat moved nearer and homed in on my position as I motioned to them. By this time, the chop in the bay was significant, and small sprays of water were spinning off the whitecaps as they approached. The operator did his best to beach right where I was standing, off the edge of the marsh.

The county vessel was a large center console sport boat with a T-top, blue lights, and a megaphone on top. There were two officers on board and two young women who had rain jackets on that read "CRIME SCENE."

One officer hopped out and the two crime scene technicians followed. They pushed the boat back out from the shore and the officer who was driving trimmed the motor up and prop dredged some seagrass as he sped off. The remaining officer was in his late twenties and wore a rain jacket zipped to the top with his uniform pants and the requisite modern tactical boots. His bulky physique and the bat belt with body armor added to his intimidation factor, even in the pouring rain.

He scanned the beach and my skiff as the rain slacked off. "Hi, I'm Deputy Mason. Are you Mr. Gonzalez? The person who called this in?"

"Yeah, that's right. I found him while fishing in the area."

"Can you show us where the body is?"

A slight break in the clouds opened and beams of sunlight and a sliver of blue sky shone through. I walked in the floater's direction and ran through the events leading up to the discovery.

The technicians went to work taking photographs while Officer Mason peppered me with questions, all the while scribbling notes.

In the distance, the sheriff's center console idled through the no-wake zone on a return trip to the island. When it arrived, there was another technician along with a larger fella who could have played linebacker for UF twenty years ago. He wore a jacket, rubber gloves, and a mask over his face. The mask covered his chin, exposing his nose, which had two plugs, one for either nostril. As the officer beached the vessel, the female on the boat kicked her legs over the gunwale and jumped, her boots sinking into the wet sand. The weight of the bag she carried adding to the thud as she hit the beach. The linebacker exited the vessel less gracefully, rolling over the edge of the boat with his gear as he sunk into the sand.

The woman who arrived with the linebacker went right to work. She wore a similar uniform to the other technicians; however, her jacket read "MEDICAL EXAMINER" across the back and "INVESTIGATOR" across the front left lapel. A flash of her blue eyes let me know I hadn't gone unnoticed. She took charge of the scene, discussing the situation with the two technicians. The linebacker stood idly by with a large duffel bag.

The day was wearing on me. I was exhausted. I hadn't planned for a dead body to invade my favorite fishing spot. Deputy Mason stepped in between me and the corpse, screeching my thoughts to a halt. "Another deputy will call you back into the station for questioning and an official statement. You can go now," he said, shaking the rain off his jacket.

Trigger emerged from the dry cover I had made for him and took his position at my side on the skiff. As the engine came to life, seabirds scattered. I twisted the tiller and aimed for the marina.

After a choppy and wet ride through the bay, I tied off the skiff to the Origin. The worst of the squall had stayed north of the coast. To the east, the shelf cloud settled in over the barrier islands. My foul weather gear had done little to keep me dry, my hands had gone cold and the aroma of wet dog rose off Trigger.

When I boarded the Origin, the door to the salon was open. Through the window, papers and charts littered the floor. As I stepped in, my feet crunched over a scattering of pistachio shells. Brightly colored flies and tackle strewn about the place, and all the drawers lay dumped on the deck. I ran my hands through my hair and shook my head. It didn't strike me as a robbery or a standard break-in. There wasn't anything missing. My saltwater-resistant marine coat shotgun was still in the locked position above the door and I had nothing else of real value onboard the Origin. I pulled out my phone to call 911, but reconsidered. I had a feeling it was the same two guys I had words with in the parking lot, but lately I had made some new enemies, so it could have been anyone.

After I cleaned up the place and took a quick shower, I queued up some reggae and sat at the chart table. I marked the location of the fish I caught earlier, recorded it in my log, and then also took time to mark the location of the dead man I'd discovered.

I fixed a rum drink and made my way up to the flybridge. To the east the sky was dark and an empty coal barge headed west toward the Origin, flattening the whitecaps on the bay as it pushed through. I kicked my feet up, gave Trigger a pat, and let the events of the day roll off me.

The next afternoon, I was working my usual shift at The Lost Republic Bar and Restaurant across the canal from Mile Marker 171 Marina. Rain had continued intermittently, and it was buffeted by periodic lightning and thunder from a spring storm lingering along the coast. The rain had driven the locals inside the restaurant and a fresh crop of tourists had found their way into the bar to hear the local minstrel, Jerry. A massive live oak tree made up the western wall and cradled the stage where he sat. Somewhere in between the flashes of lightning in the thunderheads to the west and the drinks I was pouring, my long-time friend Everett slipped in and took his regular seat at the bar beside the bartender's well. I cracked a beer and slid it over to him. Everett was a local transport captain and mechanic. Which meant he regularly took jobs that required travel to some coastal town or another to pick up a vessel and pilot it to another coastal town. When he was around, he split his time between my boat and his lady friend's apartment on the Key. The rest of his free time he spent perched at my bar.

The Lost Republic has been in its current location since after the canal was cut. It was part of a larger complex, including a fish market and commercial fishing dock.

In 2004, Hurricane Ivan shut the place down. The owners tried again after years of waiting on insurance. I came in and reworked the bar. As business picked up, it became apparent The Lost Republic had a reputation as an old haunt for fishermen. Also, as one of the last places not corrupted by the tourist machine. The place has been busy ever since.

A man in his early 30s took a seat next to Everett. Britt, the other bartender, grabbed the man a beer, and a few minutes later I stepped back over to talk to Everett.

"Hen, this is Ace." Everett said before pushing his empty toward me.

I reached over the bar to shake his hand. "How you doing?"

"Hey man, good here. I was talking with your buddy here. He says he's known you forever."

That got a laugh from me. "Something like that. You new in town or visiting?"

He took another sip of his beer. "I'm here on business. Just got off the clock and found this place."

"Welcome. There's no better bar, but I'm biased."

"Yeah, random stop, but I like it. I've been working in town for the last couple of weeks."

I raised an eyebrow. "And you found this place? What do you do?"

"Well, I work for the Feds man, mostly paperwork. That kind of thing." He quickly pivoted the discussion away from himself. "Your buddy here says this place has been here forever?"

"Yep, it's got a long history. Mostly local business and kind of a cult following around here. You found the right place to be if you want to settle into local culture."

He surveyed the place and said, "I like it, right on the water. Live music and the scenery isn't bad either." He gave a glance toward Britt.

She smiled; while he had her attention, he said, "Hey, would you grab me another beer and one for him too? I'm going to hit the restroom."

"Sure thing," she replied.

When he left, Everett said, "Cool guy, huh?"

"Only because he bought you a beer."

"Mostly true. But he seems decent." His face turned serious. "Alright, so catch me up. What went down yesterday?"

I poured a couple of beers and caught up the service well, then polished some glasses while I filled Everett in on the day with the two thugs.

Everett nodded for an acknowledgement. "Well, did you kick some ass?" he asked as he drained the neck from his beer.

"No, but they tried again. I saw them before the meeting and then they showed up when I got out. I didn't know they were there until they had me hemmed in. For a minute I thought they were going to lay into me right there in front of the County offices."

Everett took his hat off and scratched his head. "What? Weren't you carrying?"

"I had to leave it in the truck when I went into the building." I shook my head. "Anyway, that would have made things worse. A couple of deputies pulled into the parking lot, so they backed off." I said.

About that time, Hen sat back down at the bar, stopping to take in the rest of the place. Jerry worked the crowd, drawing the people on the dock into the restaurant. Everett took another pull from his beer and said, "Well shit, how did the meeting go?"

"It was more of me talking and the board members listening and that's about it. I didn't get any feedback at all. I'm still waiting for the decision, but I would say it's approved."

Everett continued. "So, I heard something about you and the cops and a dead body. What the hell happened?"

Hen's attention swiveled from Jerry back to us. "What?"

My nose wrinkled like I smelled the dead man again. "I found a body floating while I was out fishing with Trigger. That's all I know." I made a couple of drinks and came back to the conversation.

"Then I get back to the Origin and someone had broken in and trashed everything."

"Son of a bitch!" said Everett as he slapped the bar.

"Hey, do you know anyone that works at the Medical Examiner's office?" I asked.

Everett shook his head. "No, why?"

"No reason," I said, considering I may sound a little crazy mentioning that a woman I didn't know had been on my mind since the moment I laid eyes on her.

Hen said, "This town is more exciting that I thought."

"Not the right kind of excitement." I replied.

Hen and Everett continued their conversation until they wandered out after last call. When the last customer had left, I locked the doors, poured a drink and counted the drawer out.

I couldn't stop thinking about the dead guy. And then someone breaking into my boat? I knew there had to be more to it. I walked the cash drawer back to the office and locked up. From the office, I heard the old rotary phone at the bar ringing. I jogged up front, stretched across the bar and answered, "We're closed and if he isn't home, he isn't here." I chuckled to myself.

There was silence. Then a scratchy voice said, "Back off the towers project. It's bigger than you." Then dial tone, nothing more.

The hair on my neck stood up, and a chill ran down my back. I scanned the place, confident I was alone. There was no sound aside from the hum of another barge on the canal outside. Another threat, this time by an unnamed person, but probably part of the same group of thugs from earlier in the day.

I reached down and tapped the Glock hidden under my shirt, then hit the lights on my way out.

My old truck whined as I climbed the bridge to the Key. A vague outline of the island in the darkness.

As soon as we were back on the Origin,, Trigger plopped down in his usual spot on the floor and I crawled into bed. My clock read 12:47 a.m.

I was underwater. Struggling. I clawed and scratched at the arms around me, but they held me tight. The water was cold and dark. I couldn't see a face. The urge to take a breath was overwhelming. My lungs burned. I struggled for the surface. Murky water blinded me. Again, the arms like a vice closed in around my head and throat. I continued to fight, but everything narrowed.

14

With a gasp, I jolted upright, my heart thumping hard in my chest. Sweat ran down my face, I raked my fingers through my hair, then took a deep breath and pulled myself out of bed. The clock on my nightstand read 5:05 a.m.

I shuffled to the stove, only to realize that my tin of Bustelo was still empty. After pulling on a semi-clean shirt, Trigger and I headed down the dock to the marina store.

"Mornin' Sam," I said to the dockmaster at the counter as Trigger chased off Larry the Pelican out on the dock.

"Mornin' Ace." Sam was reading the paper amid a pile of invoices and brochures for new boats. A brass ship's clock on the wall showed the wrong time.

"Coffee's hot," he said. "You work last night?" His mouth shielded by his oversize western style mustache.

"Yea, it wasn't too late, though."

He gave Trigger a pat on the head while I picked up the newspaper from the counter.

Sam took notice. "Yep, they got your floater in there today. Not much information, though, and they left your name out."

"Well, that's nice." I paid for my coffee and the newspaper. "See ya, Sam."

"See ya, Ace."

Back on the Origin, I was finishing my coffee when I noticed Sam talking with a couple of guys at the end of the dock. I watched him motion toward the Origin and the smaller man tightened his grip, pointing at my boat with a handful of papers as they began heading in my direction. As they stepped out of the shadow of the awning of the restaurant, their badges riding on their belts shone in the sun.

I stepped out onto the stern, and a knot formed in my stomach. The larger of the two started questioning me before he stopped walking.

"Are you Ace Gonzalez?" he asked.

I could feel the sweat on my neck and my palms turned clammy. "That's right. Can I help you?"

The older officer nodded at the other man, and he stepped on board the Origin. As the boat rocked under his weight, Trigger emerged from the door of the salon, barking.

I held up my hand as if to stop the man and said, "Hey, you need to ask permission to board this boat, and any other, for that matter. What do you want?" All the while, Trigger by my side, growling and gnashing his teeth. With another nod from the man on the dock, the man on the boat ignored me and moved to step inside the salon. As he moved for the door, he stomped like he was going to kick Trigger, which warranted a defensive snap from Trigger. I scooped up Trigger and put him on the dock where he assumed the guard position.

I moved to the door and said to the man who had stepped inside, "Get off my boat. I don't remember inviting you and I don't see a warrant!"

The man ignored me and began moving papers on the chart table. I put one hand on the papers and he stopped. His eyes met mine, and he grabbed my wrist, twisting it behind my back and pushing me out the salon door.

"Florida Department of Law Enforcement, sir. You're under arrest for obstructing an investigation. Step up onto the dock."

"What? What kind of shit is that?" I protested.

"You're under arrest."

My knees shook as I stepped onto the dock. The other man slapped the cuffs on me as he began reading me my rights and checking my pockets.

"What? This is crazy. Tell me what's going on!" Neither offered any response. The larger officer had one hand on my shoulder and the other on the cuffs, steering me down the dock and toward the parking lot. Trigger was on my heels as a small crowd gathered.

I turned to Sam and yelled out, "Call Britt and keep an eye on Trigger for me." The officers didn't speak as they loaded me into the unmarked SUV and dropped some papers into the seat beside me. Through the back window, I could see the crowd in the parking lot in a cloud of dust. A crime scene van pulling into the marina as we left.

CHAPTER THREE

An hour later, the smell of cleaning solution and urine burned my nose as I waited in the holding cell. I was alone, separated from the other inmates. My wrists were sore from the cuffs and it seemed the only relief from the pain was rubbing them periodically. Through the wire glass window on the main holding area, there were several other people sitting in rows of metal chairs bolted to the floor. I had a feeling that Liona had extended her reach even further than I had expected, and now she was using law enforcement to get me out of the picture. I paced the room, replaying what happened, searching for anything to make sense. The clank of the door to the cell startled me. The jailer took me down a hallway through a series of security doors to a room with a table, two chairs, and a large mirror window framing out one wall.

The Special Agent who had arrested me came in and sat down.

"How you feeling?"

"Shitty, why am I here?"

"Sorry to keep you waiting, but I needed to give the team time to complete the search warrant on your boat."

I felt my head get hot and my bottom lip tighten. "What search warrant on my boat?"

"Calm down," he said. "We found nothing incriminating. We brought you in because of your involvement in a recent homicide."

"What? The guy I found in Big Lagoon?"

"We need to clear up some details so we can get you out of here. Are you okay answering a few questions?"

"I've got nothing to hide." I leaned back, crossed my arms, and let out a long sigh.

"Alright, can you tell me your whereabouts the day prior to the day you discovered the decedent?"

I searched my memory for a moment. There was some fishing involved and work, but it took me a minute to line everything up. "I got up early and took one of the regular customers fishing. We were out at sunrise and came back before I went to work that afternoon."

"Did you know the decedent before you found him in the lagoon?"

"Given that I only saw the dude floating face down, I can't say. Is it someone local?"

The Agent thumbed through some pictures in a folder, decided on one, and slid it across the table to me. It was a shot of several people in a big room, framed with palm trees and a bar.

Upon closer inspection, I realized the picture was from the night when the two goons beat me up. I was in conversation with Liona. I recognized the setting in the photo, but I did not know who took the picture.

"Ok, why are you showing me this? I was at the meeting. That's no secret."

The detective took his pen and pointed to one man standing behind Liona. "This is the decedent."

I stayed silent, my expression never changing. It was possible I had met the guy in passing. I had one mission that night, and that was to get to Liona and deliver my message.

It turned out she had already known who I was, which had surprised me. I only focused on talking with her. Once I had relayed my message, I was gone.

The Agent continued, "Why were you there?"

Pointing to Liona in the photo, I said, "She's heading up the development team for a project on the Key. I'm the opposition. That was a courtesy visit to meet her and relay some information, that's all. I didn't stop to make small talk with anyone she was with. A couple of them roughed me up later that night. It wasn't a friendly exchange."

He made some notes and was quiet for a moment. "So let me confirm, you never met this man?"

"Again, no." I stalled, more thoughtful, then I slid the picture closer, examining it with a little more detail this time. The group of thugs were closed in tight to Liona, and it was apparent that I was mid-way through the solo I had mentally prepared for that encounter. The most prevalent part of the photo was her smile, sharp and snakelike, that stood out. Everything else seemed blurry and out of focus, like someone rubbed dirt on the lens.

Frustrated and done with questions, I said, "Help me out here. You came to my boat, arrested me in front of my friends, searched my boat on a hunch that I was involved somehow. All this because you found a picture I've never seen?"

He said nothing, then reached back into his folder and extracted a form and began reading it. It was a rundown of my personal information. Once he got past the basic info, he read, "booked for murder in Key West. Tell me about this, Mr. Gonzalez."

I tensed up and then deflated. "You went way back, huh?" I shook my head. "It was nothing. Me and my friend got into a fight with some guy at a bar and then later we found his body." I stopped for a moment, the reality hitting me that the two events were eerily similar. A dead body was the ultimate conclusion in both situations. I could feel his eyes on me, watching as my mind processed the situation. I let out a long breath. "The case was closed, and we were cleared of any charges."

The Agent reviewed the paperwork. "Says here that the case was never closed, but you and your pal, Seamus," he switched back to the form, "were suspects in this case. A man turns up dead that you had an altercation with. You have to admit, sounds pretty familiar, doesn't it?" A smile grew on his face. "Maybe you thought 'Hey, I got away with it once. Why not try again and see what happens?'"

Instantly I felt nauseous, and then a wave of heat came over my body. I shifted in my seat and clenched my fists. My knuckles burning as he leaned back and observed. "But the difference is, I didn't have a confrontation with this," I pointed to the picture, "dude." I took a deep breath. "Now, if you have any more questions, I'll need my attorney."

He gave me the silent stare he had probably practiced so many times before, then closed the folder and left the room.

I sat there, trying to patch everything together. A couple of hours later, Hutch, the Sheriff's deputy who works at Lost, came in. "Hey, you ready to go?" I felt a weight lift as he checked me out and was quiet until we were outside. "Hey man, sorry about that. I didn't know you were here until about an hour ago. I called Britt. She's on the way."

"What the hell was that about?" I asked.

"Good question. FDLE is on the case, and I haven't figured out why yet."

"What did he have?" asked Hutch.

"Some picture that put the dead guy and me together. Then he brought up an old case from the Keys. That's it. I think he wanted my reaction when he showed me what evidence he had. That was about the time I said 'attorney' and he backed off."

The familiar silhouette of my pickup truck pulled into the parking lot, and Britt and Trigger rolled out of the driver's side.

Britt had been a friend and co-worker in Key West. She was a transplant from the east coast. We became pretty close friends working in the same bar. Most nights after work, a drink was necessary, which meant a stop at the Parrot or Willie T's after shutting down. A beach day wasn't uncommon either.

"Hey, you alright?" she asked and slammed the door.

"Yeah, let's get out of here. I need a shower."

She gave me a hug anyway, and Trigger nudged my leg for some acknowledgement. I shook Hutch's hand, thanking him for the help. Then patted Trigger on the head, rapped him on the side and said, "Let's go."

"Alright man, I'll see you at Lost," said Hutch.

On the ride home, Britt was all about details. I ran her through the discussion with the detective and the photo.

"Why would they have that? Was it clear they were taking the picture of you?"

"I don't know. It's hard to say. May have been a random photo taken at the event."

That night I was working my usual shift at Ozone, a pub in my neighborhood. I run double duty part time here and at Lost. This place was another local establishment and couldn't be found without trying. Nestled in the basement of an old hospital building and like Lost, was a local hub for the neighborhood.

As the night crept in, a familiar face settled in at the opposite end of the bar. It was Leah, a bartender at the Wisteria, who lived down the street. She said she was meeting a friend there for drinks and ordered a glass of wine. A few minutes later, an athletic blonde joined her. It was the investigator from the crime scene. I froze momentarily and then finally exhaled and introduced myself while she did the same.

"Can I get you a drink?"

"I'll have the same thing she's having." I let them be, but I sensed a smile when I dropped the wine.

After a few minutes of overthinking how I should approach her, I came back and asked her if she remembered me.

With a smile she said, "I'm Analee. I was wondering if you would remember me."

"Of course, I'm Ace." I said.

"How long have you been doing that? The job, I mean?"

"Oh, for about eight years."

"I bet you have some interesting stories."

"Yes, of course, but I can't talk about them," she said with a wink.

"Ah, that's right. Ok, no further questions. I'll leave you two be. Let me know if you need anything else."

A glass of wine later, they were getting ready to leave.

I had Analee's attention for a moment. "Hey, I'd really like to talk with you more."

Leah stopped me and said, "Well, we are going back to my place to have another glass of wine. You should join us."

I pressed my lips together, contemplating how fast I could get out for the night and if they'd still be at Leah's. "I have to shut down here, so it may be a little while."

"That's fine," said Leah. "I have to get home and relieve the babysitter, but we'll be up for a while."

"I'll see what I can do to leave early. Maybe I'll stop by." I replied.

An hour later, I drove up 12th avenue beneath the canopy of live oaks and turned into Leah's front yard. The house was dark, but there were voices coming from the backyard. I stuck my head around the corner and found them on the patio. The branches of a centurion live oak held strings of clear incandescent lights. They sat at a small table and chairs on the patio beneath the lights. Trigger plopped down on the patio next to us after a nudge and scratch from Leah and Analee, so I took an empty chair. "I have to admit it was a surprise seeing you sit down at my bar tonight. Leah comes by pretty often with the kids, but this is the first time you've sat at my bar."

"I've been in there before, but maybe not when you're working." She smiled.

"Do you live in the neighborhood?" I asked.

"I live on 18th avenue near Bayview."

"Ok, that's not far at all. I'm sure we've crossed paths before and didn't realize it."

"I don't get out much these days, but it's possible," she said.

"How do you two know each other?" I asked.

"We used to work together at the Oar House when we were in college."

"Ok, it's coming together now," I said.

She smiled. "Leah says you've been working at Ozone for a long time now."

"It's been a few years, but only part time now. I also work out at The Lost Republic on the Point. Between the two, I have a full-time job." then I added, "So, tell me about your job. What's it like?"

"A lot like your job. It's never boring, and it's something new every day," she said. "There's more to it than dead people. The investigation is what I love," she said.

"Pretty intense stuff," I replied.

"Yeah, I'm immune to it now. I just focus on the task in front of me."

"How much do you get from a setting like that?"

"You'd be surprised. We record the temperature of the water and the body, the orientation, even types of bugs show certain things. It's a whole rundown of the scene at hand. I rarely go to the death scenes anymore, but I had an investigator out, so I took that one."

"Ok, one more question and then I'm done." I said.

"The big linebacker guy with you the other day. What was he doing there?"

"Oh, you mean Loucious? Ridiculous, huh?"

"Um, yes."

"Ha, he's our removal guy. He hates floaters, says they stink so much worse if they've been in the salt water for a while."

"That's why he had the nose plugs and face mask on, huh?"

"I guess so. He's a big baby with that stuff. That one wasn't bad at all."

"While we're on that topic, any leads on that one? How did he go?"

"Well, the autopsy has been done, but I can't discuss until law enforcement finishes their investigation."

"I had a feeling you might say that. Turns out I may have met the guy a couple of weeks back," I said.

"Whoa, that's a little too weird. Where did you meet him?"

"There was a party for the development company he worked for. I went to hit the development team with questions. This guy was with them. I must have pissed some people off because, after I left, a couple of thugs came after me."

"Ok, so you do that stuff for fun?" she asked.

"Not exactly fun. I'm sort of a freelance crusader for the local environment when there is no one else there to speak for it. Development is eating this place up. Soon we're going to look like south Florida. We need better regulation or at least more local outcry to these Disney World projects."

Leah interjected, "He's the local bartender environmental activist. He's got that reputation now, so be careful because he's got lots of enemies."

"I wouldn't say that. I get along with everyone. Some folks don't like it when I shed light on something that they consider a guaranteed pay day. Most of these developers stand to make several million dollars off each one of these projects. That's probably what she's talking about. When you stand in the way of someone making money, they usually go on the defense."

"I guess so," she said.

After a minute of silence, Leah interjected, "Well y'all, it's been fun, but I've got to get to bed. Camp out back here if you want, but I'm done."

Analee stretched. "I gotta head out too. I have a run in the morning."

"I can take a hint. Come on Trigger, time to leave."

I walked Analee to her car out front. My palms were sweating, and I stopped for a moment after realizing it had been so long since I had asked a woman out.

"Would you like to get together sometime, just the two of us?" I asked, my voice cracking.

"Yeah, maybe," she replied. Her blue eyes returned my stare. I couldn't help but smile, and she did the same.

"Well, can I call you?"

CHAPTER FOUR

After Analee had given me her phone number, I had opted for a short drive to my pool house bungalow. I woke in the morning to a heavy fog outside. I made coffee and opened the French doors to the patio. The cool air floated in and I settled into the Adirondack chair beneath the palm trees surrounding the pool. My mind was on this new woman. It also hung me up on the past. My previous attempts at relationships had ended in shambles. I could never commit, and each time this fear I never overcame served as the wedge between me and the unlucky woman who thought I might be the one.

Trigger made a begging sound and pulled me out of the 1000-yard stare I had fallen into. He rolled onto his back and began kicking his paws into the air, his eyes still closed. I refilled my coffee and opened my laptop, skimming the local news outlets for a story covering the dead man. On the local news station website, I found it. A brief story citing the guy's name, Leonard Crews, and that he was a transplant from somewhere along the east coast. There wasn't much other information. The title read, "Missing man found in Big Lagoon. Foul play suspected." The article listed the official cause of death pending an autopsy, as Analee had mentioned the night before. There was a brief video clipped from the news coverage showing a reporter standing on the point, the island in the background. The dialogue was exactly the same as the story on their webpage.

I killed the last of the coffee and grabbed Trigger for a walk. We stayed under the canopy of live oaks before the temperature got too hot. We cut through the park on 17th, and Trigger and I finished the walk and I went straight for the outdoor shower when we got back home. When I got out, I picked up my phone and sent Analee a text. "I really enjoyed talking with you last night. Hopefully, we can get together soon?"

I lived part time here at the small mother-in-law cottage in East Hill and part time on my cabin cruiser named the Origin at the marina. I purchased the home here in the neighborhood after Hurricane Ivan, when most people were taking insurance payments and selling their properties. The main house was in shambles and had extensive damage to the roof. I liked it mostly because it was within walking distance of the restaurant where I worked. It was also a classic craftsman cottage with a rough cottage out back and a swimming pool with some unknown debris in it blanketed with green algae. It had taken some time, but I gutted the house, rewired, re-plumbed and refinished everything. The pool required some pumping, sanitizing, and all new equipment. I lived in the house as I slowly built out the mother-in-law the way I wanted it.

The mother-in-law had a small workshop attached to it where I kept my surf boards and various fishing tackle. With the pool and the cottage renovations completed, I moved into the pool cottage and rented the house to some friends of mine. I could still use the pool and had a separate entrance to the backyard. It was a perfect setup, considering I only stayed here part time. The rent paid the mortgage and also added some coin to my purse to help cover utilities, so I lived on the cheap.

After the shower, I gathered my thoughts over the last couple of days and sat down to work on my next column for the Lost Key Paper. In my spare time, I wrote a column under a pen name for a local newspaper. They distributed copies all throughout the local area. The column covered local issues that the public should know about; most of them were not public unless you did some digging or spoke to the right people. It strategically positioned me in that I worked at a couple of establishments that were frequent watering holes of politicians, local administrators, city council members, and other various local elected and appointed officials. Truth is that most of these folks would tell me willingly about something that they might have had on their mind with some idea that it might get out given that most of what they let on related to my environmental crusades. I wrote under the anonymous pen name Jiminy Cricket.

I panned over the conceptual drawings of what the development would look like were it built, courtesy of Emerald Oasis Towers LLC. The many towers and pools spanning the barrier island crowded out any of the natural vegetation. The native coastal environment replaced with concrete and decorative stonework in a variety of pastel colors. It was a caricature of reality. I made some notes on the scale of the development and how many more people it meant living on an already overcrowded island.

My phone buzzed. It was Britt at Lost.

"Hey, heads up, Jared called out tonight and I'm on a double. Can you come in early and help?"

"Thanks Jared," I replied. "Anything else exciting happening over there yet?"

"There was some guy here asking about you earlier. I haven't seen him lately. Are you expecting anyone?"

"No, what did he look like?" I asked.

"Military or cop like, short hair, polo shirt, that kind of thing. He must have left. Anyway, I gotta go."

CHAPTER FIVE

I pulled into the gravel and oyster shell parking lot. The usual fleet of beach cruisers and local license plates greeted me. The scattered out-of-town plates showed a local had informed these tourists of the location of the true capital of the Lost Republic, a name that was now used for the local area and not just the name of the restaurant and bar that was the local watering hole. I walked in and saw Britt running the locals and tourists through the wringer, making six drinks at once. Trigger sat down in between the dock and the bar. Here he could maintain his view of the docks in case someone brought in a fresh catch, or more so, another dog. The Lost Republic Bar was a squat building made mostly of pilings and marine grade lumber situated right on the Intracoastal Waterway below the bridge to Lost Key. The place had survived several hurricanes and sat in among white sand dunes covered with sea oats and beach sunflower framed out by palms and sand oaks of varied heights. A weathered sign by the main entrance read "The Lost Republic." Another over the door read "Welcome to Paradise." I was several years into working here and still enjoyed it. I believe a good bartender has to enjoy the establishment he runs. A certain level of respect for the business is necessary since it is the bartenders who run the place and also set the tone. Working with Britt behind the bar was always fun. We didn't take any shit, but also didn't start any. She was dependable, both at work and outside the restaurant.

The Lost Republic is a refuge for travelers and locals alike. It serves as a hub and a regular stop for the sailors and watermen cruising the Intracoastal Waterway. Many people arrive by boat. There are slips available for boaters and overnight dockage if necessary. The canal is a sort of highway for the stateside wandering waterman. Vessels are passing by that may seek a destination hundreds of miles away and may never stop. The patrons of the Lost Republic never stop to think about it.

Tonight, a cool breeze pushed in from the north, signaling the sea breeze effect. The evenings bring the air masses out to sea and in the morning, before dawn, the wind shifts back again. Sea breeze was a natural phenomenon that led to better air quality because of the offshore breeze that pulled much of the air from pollution out into the Gulf, so the nights were much clearer and held more crisp air than the sticky, humid days. The bar at Lost was quiet, still stocked with the usual crew of regular customers and an occasional tourist family. I noticed there was a man sitting near the dock at one of the low tables who had kept to himself most of the evening. He rattled the crushed lime and remnants of the half melted ice settling into the bottom of the glass. I was wiping down the bar and clearing empty glasses when he approached the bar. He settled into a lean with one elbow propped up, the other hand hanging by his side. He was an enormous man with one of those pastel color button-down fishing shirts half unbuttoned. As he approached the bar, the stench of a man who had been drinking for hours hit me. He had beads of sweat across his forehead despite having the cool north breeze moving through Lost.

His rounded face and the gin blossom nose were swollen from the rum drinks. He reached into his shirt pocket and pulled out a pack of cigarettes, opened them with one hand, and put the entire pack to his mouth, drawing one out.

"You ever been to Jacksonville?" he asked. The cig flapped at his lips.

"Well, Jax Beach."

"That's where I'm at. Got a place there. Hell of a view, we have BBQs, parties, all that shit."

"I've been to Jacksonville but never made it to the beach," I said.

"You're missing out," he replied, lumbering around the bar to see if anyone noticed.

He continued talking but directed his voice out into the restaurant, not really talking to me anymore.

"I'm here for business, real estate, mostly in Florida, for tax reasons, but I've been over in Alabama too." Then he stared me down.

"The name's Steve."

I introduced myself and said, "You looking at houses, condos or land? This area is still pretty undeveloped."

He squinted his eyebrows and fumbled with his lighter. "I'm open to anything that could be lucrative. There's a certain level of risk that I draw the line at."

He added, "Don't wanna lose my ass if I don't have to."

"I get it," I said. "There's a lot of opportunity here. To get things going, you need capital."

"That's the story anywhere you go," he said, rattling the ice in his cup.

My gaze settled on his cigarette. "You can smoke on the dock out there, but not in here," I said, motioning to the wide dock away from the main restaurant and bar.

"Can I get you another drink?"

"Ask me again in a few minutes," he replied as he walked out to the dock, sparking the lighter.

I washed a couple of glasses, but I could feel his stare on me as I turned my back. "Hey," he said. "You hear anything about a new condo on the beach? Supposed to be real nice, a few buildings, pools, restaurants, all that stuff."

I turned to face a crooked smile on his red face; the gin blossom nose pulsating as more sweat beaded on his forehead. A fresh cigarette crunched between his fat fingers, soggy and bent.

I paused for a minute, puzzled, then smiled back at him. "Yeah, shit project, if you ask me. It's not even approved yet, so I wouldn't put much stock in that one."

He puffed up his chest, "Is that right, huh?" He snapped back, "that's not what I hear. Those dozers are ready to level the place." He huffed, then turned and walked back out to the dock, flicking his now wet and broken cigarette into the water and retrieving another from his front shirt pocket. Larry the Pelican sat perched on a piling and, as the crumpled cigarette hit the water, he dove in and guzzled it down, assuming it was food. I watched him as he landed on the dock next to Steve. Larry's large beak pocket expelled the water trapped inside as he gulped the cigarette down. Within a few seconds, Larry began retching and in an animated motion, wings spread, beak in the air, he hacked the butt up and it ejected out across the dock. It fell right next to Steve as he chuffed his smoke. I watched as he chuckled to himself and muttered a few words, then gave a kick in Larry's direction and flicked another cigarette butt into the water.

A few minutes later, the place emptied, and Steve wandered out the front entrance. An old blue Cadillac convertible crept out of the parking lot, gravel and oyster shells crunching as it went. The glow of a cigarette from the front seat trailed off into the night.

This guy was unexpected tonight. He came in with some intention and I got the feeling he wanted to talk to me. I didn't expect an outsider to ask me questions about the towers, since there wasn't much buzz outside the local population yet. He was fishing for information; I couldn't help but wonder if he had something to do with the dead guy in the lagoon. He was certainly big enough to toss that guy in the water if he wanted to. I stopped myself; had I just had an argument with a murderer?

I woke the next morning on the Origin as the sky glowed in the east. The water on the lagoon was glassy and a long V-shaped wake rolled in the distance behind a center console fishing boat, nearing the no-wake marker. The white sand of the barrier island shined in the morning light. It was Friday, and the water would soon be busy with the weekend warriors.

On days like this, I kept the skiff tied off parallel with the Origin to face the near constant boat wake. Last night, I had tied the skiff off across the stern for an early morning run out to the pass to fish the sandbar off the national park. The trip would take about twenty minutes. I packed breakfast the night before and after our usual walk, Trigger and I set out.

The water across the lagoon reflected the early morning sky as we cut across it. Trigger perched like a hood ornament on the front of the skiff. We hugged the west side of the pass, slipped past the jetty, over the west shoal and idled along the beach. I continued, fishing that stretch of beach with little luck. I decided I would cruise west and make the wide circle back in at Alabama pass and through the stretch of protected water known as Old river. When I reached the end of the national park, I called Britt. She lived in an old two story multi-tenant house across the street from the Gulf. She often spent her mornings in the water, riding her longboard and surfing the rollers coming into the shore of the Key.

When she answered the phone, she was sitting in the lifeguard chair on her stoop sipping a cup of coffee, watching for surf, which was nonexistent. "Hey, you wanna take a morning cruise and catch up? I've got something I want to run by you." I asked.

"Of course." She replied.

"Well, I'm headed your way now in the skiff, Gulf side."

"How about you walk down to the beach and I'll pick you up?" I said.

"Sounds like the best idea you've had all day," she yelled.

I smiled and said the day was just getting started. A few minutes later, I trimmed the motor up and eased in towards the beach as she waded through the clear water. She caught the bow and turned it back toward the Gulf as she jumped in. Trigger nosed her face as she hopped out of waist-deep water. We eased down the beach beyond the second sandbar and I scanned the horizon as she shed the wet shirt and board shorts and pulled her hair up under her cap. The aviator sunglasses shined back at me as I ran through all the thoughts that consumed me with the dead guy, break-in, development project... and then I got to the woman.

"Alright, so I gave you the rundown on the whole floater situation the other day. I met someone too. She was the lead investigator on the scene, and it turns out we have a mutual friend. She showed up at Ozone the other night and we got together after my shift."

"Wait a minute, she showed up out of nowhere? And then you got together that night?"

"Yep, ordinarily I wouldn't think much of it, but it happened twice over the past couple of days."

She caught me smile, and I said, "maybe the universe is trying to tell me something?"

The corners of her mouth turned up into a smile. "Maybe so. Did you get her number?"

My smile turned to a laugh. "I did, and I sent her a text, but she hasn't responded." I hesitated, reached into my pocket, and checked my phone. Still no response. I took off my hat and scratched my head with the bill. "Do you think it's too soon for me? You know me better than anyone and that's why I'm asking. It's been a while since I've been interested in a woman like this, so I have to believe it means something considering how things played out. I'm asking you because I thought you might give me some perspective as a female."

She paused and I could feel her eyes on me from under the aviators. We were passing the State Park now, the row of high-rise condominiums looming larger on the horizon.

"If you came to me, then you've already decided. You need some distraction anyway. Get your mind off the past and the development you've been focusing on."

"Yeah, maybe I'm still hung up on the past and I needed a little confirmation from another lost soul."

I got the grin this time, and she said, "What's your plan?"

"I'm going to leave it to her for the moment. If she doesn't respond by tomorrow, I'll follow up with her friend and see if she'll put in a good word."

She stopped and said, "My advice is to be direct. I know it's been a while since you've done the pursuit thing, but if you dance around the subject, then you risk not getting your intentions out there by being vague."

"Ok, so ask for a date right off?"

"No, just try to get to the point and don't ramble on," she said.

"Ok noted. No bullshit."

She laughed, "Funny, no, be clear and see what she gives you back."

Ok, I thought, sound advice from another mysterious creature called a woman.

We were coming up on the Flora-Bama now and the beach was quiet, with remnants of the previous night scattered about. I could see the Alabama Point jetty in the distance.

Britt said, "I think you should go after this one. You need a distraction from the past, and who knows? She might be what you need."

She gave me one last smile before she flipped over to face forward and I pulled the boat wide out to the Gulf to clear the jetty. We rode the tide into the pass and under the bridge. I kept the skiff close to east beach before taking the channel to Old river. We followed the channel as a school of mullet pushed in ahead of us and a pod of dolphin funneled them towards the shallows. We passed under the Ono Island bridge, keeping to the deeper water in the channel. The sands change overnight in Old River from tides and shifting sand. I kept to the south side of the bay as we came out of Old River and eased over some grass beds towards Holiday Harbor marina. The sun was over the trees now and the humidity was rising. A short ride later, we were back at the Origin.

Britt and Trigger took a walk while I washed down the skiff. I sat down at the chart table, made some notes, and pulled out my laptop to go over what I would present for the County Commission at tonight's meeting.

The focus of the presentation was on the environment. I had some interesting arguments for the Commission not to approve a large-scale development in this area. I was clear in the presentation that I was not against developing this property; it was another oversized iteration of the common beachfront, high-rise condominium complex that is present across so much of the Gulf Coast. This one was in an area with known endangered species documented and confirmed. The developers were ready to flatten the entire parcel and pay to make up for the devastating effects off-site. A smaller, more thoughtful design would be better. The plan now would provide the developers with a huge payoff after the initial investment and years of income. I was pretty sure I had two of the commissioners convinced, but I needed the majority, and it would be a gamble to go into the meeting with only two votes against it. I checked my phone again; still no response from Analee.

That afternoon, while getting ready for the meeting, I received a text from one commissioner informing me they had rescheduled the hearing for the project on tonight's agenda for a special meeting scheduled next week. There was no explanation. My guess was they did not have the majority vote, so they needed more time to decide. I made a few calls but couldn't find any new information on the decision. I felt my stomach rumble and remembered that I hadn't eaten today. So, I took the skiff and Trigger over to Lost for a Mahi sandwich and a drink.

Distant music and a wet haze hung above the canal and in the quick trip, Trigger was panting and my clothes clung to my body. We tied off to one of the outside finger piers nearest the fish market. There was only one empty seat at the bar next to the service well.

Britt looked at me quizzically. "Aren't you supposed to be at a meeting tonight?"

"Postponed", I said.

"You need a drink?" she asked.

"Absolutely. How about a Kalik and a Mahi sandwich?"

After running through the arrest story a few times for some regulars, I focused on the upcoming piece in the Lost Key Paper. Trigger settled in behind me and scanned the floor for stray scraps that had found their way down to his level. I crushed a lime over the fish and as I took my first bite; I saw Steve across the way.

He was sitting at a table, but in much worse shape than the night before. His bloated, red face made him appear as if he could keel over and stop breathing right there. I decided he was too drunk to notice me, and my attention went back to my sandwich. A moment later, Britt shot over to the well to mix a couple of drinks.

"Hey," I asked. "How long has table 101 been here?"

She dropped a drink in front of a customer and glanced in his direction. "He came in around sunset and watched the charters come in. Then moved to a table on the dock to watch the sunset. He's downed like ten rum and sodas. Said he's staying right down the street in a rental. So far, he's keeping it together. I've been serving him lighter the longer he's been here, but I haven't cut him off yet. I bet he's smoked a pack and a half out there on the dock. You wanna know his name? I've got his credit card. He wanted to run a tab." She hit the tab button, and the drawer popped open. I took a quick glance at the Amex platinum card. It read Gulf Ventures LLC. Figures, it would be a business card. I took out my phone and snapped a picture. Then Britt returned the card to the drawer. I made a mental note to do a search on the corporation.

I told Britt the story of my previous encounter and how he took off so quickly.

"Well, he's been cool so far. He makes little smart-ass comments but hasn't even tried to hit on me, so who knows?"

"I got a strange vibe from him last night, that's all."

She shot me a smile as a customer ordered another beer.

A few minutes later, I noticed the table Steve was sitting at was empty except for an empty drink cup and a crumpled-up pack of cigarettes. I scanned the restaurant and found him out on the docks at the edge of the marina. He was chuffing a cigarette and talking with someone in the shadows. The music and the restaurant noise drowned out their conversation.

I kept watching, but there was a dock light behind them obscuring the view. Steve grew more animated as he spoke, flailing his arms and sucking hard on his cigarette. The other man in the shadows returned the energy, and they both parted ways, but as the man left, he passed under a light. I couldn't be sure, but it may have been one of the thugs that had beaten me and, more recently, threatened my life.

CHAPTER SIX

The next day I had the night shift at Ozone, so I took Trigger to the beach. We headed down towards the entrance to the National Seashore and turned before the gate, right next to the Emerald Oasis Towers property. It was an untouched stretch of barrier island that spanned about eight acres. It had waterfront on the lagoon and on the Gulf of Mexico. The developers had taken it upon themselves to install a large chain-link construction fence to stop unwanted visitors. A wind tattered vinyl sign hung from the fence reading, "now taking deposits. Reserve yours today!" Beside it was a computer generated version of the development. There was a small gravel parking area and a travel trailer serving as a sales office. The land was habitat for species like the lost key beach mouse and several species of sea turtles that nest there every year. The property was also the location of the only natural dune lake on the Key. A spring upwelling in a low point of the dunes fed the lake. The water was the color of strong tea from the tannins in the soil. At high tides and full moons, it flowed out to the Gulf in a small incised channel. It held some decent redfish and trout in the deeper areas and had the remnants of an old fishing cabin and pier hanging on to rotted pilings. The banks of the lake were pristine coastal scrub with lichen and gopher apple covering the ground below the rosemary, salt bush and scrub oak.

The wind and weather had shaped the coastal sand live oaks into the shape of the dunes. These living plants combined to give off a sweet musty smell unique to these coastal environments. Amongst the rolling scrub habitat was a small population of gopher tortoises, considered a unique subspecies existing only on the Key.

The state had listed the land as a top priority for acquisition since it was abutting state and national park lands. The previous owner passed away without a will and his only surviving child preferred to sell to the highest bidder. Here, it turned out to be Emerald Oasis Towers, LLC. The conglomerate responsible for the proposed development I was now fighting against.

I parked on the east end of the property in an oyster shell mound along the road. Trigger and I walked the perimeter of the fence towards the Gulf and sat on the low dune, where the channel cut out to the Gulf. There was a light offshore wind, and the surf had pushed enough sand up to keep the cut from opening. Dull clouds hung over the Key, and the Gulf was choppy and dirty near shore. The beach was empty. I found a sandy spot out of the wind below a hunched oak. From there, I sat back and tried to imagine the place built up with high-rise condominiums and all the wildlife and critical habitat preserved and intermingled with the development. It sounded good, but it wasn't reality. These developments are becoming the new normal across the coast. New ordinances rolling back height restrictions and density limitations are the way for developers to maximize profits and build these small, all-inclusive cities in places that don't have the infrastructure to support them. Local officials only see the almighty dollar when the increase in bed tax monies adds to their coffers for some animals being displaced and a few trees cut down.

I continued walking, and as I neared the trailer that served as the sales office, I noticed two cars in the lot next to it. I could hear voices carrying into the dunes, but couldn't make out what they were saying. Through the oaks, Steve, the drunk from Lost, was standing there. He was talking to Liona, the head developer. There was a brief exchange as Liona got louder and the conversation halted. I stayed low as I watched her get into her car and leave. Steve stood there for a moment, then reached into his shirt pocket, grabbed his cigarettes, and lit up before climbing into his old Caddy. This couldn't be a chance encounter. I was missing something, some connection I hadn't seen before. After the last sound of Steve's car faded into the rumble of the surf, I headed to my truck as Trigger trotted up caked with sand and seawater. Later at the Origin, I sat in the lounge and logged on to the State website for corporations. I keyed the name of the LLC on Steve's credit card in the search bar. A list of names ran the length of the screen. It took a couple of tries, but I found the right corporation. It had Liona's name listed as the principal and a local address. Steve was the secretary and below his name was a Jacksonville address. There was one other officer listed with a Texas address and the name Robert Mendez. This all confirmed the connections I had assumed, but this new name in Texas I had not. A quick map search of the local address showed a property off the interstate, a warehouse from the aerials. Another search showed a warehouse in Jacksonville. The Texas address was a suite in an office building in El Paso. This last one brought me more questions. I may have to ask Hutch if he could find any info on this new guy. It may help me understand how he fits into the puzzle.

Outside, a light rain fell, turning steady. The smell of fresh rain on salt water moved through the lounge and I kicked back on the couch. Trigger and I faded off to sleep.

A little while later, I woke to the boat rocking and a tanker barge pushing east, followed by a distant rumble of thunder. I checked the marine forecast and secured all the lines on both boats. After getting everything together, I buttoned up the Origin and Trigger and I headed into town. We took Old Gulf Beach highway past the back gate at the Navy base, and I watched a large cargo plane drop in the familiar approach pattern to the runway, shaking the truck as the exhaust from its engines came into view. As I passed the back gate, I noticed the familiar silhouette of Steve's caddy behind me. It was keeping the distance to follow while remaining inconspicuous. After the Bayou Chico bridge, I took a detour. I pulled off the road and slipped into a spot downtown. The car didn't follow, so I stopped at the local grocery. Trigger greeted me from the bed of the truck as I came out. I tossed him a chew stick and checked my mirrors. No sign of the car, so I pulled on to Garden street and headed for East Hill. Before I made the turn north next to St. Michaels Cemetery, I saw the same car pull out behind me a few cars back. I skirted over the railroad tracks and tried to make a couple of turns to shake the car. I decided it was best not to go straight to the house or work.

An empty lot at a church a couple of blocks away from the house provided a decent spot to park without giving away the location of my house. Trigger and I snaked through a few backyards and empty lots and came through the back gate next to my cottage. I checked the street to be sure we were clean of the tail. After the evasion tactics, Trigger and I both took a dip in the pool. I had some time before my shift at Ozone, so I revisited the byline. Analee was still on my mind, and I couldn't stay focused.

CHAPTER SEVEN

During my walk to work, I couldn't shake the feeling that there was something I was missing about the events of the last couple of days. The dead body that had washed up on the shores of my favorite fishing hole, my jail time, the media coverage was still lacking, now this new information from the corporation database.

Our corner of The Lost Republic was quiet. Rarely had something such as a murder occurred, especially within reach of my dock or my job. It made me stop and consider the link here to what I was doing. Could I connect it to the development project? Was someone after me?

I walked up to the old stone building that resembled a castle. The historic hospital building loomed over an entire city block. An hour into the shift, I was talking to some regular customers about fishing when I noticed a familiar face sitting at the end of the bar below the stairs. It was Elena Peláez, a long-time friend and a local business owner.

"Hello, Ace." She smiled.

"Hey, it's good to see you. It's been a while," I said.

"Yes, well, I've been busy running the business, trying to keep the locals supplied with seafood. We are branching out to other locations. It's been exciting, but busy."

Elena had a confidence that at first glance was undetectable, but when she spoke, it was clear. She stood about 5'7" and dressed conservatively, yet always made sure she didn't go unnoticed. Tonight, she wore a tight-fitting pair of capris and a dark blue tank top with a long golden necklace, a small whale's tail on the end. Her skin was a light tan mahogany with some golden shimmer, and she wore her hair short above her shoulders.

Elena was an anomaly. Her family had moved here back in the 90s from the Tampa area and had started a commercial fishing company that supplied fish to markets up the east coast and across the southeast. It was a business that her father had started and built from nothing. In this part of the panhandle, it was not common to have a Latino family as part of the commercial fishing game. Across the panhandle, most commercial fisherman were white, representing the usual demographic that we have here. Elena's family had survived by providing specialty seafood to high-end restaurants like local farm raised oysters and mullet to the local joints.

"For a moment, I thought you hadn't seen me," she said.

I smiled. "It's hard not to notice you, Elena," I replied.

She smiled and said, "I'll have a dark rum. Easy on the ice."

When I returned she said, "How is the case against the Emerald Oasis Towers development coming along? Are you confident this monstrosity won't be built?"

Before I could answer, she said, "I know you're working hard at this, but we need some assurance it will not go through to construction. Several of the people I represent are counting on me to see this through, which means I'm counting on you." She slapped her hand on the bar beside her drink and straightened up. "I'm doing my part. I've lobbied the commissioners. There will be media coverage coming out soon."

Her intensity surprised me. "I appreciate your passion here, but I can only tell you I'm working on the case and plan to present it to the commission at the meeting. I've got meetings set up this week and I am planning others. What else can we do from here, short of some legal action? I'm not sure we're prepared to go that route?" I wondered.

She settled back onto her stool. "It's a last resort," she replied.

"Until the meeting, I'd say we're working hard to stop this," I said.

She thawed and smiled. "Thank you. This is important to me."

"I know. It's always good to see you."

She smiled, finished her drink and stood, placing her hand on mine. "I'll see you soon, Ace."

With that, she left.

I spent the rest of the night behind the bar, my mind running in different directions. It was after midnight when I locked the door behind me and started the two-block walk home. Above me, a halo hung around the moon. A storm was coming.

The next morning, I loaded up my gear to get back to the Origin. I headed south out of the neighborhood and drove by the bay to check conditions. It was still early light and as I passed under the graffiti bridge; I noticed a familiar car parked at the 17th avenue boat ramp. It had its lights on and my eyes went right to it. The sharp silhouette and long lines of the caddy were easy to spot. It was Steve's, and the same one that followed me the day before. I circled back and pulled into the parking lot to investigate, and Trigger's nose perked up as we stopped.

Steve was in the front seat, slouched down, snoring. I wanted to shake the hell out of him and ask him why he had taken such an interest in me. Waking a sleeping bear wasn't a good idea. Maybe this guy could never pick up my trail after I lost him and he got tired and gave up, maybe too drunk to drive back to wherever he was staying. I drove to the island and ran the scenario through my head. Did I piss this guy off at some point? That didn't seem likely since I had just met him. He was a long way from the Key. Nothing made sense. A minute later, my phone buzzed. It was a bartender friend of mine and fishing guide, Chris, who worked over in Gulf Shores. His text read, "come see me today at work, we need to talk."

Stevie Ray Vaughan's "Little Wing" played over the speakers as I climbed over the bridge to the Key. The sky was orange and silver. Steel blue clouds were on the horizon, blowing out the sun as it began its arc over the southeastern sky. The lagoon was flat and shone the sky on the surface, a lone kayak cut across the reflection. That was where I needed to be. I glanced down at Trigger laying over the passenger seat snoozing, one leg twitching as if running, probably dreaming of chasing seabirds on the beach or the docks at Lost.

The trip down the intra-coastal was uneventful. I took my time and fished a couple of inlets and holes, dodging some barge traffic on the way. I began the trip early so the recreational boaters had not begun their days, but by the time I reached LuLu's, it was picking up and already jamming the Margaritaville to the tourists. Trigger stayed on the boat while I tied it off. The restaurant was buzzing with servers and the bar was full. I made for the server station and recognized one server, Jessica. She pointed to a side room. A stainless-steel horseshoe-shaped bar hemmed in by a ticket machine that spit out tickets with drink orders corralled Chris. His tall frame and brown hair hung over a sweatband and his LuLu's shirt was already showing his sweat.

He gave me a big smile when I walked in and said, "damn I thought you might make an appearance today."

"Well," I said, "I got the feeling we needed to catch up?" I said.

He laughed. "Hey, it might be nothing, but I thought a face to face would be best."

"You been catching any fish?" I asked.

He said, "I've had a few charters. I was out this morning when I sent you that text. I head down to Mexico in a couple of weeks. Last month, I went down to the Keys. I pulled some tarpon and a couple of permit, fishing at the same spots we used to."

The thought of a tarpon or permit on the line got my heart going.

"Man, that sounds good. I need to head south for a few days. Maybe I'll call Seamus and get something lined up."

He kept the conversation going, but stayed focused on the machine. During that time, he never stopped mixing, pouring, and sending those tickets out as the servers came in.

When he cleared the tickets, he slowed down and lowered his voice. "I had a client out yesterday. We were fishing off Ono and he had a couple of drinks and started talking. He mentioned this project you've been fighting against. So I started drawing him out on some things he was saying. Most of it sounded like BS. According to him, this lady in charge is connected to some guys in Mexico and Texas. That's where the money comes from and it's all dirty. He said she has a network and people are trafficked. It was a weird conversation. He talked about a bunch of girls and connections to parties here on the beach. He said the lady in charge has ties to some Mexican gangs. It sounds like the cartels are backing this shit, man, and they provide security, too. I want you to know because it sounds heavy and you're in the middle of it. Watch your back, is all I'm saying. Things could get weird."

I smiled. "The Lost Republic is weird already, but thanks for letting me know," I said.

The ticket machine began singing again, and another server came through the swinging door.

"Hey, let's get together soon and go fishing." He said. "I hear they're catching blackfin off the pier. Maybe we can go hit some on the fly!"

"Let's do it!" I replied, laughing. "I'll hit you on my next day off."

"Alright brother." And with a wet, liquor-soaked handshake, I took off. Trigger, still perched on the bow, was waiting for my return.

We cast off and idled down the canal through the narrows and past the Wharf as the boat traffic picked up. When the bay opened up, I brought the skiff on plane, and we kept to the calmest water we could find.

The story Chris had come up with did not make me feel better about Liona and her threats. The two goons I had run into recently were likely some cartel thugs hired to keep me in check.

I rounded Bear Point into the bay and the chop increased as the water opened up into Lost bay. I had to throttle down; as I did, a couple of jet skis buzzed by, catching air off my wake. I made it through the initial washing machine of waves and wake, then found a groove in the bay and continued to push towards the marina. Here, the bay opened up to the north, the highway 98 bridge visible, and to the south, a row of towering condominiums loomed on the shoreline. The chop had increased, and so had the boat traffic towards the south as a barge crested the eastern horizon.

Then, a jet ski cut through the dark water and smashed into the bow of my skiff, submerging the bow in the water. A string of obscenities spewed from my mouth as I struggled to get my footing. The skiff filled with water, and it rushed into the stern and pushed the skiff lower in the water. A rooster tail of water was visible in the distance when I regained my footing and grip on the throttle. Trigger stood frozen in a wide and low stance, soaking wet, worried. I scanned the bay for the jet ski. What the hell was that? I thought.

A moment later, another ski came alongside the skiff. It was one of the goons that had been following me. He was ridiculous in his gold-rimmed sunglasses and, thankfully, no visible weapons.

"Hey Amigo!" he said.

"You in trouble now, eh?"

"You and your dog!"

And he took off, leaving a rooster tail behind him in his wake.

I took that as a warning. It would be a rough ride, but I cranked the throttle and yelled to Trigger. "Hold on boy, we'll make it."

More determined now, I tried to steady the narrow skiff in the chop. I aimed for a barge in the distance. The motor struggled in the chop as it worked to plane out, riding the peaks and valleys but never able to get up out of the washing machine. It was narrow and flat and never built for this kind of water.

I pushed on; the skis buzzing all around me.

Through the wake, the tower of the barge in front of me kept my bearing, and I aimed the bow towards the high side of the barge, hoping to put something between me and the skis.

As I struggled to find calmer water, the buzzing slowed. Off to my right, the two skis pulled alongside one another, talking and making chopping motions with their hands. Judging by the distance now, the barge was bearing down and I would meet it in a matter of moments.

I checked again. The two goons had finished plotting and now made a wide arc, coming back at me.

I grabbed Trigger and shouted, "Hold on boy, it's about to get weird."

The barge was bearing down closer now and they may try for one last strike to put the skiff down before the barge met me. If they succeeded, the barge would overrun Trigger and me, and we would end up at the bottom of the bay. Another boater who couldn't get out of the way.

The skis completed the arc and came together side by side, full speed right next to each other. Holding my position and tucking Trigger back with my left foot, I braced myself on the poling platform behind me and gassed the engine, kicking up the bow of the skiff into the air at the last minute.

The motion sent the skis in different directions since it was obvious they wouldn't be able to skip over the top of the skiff anymore. I leaned to the left, and the skiff made a complete corkscrew turn, bow in the air and landed back in the same position with a thwack!

I gassed it and made for the high side of the barge, banging the wake as I went. A couple of warning whistles from the barge signaled they had seen me. The skiff was taking a beating, and I made a mental note to do an overhaul of the motor soon if I made it out of this. Trigger was still in his splayed-out position, clinging to some stability; I kept on my line towards the marina, now wide-open throttle and catching air on the chop as I bore down harder.

For a moment, I considered trying to lose them under docks along the point, but they had the advantage of speed and drew less water than my skiff.

I continued at full speed along the point, the no-wake signs in the distance.

There was a public boat ramp and dock inside the no-wake zone that was always busy. That was my destination. I passed the no-wake sign and held the throttle. They were in my wash and if I slowed now, they would be on me.

The dock came into view along with the silhouette of a coast guard boat. They would have to back off now or risk committing a maritime crime in front of the coast guard. I doubted they would recognize the boat, but if the crew was out on the dock, they would be official enough to slow them down.

As I closed in on the boat ramp, I noticed they must have figured out I was headed that way. They both overtook the skiff, coming around in front of me and slowing down. Trigger wore the worried face I had seen since we took the first hit. More determined now than ever, I took evasive maneuvers. I slowed to their speed and cut the tiller, skirting around them and heading for the stretch of beach beside the boat ramp pier. The nearer we came, it was clear there was nowhere to beach the skiff. By now, the coast guard crew had taken notice and so had the others on the beach. I was only a hundred yards out and they were right back on my tail as I neared the pier. The goons got the message and backed off, slowing and falling into the line of boats moving through the channel. I let up on the throttle and coasted in towards the pier; then slamming the motor in reverse, I kicked the skiff right up on shallow side of the pier.

Petty Officer Matt Moore stood on the pier.

"Ace, what the hell are you doing man?" he said.

"Sorry man, I had no choice," I said. "They were all over me."

"What? Who? Those two skis?" he asked.

"Yeah, they came close too, tried to put me the under that barge that passed. Smashed my skiff and scared the hell outta Trigger." I motioned to the bow and then Trigger as he jumped out of the boat and trotted down the pier, happy to be on a stable structure.

"They did that?" he said, pointing to the skiff. "What did they want?"

"They've been on me for the last few days. They work for a big developer here and I'm trying to stop the development. I've already had a couple of brushes with them, but this was the nastiest yet."

Matt stepped over to the coastguard vessel and got on the radio. A minute later, he was back on the pier inspecting my skiff with me.

"Smashed it up pretty good, huh," he said. "I radioed ahead to our crew out at the Pass. If they see them, they'll pick them up."

I inspected the rail and the light. "Yep, it got the rail pretty good and the starboard light. It'll take some glass work and a new light, but I'll get Everett on it."

He stopped. "What? That guy's still around? I thought he would have stayed on one of those islands down south, running boats for some boat dealer," Matt said.

I nodded. "Yep, he's still around. He's got a lady here, so he's stationary for now; he does good work, too. Lately, he's been down at the harbor working, and he still takes transport jobs when they come up. He's a solid mechanic and does good glass work, too."

"I'll keep that in mind," he said. "I've got a project I may bring him in on."

"Anyway, are you good?" he asked.

"I'm fine, but I may have some trouble getting Trigger back on this skiff."

Matt smiled. "Good luck with that. You're still floating so you can make it back to the marina."

"I'll be fine."

Matt said, "Look, if you get into trouble again on the water with these guys, hail us on Channel 16 and we'll get some help to you."

"Roger that. Hopefully, you won't hear from me."

I finally coaxed Trigger back on the skiff and we were back at the marina within a few minutes. No sign of the goons anywhere. He took his spot on the lounge floor and I made another inspection of the damage.

CHAPTER EIGHT

I had enough time to change into my bar gear and check the lines on the Origin. We arrived on the skiff and Trigger assumed his usual spot. I relieved the day bartender and went through the usual motions, preparing for the evening. It was still a couple of hours before sunset, so it was mellow aside from the usual neighborhood crowd and a few tourists from Alabama on a booze cruise. Before sunset, Britt came in for the closing shift and I noticed a few minutes after that, Steve came in. He grabbed a table by the water so he could chain smoke and watch the sunset. He didn't speak to me and only ordered drinks from Britt. After sunset he had downed more than a few rum drinks and soon began shaking the plastic cup, rattling the ice when he needed another. All the while chain smoking and knocking the drinks back. He hadn't made a move in my direction at all. Later, when the dinner rush faded and the bar cleared, he approached the service well. He squared up like he wanted to say something, then leaned on the bar and squinted. His eyes were only slits. He took another draw, resembling someone siphoning gas, his cheeks forming divots with the cigarette aiming right at me. After another exaggerated inhale, he blew the smoke in my face. He had reached the limit of rum drinks and was prepared to say whatever was on his mind.

"Where you been?" he asked.

I sensed he was going to instigate some sort of hostile exchange, so I thought, what the hell. "I've been here," I paused. "Working." I steadied myself on the bar and leaned towards him. "By the way, you can smoke outside," I said, wiping down the bar and clearing drinks. He took no notice of the direction to smoke outside and continued.

"You saw me over there, huh?" he asked. "Yeah, nice sunset today. I get to watch it set over the water here, not like at home. The sunrise over the Atlantic is incredible."

"Sure it is. You got something else on your mind?" I set the drinks at the server station and stepped to the cut through at the bar. He repositioned and steadied himself, facing me with his left hand on the bar, white knuckled and clamped down on the rail. The stench of booze and smoke heavy on his breath nearly knocked me down. I knew he was going to make a move. I am not a large man, but I handle myself well in a confrontation. Keeping my voice low and breathing steady, not getting myself backed into a corner has kept me out of most ground fights, which is where most bar brawls end up. I have a taller frame, but I can be quick when necessary. This may get tested soon. It was apparent this man was hiding some unknown vendetta against me.

He tapped his pack of cigarettes on the bar and said, "that your boat over there?"

"Which one?" I asked.

"The one back there with the funny platform on it." He turned to point and began walking in that direction, motioning for me to follow. When he turned his back, I waved to Britt and made the universal phone signal, meaning to get ready to call the cops if it gets real. Most of the other bar customers had taken notice as he approached the bar, smoking and over served. I am not a seasoned pro. I don't search out conflict. However, my father instilled in me the capacity to avoid a confrontation or at least handle myself well enough to keep from getting myself pummeled by a drunk. Steve stumbled toward the skiff using the 10x10 posts to steady himself. As he approached the dock, he slowed and Trigger scrambled to get out of his way. He stopped, turned abruptly and went into a low lunge aimed at my waist, both arms out like a defensive lineman. I was far enough back that I bladed my body and stepped to the side as his arm and left knee passed me as he stalled out. I threw a quick sidekick to his knee, and he tumbled forward, unable to maintain his footing. His trajectory carried him to the ground, his weight moving with such force that his face planted into a post with a thud and an audible crack. It wasn't clear if the crack was the post or his face, but there was blood under his head as he settled into the concrete. I could hear Britt on the phone behind me. Keeping a wide berth, I sidestepped around him, but Trigger approached the now unconscious and bleeding man with a low growl and teeth bore, prepared for a death match if needed. He stayed down for a minute, and I attempted to raise him, but the heft of a man that size, rum drunk and semi-conscious, is more than I wanted to deal with. Within five minutes, Hutch, the deputy, was there with backup. He pulled me to the side away from the other deputies, who were now helping Steve to his feet and into cuffs.

"What the hell happened, man?"

"Not sure. He turned on me and I helped him to the ground." Hutch didn't respond. "One minute he was asking me about my skiff and the next, he tried a torpedo on me. I sidestepped it and helped him down, hell he would have smashed his face even if I hadn't."

In the parking lot, Steve now had his hands cuffed behind his back and was refusing medical attention, yelling for a cigarette with blood all over his face.

Hutch said, "Well, do you wanna press charges? I got several witnesses, and the security cams should seal the deal."

I stood there thinking about it. I didn't know who this guy was or what he wanted with me. He was little more than a violent drunk and I didn't count this guy as a threat.

"No, I don't want to press charges. He's going in for the night since he's drunk, right?"

"Yeah, we'll keep him in the drunk tank until the morning and release him sometime tomorrow."

"Is there any way you can keep him longer?"

"Not unless you change your mind on those charges and even then, he wouldn't be in long, at least until he makes bail."

"Alright, there's something else though," I said. "Well, I'm pretty sure this guy has been following me. I saw his car behind me the other day when I drove into town and this morning, I found him asleep in his car at the graffiti bridge boat launch."

Hutch raised one eyebrow. "any reason he would follow you?" he asked.

"He's in with the development team." I said. I stared off into the darkness for a moment, considering what this guy's real motives were.

"Just get him the hell out of here. I don't think he knows where I live, anyway."

Hutch stopped. "He knows where you work, which might be worse."

I hesitated, then replied, "I'll be fine."

"You're sure?" he asked.

"Yep," I said.

"Alright man, it's your funeral," Hutch said.

"That dude is huge and not too smart, which tells me he'll try again."

"I'll risk it," I replied.

He shook his head, then said,

"I'll stick around in the parking lot for the time being to finish up some paperwork." I turned to walk back into the restaurant and stopped. "Hey Hutch, while you're sitting in there, maybe you could do me a favor?"

"Whaddaya need?" I handed him a guest check with the name Robert Mendez on it. "What's this?" he asked.

I gave him an awkward smile. "Let's just say when you plug that in your database, there may be connections to people I've been dealing with here. I need to know how this guy fits in to everything here."

"I'll see what I can come up with," he replied. Hutch walked over to the other deputies waiting and said a few things, then they loaded Steve into the back of a County SUV.

When I walked back to the bar, Britt said, "What the hell, dude? You know he's not done. He had those crazy eyes."

"I'm not worried about it. Hutch is going to hang around the rest of the night. I think we can agree he's 86'd from here, anyway. If we see him again, we call the law simple as that."

The rest of the night was uneventful. I handled my shift duties and set Britt up to close. After it had settled down, I clocked out and grabbed a print of the numbers for the day and a drink and sat at the bar. Trigger and I had a bite, and I mulled over the scene that had unfolded with me being the primary character. I kept going back to when this guy walked in. The way he was acting spelled nothing different from what he'd done the past few times he had stopped in for drinks. Maybe he was still mad about losing me the other night in my neighborhood? If things had turned out differently, that night may have been when he took action, which would have been worse, as city law enforcement is not as quick to respond.

In the parking lot, his old caddy was still there. I hadn't thought to have it towed, but it may be a better idea, so he had no excuse to come back here. Hutch was still in the parking lot, engine running and windows up. I could see the glow from the laptop in the console running through the less glamorous duties of the job, like paperwork and files. A few minutes later, he had gotten out of his cruiser and was standing next to it, talking on the phone. I slid off the barstool and headed in that direction around the side of the outside bar, inside the same alley that housed the bar mats, mop buckets and scrub brushes. I opened the gate that led to the parking lot and met Hutch next to his cruiser.

"How you doing?" he asked.

My face said it all. "Winding down after that night and the episode where a drunk 60-year-old linebacker tried to tackle me."

He smiled and said, "Ya, that guy was big. He went down hard, though. I think that knocked some sense into him."

I managed a chuckle. "Doubtful."

"I got off the phone with the deputy that took him in. He said about halfway back he came out of his fog and started yelling some crazy shit."

"Like what?" I asked.

"Well, at first it was gibberish, then he got into something I thought sounded a little off. He said you killed his best friend and that he owed you. He kept saying you killed him."

As Hutch ran down this new information, I could feel the anxiety creep up; the hair on my neck stood up, my muscles tensed up and my head got hot. What the hell was this guy talking about? I tried to come up with something. "I think he's talking about the floater I found last week? The body had been there for a day, and I had nothing to do with it."

"Maybe he knows they took you in for it?" Involuntarily, my hands came up. "How could I have done it? I don't even know how the guy died?"

I continued; I was pleading my case to avoid another arrest.

"This is crazy, man. I'm still trying to connect everything here. I knew the guy, and I use the term loosely. It's possible I met him at a public meeting for a big development proposed on the Key a few days ago. The meeting is the only contact I've had with the dead guy and this guy Steve, I just met. He came out of nowhere and told me he was a real estate investor trying to get in here on the Key. This is nuts man, you gotta know he's crazy, right?" I was looking for some reassurance from Hutch, but he said nothing.

"Did he say anything more about why he thinks I killed this guy? Any details?"

Hutch shook his head. "No, it sounds like he's on a rant."

Hutch shifted his belt and adjusted the volume on his radio. "Yeah, I'm sure it's nothing, but it's all recorded in the cruiser and if he's still going when they throw him in the tank, then there is more on the record."

"Well, can I talk to him, find out why he's saying these things?"

Hutch shook his head, "no. I can't take you in to talk to the guy who attacked you, not protocol. Besides, you need to be ready. It may prompt more questioning from FDLE since we have to report all this. Regardless, it's a good idea to watch your back over the next few days until this guy gets run out of town or runs out of money."

"I guess that was me hoping he would go away, huh? Thanks for the heads up."

The anxiety was still hanging around and had moved up to my head. I noticed a layer of sweat beads around my forehead. The hair on my neck had lain down and replaced with goose bumps. I stood there, trying to decide my next move.

Hutch went back to his notepad. "I got some information on the name you gave me. He's from Cuba, but he's a big shot in Texas and Mexico. He stays out of Florida best I can tell. Most of the info I found was sparse, but he's connected to a ton of people and most of them are nasty characters, gangs, cartels, ex-cons. If this guy is involved somehow, I'd say this is a good reason to back off this thing. Hey, I wouldn't want to tangle with this crowd." His tone had changed to serious with a touch of skepticism. "Anyway, that's all I got for you."

Hutch's phone rang, and he answered and waved to me as he got back into his cruiser. I walked back to my seat at the bar and went over any possibilities I may have missed. I'm going to need to do more investigation myself to know where I stand. My phone buzzed in my pocket. It was a text message from Analee. "Hey sorry I haven't replied. Been busy. Let's get together soon." My first thought was, "She sure picked the right time to respond," but then, "She may give me the update on the case and what really happened to this guy."

I was sure she wouldn't compromise her position, but I may get a status or next of kin. Then another visit from law enforcement. They would ask if I knew anything else or had forgotten to tell them something. But I may know where I stand then and what I'm in for.

The next day I headed over to Orange Beach to discuss the write up I had for the Lost Key paper with Dan, the editor. He lived over on Bear Point on one of the back streets, shrouded by live oaks and sabal palms. On the drive over, I considered making the phone call to go over the story. I thought it better to get some context in and also use it as an opportunity to get some guidance on the situation I was dealing with. A woman, a potential homicide, a strange stalker and the entire Gulf side development that I would crusade against. I was running head on into all this, and I couldn't stop. Life as it was playing out.

I pulled into Dan's driveway and Trigger scrambled over me to get out. The front door of the old house opened and out came Dan's redbone hound, Spooner. He and Trigger were soon rolling through the brush and leaves in the front yard.

"Wild dogs," I said. "How you been?"

He smiled big under his mustache and gave me a hug. "Great." He squared up my shoulders and looked me over. "Great to see you. " I smiled and returned the compliment.

We sat on the front porch and I caught him up on the story; since I had already sent it to him, he had some comments and suggestions related to the overall message. I would edit as needed and send it back tomorrow.

"If you have the time, I want to run some things by you," I asked.

He ran his hand through his hair and laughed as the dogs rumbled through the front yard. "There is always time for you. What's on your mind?"

"Well, I'm sure you know about my discovery of the dead man in Big Lagoon," I said. "The paper said a fisherman found the body, but I didn't realize that was you?"

"Yep, I am the nameless fisherman. Crazy story, but it gets better."

I let out a deep breath. "I got arrested because of it." He stayed quiet, but I could see his brow wrinkle as I continued. "On top of that, I've had these two goons trying to kill me and another guy has shown up at Lost trying to take me down."

"On the way into town the other day, I noticed a car tailing me."

"I ended up losing the guy and stashing the truck down the street, but the next morning I drove by the bay at Graffiti Bridge and there he was, passed out in his car. Then last night he came into the place and tried to bulldoze me."

Dan's eyes narrowed. "This guy came out of no-where?" he asked.

"I've never met him before he started stalking me," I said.

"He seemed harmless at first, but when he gets a few drinks in him, he gets nasty."

Dan shifted in his chair as the dogs came rolling out of the bushes and crashed into the Patio furniture.

"If you don't know why he's there and why he's acting like this, then yes, you need to be careful."

"What about these other guys?" he asked.

"Well, they work for the developer for the Towers project."

Dan's face wrinkled into a scowl. "That sounds right." He said. "That crew has some shady connections. You still carry, right?" he asked.

"Of course, I can't afford not to after this. These guys tried to put me and Trigger at the bottom of the bay yesterday. Came after us on the skiff with jet skis. I thought for a minute they might get us, too. I made it to Galvez boat ramp and luckily the coast guard saved us." Shaking his head, he said, "there are some crazy people out there."

I agreed. "I was on my way back from a meeting with a fishing buddy of mine. He got some information on the developer and says she's involved with the cartels down in Mexico. This whole thing is getting out of hand. I've never even heard of this stuff before and now it's right here in my face." I stared off into the distance for a moment and he stayed silent, watching the dogs.

"Another part of the story you don't know yet is that I met someone. When I found the dead guy, I called the law, and they sent some deputies, plus someone from the Medical Examiner out to survey the scene. I guess this is standard practice when someone dies. The Investigator with the M. E.. got my attention and since then we've crossed paths. She keeps my attention even when she's not around," I said.

"Ha, the opposite sex has that effect on most of us guys." He laughed.

"Hey man, it sounds like a hell of a time you've had the last couple of days."

"I know you've been through some tough times over the past year."

"I guess the best advice I can give is to ease into anything you do in that department."

"If she's piquing your interest, then let things unfold how they will and, if it's something worth your time, you'll know."

"These guys who are after you," he paused for a moment, "just stay vigilant. Don't let them get the drop on you." He hesitated again, then said, "Your dad made sure he taught you what he could, but I may send a friend of mine to see you at Lost. He's a local guy, but has a training facility here."

I smiled. "For what, like MMA or something?"

Dan returned the smile. "Something like that."

About that time, the dogs crashed through the bushes in front of the house and continued their jaunt.

"I'll work on the story and send it to you later."

"Sounds good."

"I should have it ready to go into the Lost Key paper next week," he replied.

I rounded up Trigger, who hadn't stopped the entire time. He loaded up in the front seat and settled in the horizontal position, front paws crossed and head laying over them, still panting from the exhaustive activity.

I took the ride down the beach with some reggae playing low while I considered the next trip I had been planning in my mind. I am a hard person to keep still and these bouts with development and the money backing them are exhausting for my mind and body. This one was even more so when you factor in the dead guy.

That night, Lost was busy as ever. The locals had the bar taken over and Jerry, the resident minstrel, was rolling through the usual classics on stage.

Early in the shift, a tall man with a manicured beard in black tactical pants and a collared shirt sat down at the bar. He was familiar, but I couldn't place him. He ordered a drink and sat. After a few minutes of him listening to my conversation with Britt, he got my attention.

"You're Ace right?"

I smiled and said, "Yes," reaching, out for a handshake.

He obliged and said, "My name is Marco and I work for an organization called International Rescue Project. We work to fight human trafficking and forced servitude here in the states but also worldwide. Our headquarters are in Orange Beach. We have a training facility and offices there. Your buddy Dan asked me to come see you."

"Oh yeah, how do you know Dan?" I asked.

"He comes and trains with us sometimes, says it keeps him young."

I smiled.

"He also filled me in on the unwanted visitors you've been getting. It sounds like you handled yourself pretty well."

Skeptical I would continue to be so lucky, I said, "I think it may have been a survival mechanism kicking in. My dad taught me a few things when I was a kid. Some of it must have stuck."

"Well, regardless, it's good to hear you came out ok."

"It may not be the same outcome next time. We have a great facility. Have you ever thought about some formal defense training?"

"I guess I haven't really considered it," I said. "Is your place open to the public?"

He straightened up. "No, it's a private facility, but we have classes for our staff and members. If you're interested, I'll put you on the list for access."

"We also have a full-service gym you would have access to."

"Wow, man, that sounds great." I knew Dan was right; I needed some kind of training and these guys seem like the real thing.

I could hear the ticket machine singing in the bar. "I appreciate you coming by here and talking with me, but I need to get back to work."

"I get it," he said. "Here's my card. The location of our facility is on the back. Call me or show up and we can get everything laid out for access. We have an extensive security network so you can get in, but we have to get you cleared first."

I took the card and shook his hand. "Thanks."

That night as I shut down Lost, I thought about what Chris and Hutch had told me about the developers, cartels, trafficking, and these goons who were after me, clearly connected to them. I knew I needed to do something more to stay safe and the opportunity to train with some professionals had fallen into my lap. I had to take them up on the offer, eventually.

Later that night, Trigger and I arrived at the marina, and I checked the lines as we stepped on to the Origin. The glow from the cabin showed that someone was on board. I slid the door open and on the couch in the lounge lay Everett, arms crossed with a can of beer wedged in the crevice of his arms. The television was on and Captain Ron was playing, likely on a continuous loop all night, committing the lines of the movie to Everett's mind. Trigger ran into the cabin and gave him the usual sniff test and lick, and he stirred. I said, "What happened? Your old lady tell you not to come home?"

"She's crazy man. I mean it, I'm done with her. I had a couple drinks after work and then called her and she goes off on this tear and I'm like, ok fine, and then I had a couple more drinks and called her back to make sure she got the message the first time," he said.

"So, you get to stay here for a while?"

"Yep, but I got a job coming up, anyway. Gotta head over to the east coast and pick up a dive boat and bring it back over to Destin. So that should give her some time to cool off."

CHAPTER NINE

I woke up the next day and lay there thinking about the situation I found myself in. I was working through all the adversity that seemed to come my way recently.

I believe that life gives you these tests, and you decide how to react to them. That response separates all of us. If I were someone else, I might relegate myself to be a bartender and not invite other calamity into my life. I could leave the place I grew up to be bulldozed and trashed by developers and greed. I could drop the crusader bit and ignore the urge to fight for something. This would eliminate much of the current tumult in my life, save for the damage that had already been done.

In a perfect world, I wouldn't need to take this role. However, there is a need for someone like me in many more places than here. There are vast stretches of virgin forests flattened every day to make way for strip malls and car dealerships. Commerce and shipping dredge seagrass beds and corals to make way for larger vessels that bring our necessary goods to these strip malls and our doorsteps. Humanity is oblivious to or chosen ignorant to the damage our way of life inflicts, which has eliminated so many of the things that we live for. There are the unavoidable incremental losses to our unique environment that are direct results of the sheer number of people our infrastructure must accommodate. Perhaps these developments are of the same blood, and we need them to accommodate the increase in population and increase in visitors, from the need for people to visit and enjoy the natural environment that makes this place so special.

I emerged from the forward berth and pushed open the vent to get some air flowing through the main cabin. There was a hum from the lounge, and I noticed the glow of the television and Trigger sleeping on the floor below Everett's outstretched leg. I made coffee and Trigger eased up from his position and performed his morning stretch, reminiscent of some dog yoga routine. He nudged my leg, looked up, and wagged his tail. After I opened the back door, he jumped onto the dock and into the boatyard. The sky was cloudy and gray, with a glow in the east. The lagoon was quiet and the clack of a car crossing the bridge began the morning. Dawn air was heavy and damp with fog. Swirls and eddies around the pilings danced with the tide.

I needed some time to think. I caught Everett up on everything that had happened last night; we took the skiff, and I dropped him at the marina down the canal.

I headed to the open lagoon and pushed into some skinny water near the seashore. My skiff only drew a few inches. The sun was showing through the clouds and a breeze kept things comfortable.

The bow up front was high enough to give me a good vantage point and provide a position for contemplating my current situation while scanning for fish.

I wondered how a woman might fit into my life. After the episode at Lost the day before, I realized I may still be a suspect in a murder case. The investigator at FDLE was sure to get word of Steve's drunken rant and start asking questions. I knew I was in for another visit from FDLE. One more thing to worry about.

The boat swung around as I dropped the anchor over a patch of sandy bottom. A breeze blew over me as stowed my rod and lay on the deck. Seabirds called as the water slapped the hull. The openings in the clouds let glimpses of blue sky show through and bright morning sunlight fall down on the barrier island across the lagoon as the clouds passed over the sun.

When I made it back to the Origin, I sat at the navigation table where I do most of my writing and picked up my cell phone. I had Analee's number saved and called. It rang twice before she answered.

"Hi Analee, this is Ace."

There was a brief pause and then she replied, "Oh, hi how are you?"

I held my breath. "I'm good." Unsure, I said. "Um, I was wondering if you might be available this afternoon? Maybe we can grab a bite or catch the sunset?"

She responded, "Ok, yes, sure, but I don't know what time I'll be off work. Let's do it like this. You call me later and we'll set something up."

"Alright, later this afternoon?" I asked.

"Sure, about 4:30."

"Ok, I'll call you then," I replied.

A twinkle of nervousness hummed in my gut. I turned my attention to my laptop. The column for the Lost Key Paper was not done, and I needed to finish up and get it sent back to Dan for the upcoming issue. After reading through again, I made some edits, then sent it to Dan and shut the laptop. It would run in the Lost Key Paper next week. I made a mental note to pick up a copy.

I grabbed up my copy of Fatu Hiva after moving over to the couch. The book chronicles a man and woman's journey across the globe to an island in the south Pacific. They opt to live off the land and escape the modern world, albeit for a short time. The book helps me put in to perspective the modern world we live in today and what I sometimes seek on my excursions aboard the Origin, though to a lesser extent. I was 5 pages in when the phone next to me began buzzing. The screen announced an unknown number. I hesitated, but picked it up. After a brief pause, a voice on the other end asked, "Mr. Gonzalez?"

"Yes, who am I speaking with?"

"This is Special Agent Crowson with FDLE. We have received some new information since we last spoke with you regarding the case. I need you to come down to my office and answer a few questions."

I gave it a good three second pause for effect and answered, "When would you like to do this?"

"As soon as possible," he replied. "You can come here or I can send a unit to come pick you up. I have your address listed as an East Hill location on Gonzalez Street."

"That's right, but I'm not home at the moment."

"Ok, well, I need you here today."

I chuckled to myself, not surprised he didn't want to wait on me. I felt sure this resulted from Steve's drunken tirade on the way to jail. Unless he had something new I didn't know about. This guy had to check the box and put some pressure on me, maybe try to get me to change my story. If it was the latter, I had nothing to hide.

"Well, I need to finish a few things up here. Give me about an hour and I'll be there."

"Alright he replied, do you know where we're located?"

"Yes. Up on Palafox, right?"

"Yes, that's correct."

I took my time and buttoned up the Origin, securing the lines before Trigger and I left.

I tried to soothe my nerves with some reggae on the drive over. What was this guy going to ask me? I felt sure that this resulted from Steve and the episode at Lost. He kept going at the station and tried to justify his actions. Though law enforcement doesn't have much sympathy for violent drunks, so I expected it to be dismissed. I tried to prepare myself for the questions and considered the routine. All the same questions I had been over when I got arrested. But did he have more? By the time I dropped Trigger at the house, it was 4:30 and time to call Analee.

She answered on the first ring, trying to catch her breath.

"Are you ok?"

"What me? Yes, I'm good. Just got to my car. I take the stairs instead of the elevator." She said.

"Ok, that explains it. I thought you may have finished a run or something."

"No, I'm just out of the office."

"Ok, well, if you don't have any plans, do you want to get together?" I asked.

"Sure, but I'm on call, so if someone dies, then that's it."

"Ok, how about I swing by your place and pick you up?"

"Better not. If I get a call, then I'll need to leave."

"Ok, well then, let's meet at the Oar House?"

"Alright, see you there about 5:30?" she said.

A smile came to my face," Ok, see you then."

I pulled up to the old building on the high end of Palafox. It was institutional, covered in brick and windows. Pine trees dotted the hill it sat on and a parking lot backed the building. I parked in the lot and as I approached the back doors, the cameras and security measures came into view. I pressed a button on the wall and said, "Ace Gonzalez here to see Special Agent Crowson." A couple seconds passed, and a loud buzzing came from the back door. It gave way, opening to a large hallway with an administrative desk at the end. Special Agent Crowson was waiting for me there. He had a file in his hand and didn't offer a handshake or a smile. The Special Agent led me to a room trimmed in old lacquered pine, with tile floors and an old steel table and chairs. He motioned for me to sit and said, "I'll be recording this for the file," and set a digital recorder on the table. He spoke toward the recorder and stated the date, time, case number, his name and my name.

"Mr. Gonzalez, I asked you here because we received some new information on the case and I need to ask you a couple of questions. It shouldn't take long."

I stopped him and said,

"Before we get into that, I'm curious about something. Last night I had an encounter with a man at my bar who got pretty drunk and we had to call for help because he got violent."

"He got hauled off to the drunk tank, but later I got word he was accusing me of being involved with this homicide."

"Is that why we're talking? I want to know if this meeting is because of some guy going off in a drunken tirade?"

He paused, as if annoyed by the question.

"Ok, let me start from the beginning of your question or statement, or whatever that was."

"I caught wind of this guy and the events leading up to his drunken accusations. This renewed our interest in you as a suspect."

He continued, "Regardless of that situation, we planned this anyway. We always conduct multiple interviews in a case like this and I always try to explore every possibility. The events leading up to the discovery of the body are what I want to hear from you."

He settled in and opened his notebook.

"Now that we got that out of the way, please proceed."

"Sure, well, we've been through all this already, but I spent that afternoon fishing in Big Lagoon. Besides my dog Trigger, I was alone. I caught a couple of fish and watched some weather move in. The wind picked up, and the bay got rough, so I packed it in and headed back to the marina. I'd say it was about 4 p.m. at that point. The tide had pulled me near the island. I smelled it before I saw it. The body I mean. I called it in and the person on the phone asked me to stay put, so I sat in the skiff and waited. I'd say maybe half an hour later, I noticed a deputy parked at the end of the empty lot by the marina. A little while later, I spotted the sheriff's center console headed my way, so I waved them in."

"They showed up with the crime scene and the Medical Examiner's people."

I noticed that throughout the story, Special Agent Crowson was making notes and nodding when he thought something was interesting.

"The investigators asked me some questions and let me go. That's all I have. There wasn't much to it."

"Ok, great, that was abbreviated." He continued to write. "I usually get more if I let you finish and then follow up with some questions. Do you mind if I run through a few here?"

"No, go for it."

"Ok, you mentioned you were out fishing. Is that something that you do often?"

"Oh, I do this most days when the tide is right."

"Ok, do you recall if anyone saw you leave the dock?"

"I don't think so. There are always people at the marina, but I didn't notice anyone. I can't be sure, though."

"Can you tell me what you were doing the night before?"

I stopped and considered what the previous night was like. "Well, I had the early out shift at The Lost Republic. It's out there on the Intracoastal, under the bridge to the Key."

He made some notes as I continued.

"It was pretty slow, so I worked until about 8:30 and since I was expecting to go fishing, I was outta there by 9. I keep my boat across the canal at Mile Marker 171 Marina so I didn't have far to go. I took the dog for a walk to check the wind and conditions in the bay and then I was on the boat the rest of the night, prepping for the next day."

"So you never left the marina after you got off work?" he asked.

"No, I was there and went down early."

He continued, "Well, that helps with the investigation. There was a gap in my timeframe there and you filled it, although it would be nice to have someone to confirm."

Smiling, I said, "Yeah, I don't have that."

He shuffled some of his papers and read through his notes as he clicked his pen.

He reached back into the folder and pulled out a couple of receipts. They were from Lost, covering a couple of nights the week following the meeting. "Can you explain these? We pulled them from the victim's apartment. He liked the place."

I took a moment and examined the receipts. They were all from Lost at random dates from the last few weeks. He did like the place. For a moment, I thought maybe I had met him, but it was possible he never made it to the bar or came in when I was working. It wasn't enough to go on for these guys. I know he wanted my reaction more than anything.

After a few drawn out minutes, I continued, "If he was there, I never met the man, nor did I speak to him. He could have easily been there while I was working. He must have sat at a table or something." I read over the receipts to see if it was a night I was working. "It's impossible for me to remember every person who walks in the door."

He stared me down for a prolonged moment, trying to read me. Then he stopped, gathered the papers and shifted them back to the file.

"Alright. I have your number, so if anything else comes up, then I'll call you." He said.

I finished my coffee and stood. "I've got a question for you, out of curiosity. Do you have any credible leads? I want to know since I know I didn't do it. That means there's someone out there, still on the loose."

He smiled and said, "I can't discuss those details with you at this moment. I have other individuals I've got to interview regarding this case, but that's all I can state at this moment. I appreciate your time and the accommodation on such short notice."

It was still about half an hour before I was going to meet Analee, so I had some time to cover what I learned from the interview. The Special agent did not appear to have other leads, or if he did, it wasn't coming out at all. Knowing what I knew about the dead guy, there wasn't much to go on. Anyone he knew here was probably involved in his death, so they weren't talking. My old truck shuddered to life and then leveled out to a low purr. I headed towards the Bayou.

The Oar House was on the edge of the old causeway. This was the original path before the main road was redirected up and over the Bayou via the Barrancas Bridge. The restaurant was little more than a large palapa over a glorified deck that was all open-air. It was a great place on the bayou to have a few drinks or grab a sandwich. There was a volleyball court and slips for the neighboring marina guests used by transient vessels. The Bayou is one of the most polluted waterways in Northwest Florida and even the State. The history of industrial development on the Bayou has led to a decline in water quality and diversity of marine life over the last several decades. Industry is still a heavy presence here on the Bayou. The location of rail and marine-based shipping was an advantage for any large-scale business to locate here so many years ago. Much of the shipping operations are now based out of the port. The Bayou itself is the subject of a pending large-scale contaminate cleanup that has the hopes of removing much of the deposited pollution in the bayou's bottom and also improving the water quality hoping to restore some habitat and encouraging the marine life to move back in. The plan is ambitious, and the community is behind it, along with a great effort by the county. If successful, the Bayou could again be a vibrant waterfront community.

I walked through the gravel parking lot and stopped to admire the boats in the marina. There was an open table near the windows on the water. On the Bayou, kayakers from the rental business across the way dotted the channel. A few small fishing boats motored to and from their slips and several pilings emerging from the water had large brown pelicans perched atop, watching each vessel passing. I noticed Analee had walked in and was talking to the bartender at the outside bar. Soon after she stopped, two more servers were there in the conversation. She saw me and headed my way.

"Hi sorry, I was catching up with some old friends. I used to work here throughout college, and this is where I met my friend, Leah."

"Oh right! I remember her telling me she used to work here. I thought this might be a good spot to catch up, and the weather is about right."

She smiled, "it is getting pretty nice. Even if it's a little cool, the deck is perfect."

After a moment, I said, "So you used to be a server here, huh?"

"Yep, back in the day. It was a ton of fun, but I realized I needed to focus on other things like life, and once I got the internship, I went to part time and eventually walked away. It was so distracting from what I was trying to do. I found something I was good at and the restaurant gig was not doing me any favors with sleep and focus."

"I get it. I struggle with that sometimes too, but I have a lot of freedom where I work, so I try to keep things in perspective."

We ordered a couple of beers and fish sandwiches. She sat across the table from me and took small sips from her beer while smiling, though her eyes stayed focused on me. I could tell she was happy I had asked her to get together. It had been a long time since I had been in that situation. She must have sensed my awkwardness and said, "Ok, so changing the subject, tell me about your boat?"

I laughed and said, "Ok, well, I have the Origin, which is a trawler or cruiser, whatever you want to call it. Then I have the skiff that I use for fishing. They are both down at Mile Marker 171 Marina on the intra-coastal. I spend most of my time there, but also because I work at The Lost Republic. It's across the canal from my boat. It's the perfect spot to watch the sunset."

"Well, let's go."

"Great, I'll tab out here and maybe we can catch the sunset."

I paid the tab and after she said goodbye to the staff; she followed behind me on Old Gulf Beach Highway. We crossed the bridge as the sun was about right for a quick trip on the skiff out to the four sisters islands for sunset. We parked in the gravel lot behind the marina and Trigger raced to the dock, seemingly aware of the plan. I gave her a quick tour of the Origin and we grabbed a couple of drinks and boarded the skiff. Trigger held his spot on the bow as we eased through the no-wake zone west towards the islands. In the distance, an empty barge riding high in the water was motoring along. The sky turned a peach-colored marble and contrails cut the blue-sky haze. The sky and sun reflected on the water. A string of gulls cut a path above the surface of the water through the canal to the west. I beached the skiff on the third island and roped off to a pine tree. Trigger was off chasing gulls, and Analee grabbed the oversized beach towel and laid it out on a dry spot.

"It should be a nice one today," I said as I gave the skiff another push from the stern.

I sat down beside her and rattled the ice in my drink.

"Alright, so tell me more about you and something no one else knows."

She laughed. "Pretty direct, huh?"

Then she added, "Well, I grew up down the road from Lost. I still have a lot of family out here."

"My grandmother lived on the point for 80 years and raised a bunch of kids there. We lived down the road towards the narrows and went to school out here growing up."

Surprised, I said "Wow, and we didn't meet until now. I spent some time out here when I was a kid, but I spent most of my younger years split between Tennessee and Pensacola."

"I guess it was time for us to meet," I said.

"I'm sure we were both busy with other things, anyway," she said

I turned to see the sun dipping below the horizon and the color show in the sky growing more intense.

"So, you studied in North Carolina?" I asked.

"Yes, and down in Gainesville, too. I got my undergrad at NC State and then my masters at UF. I never got much into the college scene. I kept focused on my classes. It was easier to do that than party my days away."

I smiled. "Well, I sure had some fun, especially down in the Keys. It's a way of life down there and when you're immersed in it, there is only one response."

"I can imagine being there and living on a boat. It must have been an experience," she said.

Laughing, I said, "It was, but somehow I kept it all together."

That drew a laugh out of her, and we paused and admired the sunset. Trigger joined us, caked and matted with sand, tongue dangling from his sandy jowls turned up in a smile.

I leaned back and enjoyed the moment.

Years back, I learned that stopping to recognize the end of another day is necessary to appreciate the complexities of life. The world never stops moving, but we all can be grateful for the time we have. This was an exercise in being thankful for the days we get on earth. Another day on this trip around the sun.

We stayed in that position for a while longer without talking, just taking it all in. I thought about the situation I was in with the floater, the development project I was rallying against, and the cruise I was planning after the decision on the development was final. I would repeat this sunset ritual on some unfamiliar beach or body of water with only my dog to talk to and a similar picture in the sky.

She was silent as well, and I could only guess at what was running through her mind. She was sitting on an island with a murder suspect she had only just met. There was a distinct feeling here, though. We weren't sitting through that awkward silence. It was comfortable. I felt the attraction and watched the sun cast golden shades across her face as I felt the urge to lean in and kiss her. She turned to face me and as I leaned in, Trigger inched his way towards her and nuzzled her hand. She laughed and said, "perfect timing buddy," shaking her head as she scratched his head and brushed away the sand on his snout. "Yeah buddy, perfect timing."

When the last light of the sun had faded from the western sky and the lavender color in the east was a dark violet, we made our way back towards the Origin and stopped at Lost.

We tied off in my usual spot and grabbed a couple of stools at the bar. It was quiet, and a cool breeze moved through the place.

As we sat down, Britt dropped a couple of drinks at the service well and shot me a smile. "Hey, what's happening?" she asked as she introduced herself to Analee.

"We caught the sunset on the islands," I said. "Can we get a couple of mojitos? And we'll have some food too."

"You got it. I bet that sunset was nice out there," Britt said as she made the drinks.

"Yep, perfect," I said. Analee agreed and sipped the mojito.

"We needed to get out. How has your night been so far?" I asked.

"All good man, nothing exciting, yet."

"Good. I was hoping for mellow when we pulled up," I said.

I noticed a local County Commissioner sitting across the way, talking with his assistant, who also had aspirations of being a politician.

They both gave the wave, and I fired back with an abbreviated salute and a smile.

Analee said she needed to find the ladies' room and, as she got up, the Commissioner gave me a wave over, motioning to the barstool beside him.

I obliged and leaned over the stool, not wanting to give the idea that I was staying.

"Ace, it's good to see you," he said. "We stopped by, hoping to catch you, but really needed an excuse to get a drink."

He took another sip from his drink and then asked, "How are things going?"

"Ah, not too bad. I'm here with a friend and grabbing a bite and a drink. Could be worse, right?"

"You got that right," he said.

His brow wrinkled. "Do I recognize her from somewhere?"

"Maybe so. She works for the M. E. Here." His mind seemed to acknowledge the connection.

"Oh ok, good work my boy. Get one with brains. She'll steer you in the right direction every time," he said.

My eyes shifted to his assistant, who was silent and remained that way.

"Ace, I wanted to let you know I think the Emerald Oasis Towers project coming up for approval is going to get voted down."

"Because of the work you and your local coalition of folks have been putting in. I think you've sold us on the downsides vs. the benefits of the whole thing. We are going to spend some lobbying dollars to help get the property annexed to the state so that it will be conservation land and not a resort, of which I am not opposed to. I think there are better ways to do it."

The assistant nodded in agreement.

I returned the nod and said. "I appreciate your efforts on this, and I'm sure you put some work in on the commission getting the tide to turn." He smiled and took a healthy pull off his drink as if to say you're welcome.

I continued. "Everyone is excited about any development, especially on the beach, what with tax revenues and all."

"Well, it wasn't an easy sell, but since it was in my district and it wasn't part of the approved master plan, I think it's something they can get behind, even if it means lost tax revenue."

"There was an excellent case from the developers for the project and when questioned about the wildlife and critical habitat, they gave us a general not much to worry about response."

"Because of your reports, we knew that was not the case, so there was some cause for concern there."

"Which, if you have some time in the next few days, I would like to get out there with you and put my eyes on it, to see what will extend the national seashore lands one day."

"I've seen it from the road before, but I have not walked it."

" Sure, I can find the time. I'll contact your office and get on your schedule," I said.

He took another pull off his drink and said, "I see your dinner companion has returned, so I won't keep you."

I shook his hand. "Likewise, sir." I gave his assistant half a smile and took my seat next to Analee. "Always working, huh"?

"Yeah, I guess. He wanted to chat real quick about the development project that I'm fighting over here on the Key. It's a monstrosity in so many ways and it looks like my efforts paid off. He says they are likely to vote it down, but I won't believe it until it happens. There's too much at stake with tax revenues and who knows what else the developers are promising."

She looked quizzically at me. "Looks like you've got the politicians' ear, so you must know what you're talking about."

"The property speaks for itself. I have to show the right people the value. I've been working with the National Park Director here as well, but the asking price was too high for them to get the land. It may work out if the development gets voted down, then the asking price may drop to within the government's range. That's a best-case scenario, assuming they put it up for sale. Anyway, you can read about it all in the Lost Key Newspaper pretty soon, so we don't need to get caught up in all this."

"The paper is covering it?" she asked.

I smiled. "Well, sort of. I write some small opinion pieces for the paper."

"I believe we should all be aware of what is going on here and if it continues like this, then the northern Gulf coast will resemble South Florida pretty quickly. I try to be the voice for the voiceless."

I took a drink from the cocktail in front of me and, about that time, Britt brought over our food. "We'll need some hot sauce too, please."

"Got it." Replied Britt.

We both devoured the food and drinks and after a few minutes of the local acoustic minstrel, we paid out and eased across the canal to the Origin.

"That's a great place. I see why you like it so much," she said.

"Yep, it's a pretty unique spot. When you walk in, you're in a different world. I felt it in a few other places and I guess that's why the place resonates with me so much."

"At the time I didn't realize it and maybe you never do when you're in it, but I was that person then too. I had other things in front of me. There are special places and moments in time that define a place or even an era. The great ones write about it, and sing about it. Those moments happen in places like this."

That garnered a laugh, and she steadied herself as we navigated the brief stretch of the canal to the marina.

We made it to the Origin, and she helped me tie off to the stern and face the bow to the tide. The clear, cloudless night gave a perfect vantage point for the moonrise.

"I'm going to grab one more drink to finish the night. Can I get you one?"

She hesitated, then said, "Sure."

"Is rum ok?"

She returned a smile and said, "make it a small one."

We made our way up to the flybridge, and I pulled back the canopy so we could see the sky. A glow shone to the east and far off to the west another.

"It's pretty clear from here that's the light from Pensacola and over there from Mobile. Light pollution, huh? No wonder the turtles get confused," I said.

"That's a thing?" she asked.

"Yes, sometimes the hatchlings go the wrong direction. If it weren't for the volunteers on the beach, they would never make it."

"Wow, that's sad." She said.

"Human intervention whatever way it comes, right?" I said.

I noticed a couple of falling stars while we sat in silence for the next few minutes, our heads angled up to the heavens.

After a moment she said, "Alright you've gotten the quick and dirty on me, so tell me about you."

"Alright," I paused and took a sip from my glass. "I spent most of my childhood in Tennessee with summers here fishing and running around in the woods. When I was sixteen, I moved here. Later, I moved to the Keys to study marine biology and find a job on a dive boat or research vessel."

"So I get there and work through a couple of years in school and decide that I want to focus on conservation, so I do some research and find a school out in northern California that specializes in that and pick up and move that way. Turns out I love the Gulf and I came back here to finish my education. After I got out of school, I worked for a couple of state agencies and I guess I got disenchanted with the lackadaisical way of doing things there, so I focused on bartending, which I had been doing all along. The more I watched the place grow, the more I thought I needed to be more in tune with what's going on. That's when I started getting active in the community and going to public meetings, reaching out to politicians and developers and making sure that the public has some knowledge of what's going on in their natural world. I also like to fish, a lot. That wasn't too long, was it?"

Laughing, she said. "No, it was good. Now I know you're not a serial killer."

She added, "I noticed there was no mention of a woman."

I said, "No, I was in a relationship for a good while and things didn't work out. Not much else to say."

I asked, "What about you?"

She hesitated. "My history," she deflated. "It's complicated, and I'm not quite ready to let you in on that."

"Ok, fair enough. I'm sure it'll come out with time."

By this time it had gotten late and the moon was much further to the west. There was a slight north wind, and it raised the goosebumps on my arms.

The temperature had dropped, and a breeze picked up. She gave a slight shudder, and I knew it was time to head in. "It got cold pretty quick, didn't it? Let's move down to the lounge and out of the wind. Are you up for another drink?"

"I may have had enough already," she said.

"Alright, well, I'll dial up a movie and we can kick back for a while until you feel like driving home."

She yawned, "Ok, sounds good."

I rustled through my DVD collection and found a good Bogart flick called Key Largo.

She sank into the built-in sofa and kicked her legs up on the table. Trigger eased in under her legs and I sat beside her and wrapped up in a blanket. A wake in the canal bounced off the hull of the boat, causing it to rock. The only remaining light was the television and the moonlight beaming down on the deck outside. The movie began with that familiar scene of the bus racing down the bridges. "You know that's the only scene that was filmed in the Keys?" I said.

"The rest was in a studio in Hollywood," she replied with a hum and another yawn.

A few minutes later, she made a light purring sound, and I was out before Humphrey Bogart met Lauren Bacall.

CHAPTER TEN

The next morning I woke to Trigger stretching out on the cabin floor. I wrenched myself from the sofa, careful not to wake my companion. A crack in the door and he was out. I stood there trying to stretch my neck and work the kinks out. She stirred when I opened the door, straightened up and asked for the time. The clock above the navigation table read a few minutes after five. After a good stretch by the light of the TV screen, she got up and grabbed her things.

"I've got to go. Thanks for a great night and not taking advantage of me." Managing a sleepy smile, she said, "It would have been easy."

I returned the smile, kicking myself for not stealing that goodnight kiss. She leaned in, gave me a hug and a light kiss on the cheek.

"Maybe we can get together again soon?" I asked.

As she was sliding out the door of the salon, she said, "Call me. I'll be around."

I tried to mute my smile, but the result was a goofy grin.

A second later she was on the dock, moving through the scattered circles of the orange lighting. I watched her walking, and she reminded me of a gymnast. When is too early to call? I thought.

After checking the tides, Trigger and I took the skiff out before the sunrise. A shallow inlet off the lagoon held some emergent vegetation and, usually, some fish. It was a productive spot when conditions were right. I came to the cut at the inlet and I didn't have enough water to get the skiff in. I beached the skiff and grabbed my 8-weight sage, a fly box and hemostats, and waded in. After the exchange with Analee, I was still flying high. I kept thinking about the next time we would meet. After a few minutes of wading, I noticed the motion of water and tailing near the marsh grass on the southwest end of the inlet. The fly landed and descended below the surface, only inches from the fish.

In the next instant, the fly disappeared, and the line was tight. I strip-set the hook, and the redfish went nose down into the grass; I had to step high towards the fight to keep the line high. A trail of mud followed the fish as it made its last efforts to escape. I took a knee, tucked my rod under my arm, and retrieved my hemostats for release. As I moved the fish back and forth, forcing water through the gills, a salty wind picked up from the southwest. The sun warmed my back as it rose higher. I closed my eyes and took a deep breath, tasting the salt and the sweet smell of the rosemary and dune grass. The surf was crashing on the other side of the island. This was the moment I needed when I left the dock.

I thought about all the people only a short distance away who don't get the chance to experience this while living moments from the coast. Caught up in the same thing every day with no idea of what the natural world can provide. A dose of this each day might be the cure for anything. It certainly couldn't hurt. Instead, they go on never knowing this wind or the mud and sand under their feet. A lost way to live in view of the American sea.

I eased the skiff back through the lagoon towards the Key, following the shoreline. The grass beds were in great shape and had grown since last season.

The developers proposed to locate the marina on the bay side of Emerald Oasis Towers. Seagrass was thick here and baitfish shimmered below the surface as I approached. The development plan was to install a large marina with 100 slips to accommodate the vessels of all the new condominium owners. They would have to dredge and would need to remove most of the seagrass in the otherwise untouched area of the bay. They would remove and transplant the grass to another area that had some decline of grasses. In this scenario, they were not destroying the grass beds, but moving them to an area that needed them. They claimed the permits were pending, waiting for environmental reports confirming this would be beneficial to the aquatic environment in Big Lagoon. I was skeptical.

Back aboard the Origin, I sat at the navigation table, which doubles as my desk. After recording the location of the fish on the chart and in my log, I ran down some emails. One of them was a notification: the commission meeting to hear the Emerald Oasis Towers project. I made a note to call the commissioner's office and get that on-site meeting scheduled sooner than later.

I picked up my notes and under them lay another chart, this one covering my roughly charted course east towards the Forgotten Coast. A large development was in the works, and it was affecting much of a unique estuary. My plan was to pull the skiff behind me and get some time to fish the area, do some recon on the site and get the feeling from the public. Then my phone buzzed. An unknown number showed on the screen. I answered, and it was quiet. As I listened, a low breathing came through.

"Hello," I said. "Hello?" No response. I kept listening, only the breathing, and what sounded like a drag and long exhale on a cigarette followed.

"Hello? Who is this?" A second passed and then nothing; call ended flashed across the screen.

Later that afternoon, I was sitting at the chart table writing when I felt the Origin shift and that familiar toss when someone stepped aboard. I came out of the lounge and Analee was standing there with Trigger by her side. She wore her hair in a ponytail and a pair of dark tortoise rimmed glasses, a darker mustard colored t-shirt and a pair of jeans that fit her curves. She kicked her flip-flops off and, after a smile, gave me a hug. Her expression changed and she took my hand as she spoke.

"I came here because I have to tell you something. It's kind of my history and I think you need to hear it so you know what you're in for." I stopped for a moment, considering what I had gotten myself into.

I scratched my head and said, "Ok, do you want a drink or something?"

"No, can we sit and talk?" she asked.

Her expression was worried but calm. We sat on the stern, our backs to the canal and the passing boats.

She crossed her arms, seeming to hold herself as she spoke. "I need you to know why I've been distant since we met, and it has nothing to do with you being a suspect in a murder case. Yesterday when we watched the sunset, it was the best day I have had in a long time."

Smiling, I said, "I would have to agree with you."

She said, "I have a boyfriend. Sort of, I recently broke things off with him." There was a silence as she let it sink in. "He's in Chipley."

"Ok, so he lives there and you see him sometimes?" I asked.

Her face changed to worry. "Kind of. He's in the prison there."

"Oh, I didn't expect that."

There was an awkward smile and then she said, "Yesterday morning when I left so early, I went to visit him. I thought about it, but got up and left because I couldn't decide. He's in for another four years at this point. I go to see him sometimes and he sends me letters, but that's what our relationship is now." She stopped again and stared into nothing.

"Ok." I hesitated for a few seconds, considering what this meant for the two of us. Then a thought occurred to me, "Do I need to know why he's in? " I asked.

"He doesn't know about you and I'm telling you this because I feel like there's something bigger between you and me and I need you to know my story so you can decide about continuing this or walking away—"

I stopped her. "This changes nothing for me. This is more than a friendship."

She smiled. Then let out a breath. "Ok, I feel better."

I was curious about the circumstances. "Can you tell me more? What is he in for?"

"Well, he's in for manslaughter. But violation of probation. I guess I'll start from the beginning."

"We were on the beach one night with a couple of friends and we had been drinking. He and I were walking to our car when a couple of guys tried to rob us. He fought back, and he punched one of them in the face. It didn't even seem that bad, but it knocked the guy out and when he fell, he cracked his head on one of those parking curbs next to our car. I still remember the sound of it, like a melon dropped on concrete. The other guy took off and then there was all this blood. I called the cops, and they sent an ambulance, but later I found out the guy got a brain bleed and died. He got charged with involuntary manslaughter and the family of the guy he hit sued him because he had been drinking. The jury decided he was guilty." Her jaw tightened and tears streamed down her face. She wiped them away and then balled her fists. Stopping, she closed her eyes and caught her breath. "The judge assigned him some jail time, alcohol counseling, and gave him probation. He was supposed to stay off the booze and go to the classes while he was on probation." She cleared her throat and swallowed, then said, "and he did that to begin with, but the whole thing got to him and he started drinking again, behind my back." She paused and caught her breath again. "It got pretty bad. He failed multiple breath tests and his probation officer had to report him. At that point, he kept drinking and fell into this bender since he knew he was going in. I couldn't believe he would give up like that."

She wiped the tears again. "It didn't go well when he fought it in court. He went in about a year ago and now our relationship has been reduced to periodic visits and letters." I handed her my handkerchief from my back pocket and she used it, taking a moment to straighten up.

Tears continued running down her cheeks from under the sunglasses.

She stopped and said, "Please don't get this wrong. I'm not trying to scare you away. I want to be clear. A couple of months ago, I decided it wasn't realistic for me to put my life on hold for him. That's why I told him I couldn't do it anymore. It's also why I'm drawn to you, because everything is so easy. I feel different when we're together. It all sounds so surreal when I say it out loud. It's some alternate reality that I've made for myself." I saw the tears welling up, "You can walk away, I wouldn't blame you. I'm here because I think there is something between us that's more than a casual thing."

I reached for her hand. "We all have some story to tell. I don't expect a commitment from you right away." I said.

"It's been a long time since I've been in any kind of relationship. My last attempt scarred me for life. After that, I thought I would hold back for a while and focus on myself. I'm far from perfect and I don't expect you to be. Let's take it as it comes." I said.

I could see the tension fall away. She gave me a smile and said, "I feel better."

We embraced for a prolonged moment and my nose settled in her ponytail. Her hug was strong, and she smelled incredible, and I wanted to hold that moment for the rest of the day.

We both noticed the buzzing from her phone.

She answered and said, "Medical Examiner's office, this is Analee." She stopped and pointed to the dock and stepped off the boat, talking low and strolling towards the marina store.

A minute later, she was back. "I have to go."

"It's a Special Agent with FDLE and he's asking some questions about your case. "

"My case?"

"Well, the floater case over here. I've got to meet him at the office and go over the file with him. He wants to discuss the cause of death with the Doc."

"Can't he read the report?" I asked.

"He could, yes, but I think he needs some clarification on a few things. It happens all the time. An Agent wants all the information they can get, and a small percentage want to know the details on how we determine the cause and manner."

"Ok, well, maybe we can catch up later?"

"I'll call you when I'm done and see what you're up to." She leaned over the dock as I stood on the stern of the Origin and gave me another hug, this time with a kiss, as she grabbed my shirt and pulled me closer. Our eyes met as she rested her forehead on mine.

CHAPTER ELEVEN

Later that night, I worked the late shift at Lost. Despite the busy night, I couldn't get over the fact that this woman I was interested in was also part of a murder investigation and I may be the prime suspect. At a certain point, I got lost in the work and once I got in the weeds; I had no time to consider the reality of the murder investigation. This was the beauty of working in this industry. No matter the day's events before coming in for my shift, when it got busy, I could get lost in the moment and forget anything that might have been on my mind.

The bartender aspect is but a small part of the job. I was many people to the customers; some nights, I serve as a marriage counselor, others a spiritual guide, a tour guide, a historian, a film critic or aficionado, an expert in the opposite sex, a connection to local events and meetings, and sometimes, a politician.

Britt and I were wrapping up the closing side work and locking things down when I checked my phone. I had one text from Analee that read "call me". I stepped out onto the dock and dialed her up. She answered on the second ring.

"Hey are you ok?" I asked.

"Yes, I'm fine," she answered. "I need to talk to you, and it needs to be face to face for this. Are you coming to town tonight?"

"I was planning on staying on the boat, but I can grab Trigger and head that way."

"Ok, that's best," she replied.

"I've got a little while longer here and then I'll head out."

"Ok, text me when you're leaving, please."

"Alright, see you soon."

Britt gave me a knowing smile.

I laughed. "Analee wants me to stay in town tonight so we can get together."

"Ok, well, that's promising, right? Is this a late night rendezvous?"

"I didn't get the feeling that's why she wanted me to come over, but who knows, maybe I didn't read it, right?"

She smiled, and we finished cleaning the place up.

I skipped the usual closing drink, considering the drive to town and an impending conversation of an unknown topic.

The drive was uneventful, and I cranked up the JJ Grey and Mofro and cued up Lochloosa while attempting to clear my mind of the jumbled mess of possibilities that had come up since she and I spoke. I rolled the windows down and the air rushed in and brought me back down to earth. As I crossed the Barrancas Bridge into town, I could smell the brine and the sea breeze in full force. I went straight to her house. It was a small two story old style craftsman cottage recently renovated. It had a weathered navy blue coat of paint with white trim and modern windows and doors. The yard had been landscaped and despite the late hour; the house was well lit, a welcoming sign.

When I pulled up, she met me at the door.

"Nice place. This is one of my favorite streets in East Hill," I said.

She smiled. "Yep, I like it because it's next to the park, and it's not too big."

I opened the French doors in the back and shuffled Trigger out into the backyard.

"It's fenced, so he's not going anywhere," she said.

She gave me a stiff hug, and after a brief hesitation, I returned the squeeze.

"Is everything ok?" I asked.

"Sorry if I came across a little intense. I met with the investigator working on the floater case earlier and I have some information that should clear you, or at least give you a solid alibi. I've been trying to figure out how to tell you without compromising the code of ethics I have to operate under, but still get the message across. The best way to approach it is to tell you to get your story straight the couple of days before you found him. If you have a solid alibi with witnesses to corroborate, then you've got nothing to worry about, even though some drunk sang you were involved."

I had already covered that with the Special Agent, but now I stopped and considered what that meant; where was I? I put it all together and she watched, as I thought it over.

"Ok, I think I've got it covered," I said.

"That's all I can say. Be prepared to go back a little further than a day. You can expect a call to confirm all this."

I heard a noise and turned to see Trigger scratching at the back door. She reached to open the door, and he trotted past us both and assumed his spot on the couch as he had on the Origin so many times before.

I smiled and said, "He's ready for bed."

She yawned and said, "Me too. You can stay here if you like. I don't mind." She nestled herself into a hug, her head on my chest.

"Ok, could I borrow a shower?"

"Borrow?" She laughed. "Sure, go ahead. Towels are in the closet and everything else should be there as well."

"I think I have a pair of clean board shorts in the truck. I'll be right back."

When I came back in, she was getting the coffee ready for the morning and had set out two cups next to the pot. I caught a glance from her and I went in for a kiss on the cheek as her head turned in time for the real thing. It caught me unprepared, but also made me wonder what might happen after the shower.

The shower was necessary. I still had the smell of bar and fried food on me from Lost and a layer of salt from the air off the Gulf.

After the shower, I opened the door to find her laid out on the bed, her back to me. A triangular sliver of light shone on her rump as I opened the door into the darkened bedroom. I could see the rhythmic breathing of sleep as she lay there. I eased in behind her, the big spoon, and soon after I had shaken the day, I was asleep and dreaming of the incoming tide on the grass flats.

I woke up in the morning right at sunrise. I eased out of the bed, careful not to wake her, and made it downstairs to the coffeepot. She must have set the timer, as the pot was hot and full when I checked. I poured a cup and opened the front blinds. The live oaks across the street hung down low over the sidewalks in the park. Orange lights were ghostly orbs through the early morning fog. There were photos on the bookshelf of her with what looked to be her grandmother, some of her with an older man standing in front of a small airplane, and several others of her with a group of ladies; even more still of her with one guy. I assumed this was the ex-boyfriend. I thought about his reaction. If he knew I had slept in the same bed with her last night; although nothing happened, it would still be a hard one to swallow. There was a rustle behind me and she hit the bottom of the steps, came over and gave me a long hug. Her hair smelled like lavender and honeysuckle and was still strewn about her head.

"Good morning," I said.

She returned the welcome with a yawn.

"Sleep well?" I asked.

In a foggy response, she said, "I haven't slept that good in a while. It's the first time I've had someone in the house in a year at least."

I poured a cup for her and slid it in her direction.

"I'm glad you came over last night. I hope I didn't worry you too much."

"No, I'm glad I did," I replied. "I appreciate the warning. I'll expect a call from the investigator."

She sipped her coffee and paused for a moment, her eyes still closed. The sleep was still hanging on. She took another sip and said, "I have to get ready for work. Stay as long as you like."

"Ok," I replied. "I'll enjoy the coffee for now."

As she was climbing the stairs, she said, "Make yourself at home."

I sat on the couch and picked up a copy of "Flying" magazine and thumbed through it. Trigger had risen when she came downstairs and was scratching at the back door again, requesting entry. We both found ourselves on the couch and a few minutes later, she was in the living room with her gear like the first time I met her; boots, BDUs, and a shirt labeled with her title. There was little if any makeup on her face and the black-rimmed glasses and a loose braid rounded out the effortless style. She needed little to get moving, and she knew it. For a moment, I thought to myself, she was out of my league.

I shook that thought, turned up my cup, drained the dregs, and said, "Thanks for the warm bed to sleep in last night."

I smiled, and she returned it.

"I'm glad you stayed," she said.

"I am too, though I have to admit I was a little sketched out by the late invite. I guess unsure of the intent, but it came together."

I gave her a hug, and we both walked out together.

"Is it alright if I call you later? I work at Ozone tonight and I have a few things to take care of today in town."

"Sure, I have a run this afternoon, but that's it after work," she replied.

I bent to give her a kiss, and she leaned in, so I wrapped my free arm around her. It was a good sendoff for the day.

I headed to the Gonzalez Street house and grabbed a coffee and biscuit at the corner store. The oaks and the palms were perking up, signaling the coming heat of the day. It was still early, so Trigger and I went for a quick run before the humidity set in. A good sweat and some air helped clear my head as I attempted to run through my story and plan my alibi. As we turned onto Gonzalez, a car headed in our direction. It slowed about 50 yards away, right in front of my house, and then continued towards me. We passed the car and Steve, the drunken real estate investor, glared at me. Our eyes met, and he continued, not slowing at all.

Immediately, I went on the defensive. My grip tightened on Trigger's leash and my free hand went to my hip, where my blade was clipped.

He must have seen my truck parked out front, but I kept running and made another lap around the block. I cut through some yards behind my house and used the back gate. My keys hit the ground as I fumbled with the door handle, then checked the street. No sign of the car or the drunk. How had he found me? I checked all the locks and made sure the Glock was at arm's reach, then I grabbed a shower. My next move was to get out of the house and redirect this guy's attention. After I cleaned up, I went to the county offices to catch one of the other commissioners to gauge his vote on the Emerald Oasis Towers Project. It was coming up, and I had only an idea of one vote, though that vote might sway most of the others. After checking for the blue Cadillac on the road, I headed downtown. The county commissioners' offices were downtown in the old courthouse building. I didn't have an appointment, but they took walk-ins if they were available. I parked in the four-story parking garage and tucked the pistol under the seat, knowing I couldn't get past the metal detectors. The offices were on the third floor, and I approached the front desk receptionist and announced my intent with a smile.

A woman nearing retirement returned the smile. The nameplate on her desk read 'Mrs. Handy'. She said, "Yes, I know who you are."

Surprised, I said, "Ok well nice to meet you. Have we met before?"

"No, but I know that you're the local guy who fights for the animals and the fish, right?"

I laughed to myself and said, "Yes ma'am, that's right, only part of the story though."

"Well, I like what you do," she said. "They have no voice and you're doing the right thing."

About that time, Commissioner Riggs rounded the corner from the elevators and I caught up to him.

"Commissioner, I'd like to speak with you if you have a few minutes?"

He continued to walk to his office.

"Mr. Gonzalez, what is it you need to speak with me about?"

"I'm sure you know the Emerald Oasis Towers Project is coming up for approval."

"Yes, I'm aware," he said. He paused before he entered his office.

It was clear I wasn't getting in this morning.

"Mr. Gonzalez, I know your message and I understand the intent here. However, I have found little that I don't like about the project. As you know, it has moved through the review process with planning and zoning and the board rarely goes against their decision. You still have a lot of work to do to convince me I shouldn't approve the project. And I don't appreciate you showing up here with these intentions and no appointment. I have the information you provided to the board, referring to the info packet I put together for staff on these projects. I have done my research here for my peace of mind. As you know, we are one of many approvals for this project."

By this point, I could see where he was headed, so I stopped and nodded my head to show my agreement to continue his explanation.

When he finished, I reached out for a handshake, thanking him for his time.

As he shut the door to his office, I thought to myself, that was the quickest meeting I've had with a commissioner.

On my way out, I slowed by the reception desk and Mrs. Handy smiled and said, "Don't stop what you're doing, son!"

"Thanks ma'am, I appreciate it. Enjoy your day."

On the way down the elevator, frustration set in. I couldn't blame the guy. He had the developers in his ear, and he had the budget in mind. The taxes on this property would be an enormous boon for the county and would bolster his budget in the long run. You can't fault a guy for trying, I thought.

CHAPTER TWELVE

I got back to the truck and tucked the Glock back on my strong side. There was a place I wanted to visit on the bayou. A patch of grass that was sometimes successful at the right tide and was an easy hike over graffiti bridge.

The tide was coming in, and the bayou may be productive. I parked at the 17th avenue train trestle, also known as graffiti bridge, and began the short hike over the bridge to the east side of the bayou. There was a trail that wound around the shoreline and at low tide, I could wade in and fish the marsh along the edges of the bayou while Trigger ran around the beach. I found a good cut in the vegetation along the reeds and settled into a thigh deep section of the bayou, careful not to submerge the pistol tucked into my waistband. I took aim at the far side of the marsh island and kept my eyes on the surface, searching for the telltale streak, telling me that a decent fish was working in the shallows for a meal. As I watched, my mind wandered to the Commissioner and the one-sided exchange we had. This may be the consensus for the board, with one or two others voting with Castle since the project was in his district. After about a half hour of wading and stopping, I called it. It was nearing midday and not much would happen until later that afternoon. I followed the goat trail back up to the train tracks and halfway over the trestle I noticed a familiar car parked amongst the boat trailers. I knew Steve had been watching me the entire time. His car was there, but he was nowhere to be seen.

I slowed my pace as I approached the end of the trestle and scanned. Nothing. Where was this guy hiding? I skidded down off the tracks and ended up below the bridge over the bayou. The breeze carried the smell of cigarette smoke, and I knew he was right behind me, standing under the bridge. He had waited until I passed overhead, not wanting to scare me off. I was holding my fly rod, which could provide some distance between the two of us if needed.

I said, "Why are you following me?" He said nothing, just stood there with an evil smile, chuffing his cigarette into a pointed glow of embers.

Through the smoke, I saw a grin. "I told you I was going to get you."

I could hear Trigger rustling around in the reeds by the beach, but he would not make it out in time to cause the distraction I needed. I suddenly became aware of the pistol on my waist.

"You got lucky last time, not now," he said.

By sidestepping, I had created some space between us and now I was prepared to sacrifice the nine-foot sage maverick if needed. It wasn't the best weapon; however, I was only going to draw the Glock if I had to.

"Hey man, I don't even know you or why you think I killed your friend. This is crazy," I said.

He took another drag and then flicked the butt in the sand at my feet, splashing embers across my legs. He closed the distance between us, swatting at the rod as I moved away.

He seemed to swell even larger as he psyched himself up and prepared to go into combat mode.

A couple of bystanders kicking around the water's edge noticed the confrontation and hurried away.

Steve's hulking, swollen presence was enough to sell his intent.

He was a few feet away now and the vein on his forehead was bulging to the point of rupture. I thought there may have been some other chemical influence at work to get him so excited.

Then, he turned towards the parking lot and seemed to deflate. I repositioned to keep him in my line of sight but also give me a scan of the parking lot.

A sheriff's deputy had pulled in and parked next to the boat ramp for no particular reason, but it was a welcome sight.

He snarled at me, "you lucky bastard, I should pound you anyway."

He continued, "He was my best friend, you son of a bitch, and I know you did it. Somehow you got to him." His eyes turned red and bulged out of his head, further enhancing the roadmap of blood vessels in his face. He tried to hold it back, but he broke down crying and dropped to his knees. For a moment, I felt sorry for him; if it was true, he had lost his best friend and still had no answers. He was trying his best to get those responsible and, unfortunately for me, that meant any means necessary. I kept my distance and watched him there for a moment, a grown man crying in the dirt.

I side stepped toward my truck and said, "I don't know why you think I had something to do with your friend's death, but it's not me. I didn't kill anyone." His bloodshot eyes seemed to pulse with his breathing.

He stared as I walked away and then I hesitated and said, "I'm gonna find out what happened to your friend. I'm being blamed for it and I'm not a murderer. But this doesn't change things with us. Don't follow me anymore and stay away from my fucking house," I said.

I didn't get a response, only a maniacal stare while he fished out another cigarette. When I got to the truck, I tossed my fishing gear in the back and Trigger loaded up. I made a mental note to text Hutch and let him know I had another encounter with Cadillac Steve.

I got back to the bungalow and hosed down the rod and set it out to dry. I hadn't lost this one to a maniac trying to kill me today. After opening my laptop, I contacted Commissioner Castle to set up a time to meet at the Emerald Oasis Towers site for the next day. Assuming he would take a while to get back with me, I went in early to work at the bar at Ozone, the local pub down the street. Trigger posted up outside and stood guard while I worked. The night was quiet, and business was steady, which kept my mind off most of the madness I had been dealing with. The bar business had peaked earlier in the night, and I was winding down when Elena walked through the door and sat down at the bar. I had not heard from her since she had been in last.

She was wearing a formfitting black cotton dress that showed off her curves; cut like a tank top and ending just below the knees. She covered her shoulders with a light denim jacket. Her cinnamon skin glistened, and she smelled of coconuts and some other sort of tropical scent. Her hair was up, and some strands fell down to the side. A gold necklace and a shell pendant fell between her cleavage. She overdressed for the establishment she had made her way into.

"Wow, what have you been up to?" I asked.

"Ugh, thank you. I just left a benefit for the Mayor. He's already campaigning to run again, and he asked if I would go with him. Since we supply most of the restaurants in town, I thought it would be a good idea to attend."

"So, how did that go?" I asked.

"It was the usual smiling, talking and dealing with old men who stare too much. I ended up being arm candy for him." She shivered and said, "I couldn't get out of there quick enough. How have you been?"

"I think crazy would be the right word to describe it." She stared back at me quizzically. "Where do I start? Well, I've been accused of murder, had my life threatened and nearly beaten, but you know, nothing I can't handle. Can I get you a drink?" She sat there, confused.

"Yes, rum please. You know what I like." When I returned with her drink, she was shifting in her chair and straightening her jacket. "What's been going on? What's this murder thing and why was your life threatened?"

I caught her up on my recent encounters with the developer's henchmen and the guy that wants to kill me. When I finished, she didn't act too surprised, which was odd to me. I didn't dwell on it as she went right into why she came to see me.

"Well, I'm here tonight because I want to get an update on the Emerald Oasis Towers Project." She took another sip of her drink and focused on me.

"Ok well, it's through development review and on the agenda for the next commission meeting. I'm still working on the commissioners to get an idea of their votes. Right now, it's a toss-up. There's too much at stake. Most of these guys only see jobs and tax revenue even though the higher paying jobs dry up pretty quick and most of what's left is catering to the service industry." I said.

She nodded. "I had the feeling that would be the biggest issue."

"It's hard to argue with them about that, too. They think they're doing the residents a favor by bringing in jobs for construction, but most of those are workers that come in from out of town and they send that money home. It's an ugly cycle and helping them to understand it is one of my biggest challenges. It's tough to argue the bed taxes too. If these towers are full even part of the year, revenues would be substantial. My angle is to have them weigh the loss of what's there to what we gain. To me, it's simple. We never get that back. That's a hard message since they'll be gone for the reality of it all. The wildlife might make a recovery, but when the last bird or fish is gone, we will ask ourselves, was it worth it?"

We both considered the reality of the situation.

The last customers were shuffling out and one server followed them, locked the door and turned off the "Open" sign.

Elena said, "I know you need to close. Can I stay and maybe we can talk more after you finish up?"

The servers were preparing to leave, and the kitchen manager stepped out and grabbed a couple of beers from the cooler.

Unsure of her motives, I said, "Sure, I don't have too much to do."

After I had wrapped up the closing duties, we stepped out into the night air and I locked up the building. It was a clear night, and the moon was bright overhead. The old stone building towered over us and the empty parking lot. One light cast a yellow glow over the end of the lot. I scanned the street and immediate area for threats, namely Steve the drunk. I reached around my side and tapped the Glock on my side as a reminder it was there. We sat down at the old church pew outside the building, and I felt the cool breeze from the north hit the ivy-covered walls of the old building, pushing down on us.

I could see by her expression she wanted to say something. "So, what else is on your mind?" I asked.

She took my hand and faced me. "You have been on my mind a lot lately. We have known each other for a long time and in my mind, I have always thought that we may one day connect on another level. The last few weeks that we have been working against this development have shown me more of you and who you are." She paused for a moment, and I thought of the woman I had been with only hours before who was already consuming my thoughts.

She continued, "I knew it was time to tell you how I feel and see if you might feel the same way. I am a complicated woman and I put up this shell all the time, projecting a tough exterior, but it's exhausting always doing this." Her grip tightened on my hand. "I need some companionship and I can feel this attraction to you I don't get with any other man. It's so strong that I can't ignore it."

She straightened up and said, "I also feel like we want the same things. We fight for the same things. We could be so much stronger together. I need someone that strengthens me so I can let my guard down sometimes."

I turned to face her as a car sped down Gonzalez Street; the lights streaking across our faces as it made the turn.

"I don't know what to say. You know my history and you know that work and my side projects have consumed most of my life over the past few years. I've kept my distance from any relationships for a while because I've had trouble getting over my past."

"Yes, and this is me hoping that you have come to a point now or soon that you can move on."

It was a welcome thought. I smiled and stared back into her eyes.

"There's something else. I met someone recently who I feel like there may be a future with. I'm not sure if it will go anywhere, but I wouldn't want to jeopardize that or the friendship that you and I have."

She reached for my hand, pulling me closer to her.

The breeze from the north continued, and she shivered. From where we were sitting, I could make out headlights from time to time heading south on 12th avenue, the street running perpendicular to my street, Gonzales. At one point, I thought I noticed the familiar silhouette and sound of the Caddy that Steve drove.

"I should get home," I said.

As she stood, gathering herself, she asked, "Would you mind if I came over? I don't want to be alone and it might give us some time to talk more."

I hesitated.

"Sure, that's fine, but be prepared. It's modest."

She smiled. "I'll drive." She motioned towards a blacked-out Mercedes sports car with the word 'EL' on the license plate.

I moved towards the sidewalk. "Why don't we walk? It's a couple of blocks, and I get to unwind after my shift. I'm a creature of habit, and this is one of my rituals."

She smiled. "Ok, sounds great." She nestled into my shoulder and took a firm grip on my arm as we walked under the moonlight. I kept scanning for the caddy, but no headlights during our walk.

We reached the bungalow; the thick vegetation and landscaping lights framed the gate to the pool deck and my one-room pool house. The reflection of the pool lights on the palm trees danced over the fence, the stars dotting the sky above. It was quiet, with no sign of any action or a visit from an unwanted henchman. I opened the gate and the smell of pool and tropical plants hit me. Mist was rising from the heated pool. Trigger greeted us as I turned to lock the gate. It was late and the renters in the main house had already retired for the night. I opened the French doors to the bungalow and dropped my gear on the sofa. Everything was as I had left it, so I didn't mention the maniac who was stalking me.

"Well, this is it."

She settled into the old chaise lounge that doubled as my couch. "I love it."

"I stay out here and rent the main house out to some bartenders that work downtown. It's a good setup for my lifestyle. When I work out at Lost, then I stay on my boat so I don't have to drive into town. It's me and Trigger, so we make out pretty good on the deal."

"I knew you went back and forth." She moved towards the pool and kicked off her sandals, testing the water.

"Would you like a drink?" I asked.

Smiling, she said, "Sure, a small one."

I stepped inside and grabbed a couple of lowballs, splashed some El Dorado and cut a key lime to squeeze. I shed my work shoes and pistol but kept it nearby.

When I came back out, she had found the hammock and was sitting in it like a chair swaying slowly, facing the stars. I joined her and enjoyed the warmth of the mist from the pool and the protection from the breeze the travelers' palms and key lime trees provided.

We spent the next half an hour talking in the hammock and pointing out constellations in the heavens. She disappeared inside and I found her passed out in my bed, Trigger asleep at her feet. I killed a bottle of water and took the empty side of the bed, pulling the covers over both of us.

I woke up the next morning before sunrise to a text from Elena.

It read, "No obligations, no pressure. When you're ready, let me know."

CHAPTER THIRTEEN

I took Trigger for a walk to sort out all the thoughts running through my head. The walk turned out to be a run. Trigger began pulling me, and I overtook him and made it about ten blocks before turning around and heading back. I was still trying to sort out the events over the last few hours; working on the plan for the rest of my day was as far as I got. The run helped me prioritize and sweat out some of the rum from the night before. My meeting with Commissioner Castle was mid-morning, so I had about two hours before I had to be on site. There was time to get cleaned up and head to the marina, check the lines on the Origin and the skiff before the meeting. I also considered the facts in front of me regarding the murder charge. The players seemed to be the same ones involved in the development I was fighting against. I knew there was more. I had to keep digging.

A stop at the marina and a few minutes later, I was on the seashore to meet with the Commissioner. My plan was to walk the site, give a brief history of the property and try to throw in all the reasons this is such a unique place and should extend the seashore and not another monstrosity on the beach. I got the feeling that he understood most of this, but I respected the need to see the property and confirm these things for himself.

He could also say when asked that he had been to the site and witnessed these things for himself. I parked on the main road off the shoulder in an area of gravel and oyster shells the public had been using for years to access the beach. On the other side of the construction fence, there was a goat trail framed by sea oats that wound over and through the dunes to the beach and the Gulf beyond. I was only a few minutes early and went north towards the lagoon. A sidestep around the construction fence, and I was about fifty yards inside the dune line when I crested a large dune and noticed a black SUV parked behind my truck. A man was out and standing next to the driver's side door talking on his phone; I recognized him to be Commissioner Castle. I headed back to rendezvous there, planning to backtrack when he and I continued.

"Good morning, sir," I said, disturbing him from his phone. "Solo trip for you today?" I asked.

"Yep, I asked my assistant to come along, but he had a meeting."

Smiling, I said, "Hey thanks for taking the time to come out here with me. I think you'll get a clearer picture of the property and better understand what it is we are trying to do here. I was heading north to the gopher burrows and to confirm the sea grasses along the shoreline. We can head that direction unless there's somewhere specific you'd like to begin."

Shaking his head, he said, "No, that sounds great. You are the tour guide here, so hit the chief points and I'll ask questions when necessary."

"Great, let's get moving. Don't mind the fence, it's only here for show," I said.

We skirted between two sections and followed the same path I had been on.

"Each time I'm here, I find something else that further reinforces our efforts here," I said.

We stuck to the saddles of the dunes and, about 100 yards in, we came across the first burrow. The apron was stark white sand with some darker material showing, likely as the tortoise moved nearer the water table. It spread out wide and there were fresh tracks going on.

"Well, this is a great example of one resident here. The Gopher Tortoise in this burrow, judging by the opening, is an adult and if we keep moving, there's more around here somewhere."

We eased over the next rise of the dune and a large diamondback rattler spotted us and moved towards another burrow.

We both froze and allowed the snake to move on.

"No worries. This time of year, they are just emerging, so they are still lethargic. There are several species of snake that share the burrows." I said.

"These guys don't run them out?" He asked.

"Not typically. There's room enough in there for both and there are more critters in there too. Provided the burrow doesn't get flooded, the rattler can stay in there all winter. These burrows move more horizontally into the dune instead of down since the water table is so high on these barrier islands. There are gophers all over the property."

By this time, the sun was high above, and scattered clouds dotted the sky. A breeze blew in off the Gulf and the sweet smell of beach rosemary and sand live oak dominated the landscape. We made our way to the shoreline, big lagoon and the seagrass beds where the marina would be.

Motioning to the lagoon, I said, "If this development moves forward, they are proposing to build a large marina

here and dredge most of this seagrass for access and suffi-
cient water depths."

"This is a great fishing spot now, but if that happens, it could
mean disaster for the recreational fisherman here in the lagoon."

"Do you think the State and the Feds would allow
that?" he asked.

Nodding, I said, "If the developers check all the boxes, then
they will issue the permits for the activity. It equates to more
time and more money, is all."

"These guys have deep pockets and the experience to get
it done," I said.

Just then, a school of mullet moved through the grass beds
and a glimmer of something larger came in pursuit. I pointed
to the ripples in the water. "These grasses are important to the
juvenile fish population. They grow up here and in the marsh-
es. These grasses also hold sediment in place and provide oxygen to the water. Losing this habitat would be devastating
to the lagoon."

I turned south into the breeze. "Let's head to the Gulf side.
We can take the long way round the outside of the fence to the
beach and then cut back in at the dune line." I said.

As we navigated the goat trail through the dunes, I said,
"One of the unique features of this side is the lake. These only
exist in a few places in the world. It's fed through groundwater
seepage, and it opens to the Gulf during storm events."

We walked from the beach, ducking under the fence at the
cut in the dunes where the two waterbodies meet. It was dry at
this point and as the lake came into view, the brown tea-colored water and the same sweet smell enveloped our senses.

Similar vegetation to the north side but with more unique
ground cover shrouded the paths. Coastal sand live oaks seemed

to hug the dune crests and mimic the contours formed from years of sea spray and winds. The dunes and the trees formed protected thickets taller than a man. They allowed for the water to remain flat while a steady wind blew in from the south. A layer of dark organic matter was visible at the bottom, along with a shimmer of fish in the deeper areas.

"This lake is the only one on this island like it. There are smaller pools on the north side of the road in the saddles of beach ridges. I've seen similar further east in neighboring counties, but not like this. The developers are planning to turn this into an amenity with the major development rising around it. Any alteration to the groundwater regime will affect this lake and pounding massive pilings into the ground and installing parking lots all around while not allowing the rainwater to percolate into the soil will disrupt the natural recharge cycle here. It's going to be a slippery slope if approved and could be impossible to undo once done."

His brow furrowed, a thoughtful expression on his face. "Sounds like it would spell bad news for this lake."

"I didn't even know it was here."

He added, "Tell me something, wouldn't this development have to adhere to all state requirements for stormwater treatment? It's not like they are going to be allowed to channel all the drainage to the lake unchecked, right?"

I replied, "That's correct. However, as I mentioned before, when you install foundations and level the dunes to build parking lots, it proves to be problematic for that rainwater to filter through the soil back into the ground."

"Ok, I understand. It's clear that this is a unique place, and you know it well."

"I was hoping my assistant could join us, but he had a prior engagement. He mentioned something about you living out here?"

Nodding, I said, "Oh, I keep my boat out here at the marina and spend most of my time there when the weather is right for fishing."

We crested a dune, the Gulf above the scrub oaks; blue sky above scattered with streaks of white clouds higher up. I watched him take it all in, then he turned to me. "He also said that you were a prime suspect in a murder investigation right now." Commissioner Castle stopped to watch my reaction. "Any idea what he's talking about?" His left eyebrow raised as he shifted his weight and placed his hand on his hip, where I knew his concealed sidearm was located.

I smiled, and shook my head, thinking to myself, *your assistant sure talks a lot.*

I hesitated for a moment. "My opinion is that I am a suspect only because they have no leads. I found the body over here on the lagoon. I didn't murder anyone."

He smiled. "It's not every day a guy can say he spent the afternoon with a suspected murderer and lived to tell about it. This may help your case."

I snapped back, "you don't need help when you're innocent. Wasn't it Twain that said, 'If you tell the truth, you don't have to remember anything'? I've got nothing to hide. The cops know everything I know."

I paused for a moment, thoughtfully. "Out of curiosity, where did your assistant get this info?"

"He has a contact with FDLE," He replied. "A buddy who was in his unit in the marines."

"Your assistant is ex-military?" I asked.

"Yes, that's one reason I hired him. I try to hire veterans when I can," he said.

"What was his role? Did he do any tours?" I asked.

"Yes, I believe it was four tours in Afghanistan. He was a demo expert. He would make the bombs and then go set them on the IEDs and blow them up," he said proudly.

"Four tours? That's no joke," I said.

"He was a contractor for a couple of years after that. I'm trying to prepare him to take over when I'm done."

"Oh, so you're not running again?" I asked.

He paused, thoughtfully. "I haven't decided yet. It's a day-by-day situation now."

"Ok, I always thought you'd be in it for the long haul."

He laughed and then paused. "It's been three terms so far; that's not too shabby, right? What about you?" he asked.

I returned the same laugh. "Fair question, since I hit you with one. I'll be doing it until I either can't or don't want to anymore, or there's nothing left to fight for."

He continued with an awkward chuckle. "It appears when someone drowns a guy out and dumps him in your backyard in some attempt to frame you, that may open your eyes enough to ask yourself that question?"

I stopped and thought about it. "I guess that's a good point. It never crossed my mind."

"Hold on a minute. How did you know the guy drowned?" I asked.

He paused. "Wasn't that common knowledge?" He shook his head and said: "Anyway, I asked my assistant to pull the file. Funny thing is, he already had the file. That's why I like him; he's always one step ahead of me."

I was doubtful about his response. I shook my head. "This keeps me diligent. It's a sign that I'm doing something right here since I've gotten the attention of someone that sees me as so much of a threat, they will try to frame me for a murder."

I felt the weight of the Glock on my hip.

Was it worth it? I thought to myself.

My life being threatened because of my actions on this development project? A question I would have to answer later.

He made his way towards the road. "Ace, I need to head out. Thanks for taking the time to meet me," he said.

"Hey, this is what I do. Regardless, I enjoy getting out here."

"I think you know where my vote stands, but I can't speak for the other members. I have my assistant and a couple of others working on getting the property moved up on the Florida Forever acquisition list. It may not happen until the next session. If anything else comes up, reach out. You know where to find me."

"That I do," I said.

He smiled and reached out for a handshake. "You'll see me soon, on the right side of the bar."

When he turned on to the beach road, I could hear the drone of his SUV. He would be an asset in saving the property from development if I could keep him on my side. But I had a feeling some of his tactics and approach were not what I agreed with.

I took another look back at the dunes and a glimmer of the lake through the oaks and sea oats. The chain-link fence surrounding everything was a satirical picture of the whole thing. Another fenced and gated community in the sunshine state. A picture so common and was becoming even more so here in The Lost Republic.

I still had some time before my shift at Lost, so I headed back to the Origin to wash down everything and clean up since

I had been away for the past day. I was at the navigation table making notes when a voice called out from the dock. It was the Special Agent I had met with back in town. He dressed in the same tactical polo shirt with the FDLE logo, combat boots, and khaki tactical pants. He was roughly the same build as me, height wise. In the sun, his beer belly was more pronounced and his pocked cheeks gave him a gritty complexion. The high and tight haircut with oversized black sunglasses rounded out his greasy smile. He didn't come aboard.

"Mr. Gonzalez, I'm sure you remember me."

"I do. What can I do for you?" I asked.

"I had some other questions as a follow up and I wanted to see if I could catch you here instead of a phone call," he said.

I checked my phone.

No missed calls, but a text message from Analee. I didn't read it.

"Yes, well, a phone call would've been nice, but you're here now. Would you like to come aboard?" I asked.

"Sure, if you have a few minutes to talk."

He stepped aboard and the boat rocked under his weight. I leaned on the stern, and he stood under the awning, taking notes.

"Mr. Gonzalez, I'm here because I need to ask you some more questions regarding the dead body you found and also about your past arrest record."

I crossed my arms and said, "Ok, what is it?"

"We received the report from Monroe County Sheriff's department today, shortly after we last spoke. You were brought up on murder charges a few years ago. They were later dropped, it says here, but the case was never closed. We can't help but find some similarities to this case."

My past was always one step behind me. The acid crept up in my throat. Without thinking about it, I took a defensive position. "I don't see what that has to do with any of this," I said. "It was all over years ago. My friend and I caught the charges because we had an argument with the guy."

His smile got bigger as he thumbed through the papers he was holding. "The report says they cleared you, but the case was never closed. There are some other notes here about a witness, but they disappeared before they could testify. Sounds like there may be some missing pieces that never came together back then. His smile grew bigger."

He shuffled the papers from the folder and closed his book, securing it with a rubber band. "Thank you for your time, Mr. Gonzalez."

With a hint of sarcasm, I said, "Thanks for coming in person to ask these questions. I bet you would glean more from someone in person anyway, if only from their body language."

"I prefer in person questioning." He said.

I thought for a moment and said, "I have one more question if you have a minute before you go," "What kind of access does the public have to this investigation file? This is an ongoing investigation, right? So how would, say, a politician or their assistant get information specific to an ongoing investigation?"

After a pause and a wrinkled forehead, he said, "Well, that's a good question and I can't answer that right now. Further, I don't appreciate your insinuations that I may work with or may be influenced by a politician in this investigation. This is all confidential information until the case is closed and even then, it will need to be accessed through the proper channels. Now, if you're done, then I have some pressing investigations to focus on. I will let you know if I have any more questions."

It was clear I had struck a nerve. "Ok, I would appreciate a call first next time, if possible." After he was gone, I was pretty sure I struck some soft spot with the investigation file and, based on his reaction, this would need some further investigating.

CHAPTER FOURTEEN

Later that day, I checked in at Lost about thirty minutes before my shift. I hit the kitchen for a grouper sandwich. I had to take inventory behind the bar and run some numbers. The usual regulars and tourists filled the bar. I noticed that the Commissioner's assistant was sitting at a table by the canal. A man was getting up from the table with his back to me; as he turned, I spotted a familiar face. Steve, the drunk stalker, was walking out. I stepped back for a minute, assuming he missed me standing there. What was he doing here with this guy?

The kitchen bell rang, and I heard my name. The sandwich didn't last long and as I ate; I ran over the numbers for the night, but my head was spinning. I didn't know the Commissioner's assistant, but he had ties to this guy who wanted to kill me and also an ally of mine with the Emerald Oasis Towers project. What the hell is going on? Just then, the roof rattled, and the scream of the deep blue hornets flying in formation overhead was the only sound. All the tourists in the house ran out on the dock to catch the show. The locals stayed put and waited until the sound passed to pick up their conversations again. When I got back to the bar with my food, they were both gone. Hutch, the deputy who'd arrested Steve, was standing by the service well and gave me a nod.

I stepped to the side to talk.

"Hey man, what's happening?" I asked.

"Not much. I'll be making patrols in the neighborhood tonight. If you need me, I won't be far away."

I laughed. "Ok, well, you missed the drunk guy who tried to kill me."

"Here?"

"Yep, he was here, left a couple of minutes ago."

"Did he say anything to you?" he asked.

"Not me, but he was having a drink with the Commissioner's assistant."

"Ok," his eyebrow raised. "What the hell is that about?"

"Who knows?" I responded. "Well, I'll watch for his car. You can't miss that thing. Any idea what they were talking about?"

I shook my head. "No none, it's a strange match up to me, and why did they choose this place to meet?"

"Who knows man, the assistant is weird too. About a year ago, I had a run in with him. He wanted info about a break-in we worked. There was some link to the military, I think. He came in all entitled to the info. I told him it was an active case, and gave him some basic info, no details. He didn't like it, but let it be anyway."

"Hey, I wanted to ask you. Has Special Agent Crowson been hounding you?"

"He's questioned me a couple of times about the floater. Won't let it go."

Hutch nodded. "Ok, well, have you been talking to Analee at the M.E.'s office?"

"Yeah, we've been seeing each other off and on for the last few days."

"Ok, heads up, Special Agent Crowson has been working on her for the last year and she's not interested, but he's still on this kick where he thinks she's his or something. She's given him the brush off more than twice and he's still not backing off. If you're in there now, he's probably not too happy about it."

I shook my head. "That's why he's on my case, huh? Well, I'm not worried about it. If he's not backing down from her, then he won't back down on me either. I'll keep my eyes open for him and let her know to do the same."

He laughed. "Of course, we all work with her and we know this dude is no good, so it shows good judgement by her which we already knew was there since she's letting you in the door."

I smiled and said, "thanks." His radio squawked some inaudible noise, and he acknowledged with a squeeze and a similar inaudible reply.

"Gotta go man, good to see you and holler if you need me."

The band was warming up and a new crop of boaters had pulled into the open slips at the marina. The afternoon heat stirred up the sweet musty smell of beach rosemary and oaks mixed with fried snapper, beer, and brine. A light southern breeze brought in the salt air. Further out on the dock, a great blue heron perched on the last finger pier, scanning for a meal. It was a great time to be working on the water. Britt gave me a smile, and I focused on the shift that night and worked on a plan of action later. The meeting on the Emerald Oasis Towers project was coming up soon, and I still needed to prepare.

Later that night, I finished the shift and locked the place down. There was a mist across the canal and during the quick trip to the Origin, my clothes were damp from the night. I pushed the skiff against the stern of the origin and tied off to the port and starboard cleats. The tide was coming in that morning, so I pointed the bow of the skiff towards the lagoon to take the current as it pushed in. I kicked on the dehumidifier as I walked in. Everett was asleep on the couch in the usual position. After a quick rinse off, I made some notes on the project and responded to a text message from Analee. Hopefully, I would see her tomorrow.

The morning was cool and damp, and I woke as usual before first light. I got up to make some cafe Cubano and let Trigger outside. Everett didn't move an inch. I pulled out the charts for the ICW east and began mapping my route east along the Intracoastal. There was a large development proposed that would alter the course of a river, which was a migration route for an endangered species. The trip all together would take four or five days. Sitting out on the Origin in some of the remote areas along the ICW, where the stars beat out light pollution and the sound of wildlife replaced the noise pollution, was like going to church for me. Everyone gets it, but it's not always the same for everyone.

A little after sunrise, Everett rolled off the couch. He grunted and then grabbed his hat off the floor, then his cigarettes and lighter off the table. "What time is it?" he asked, fishing a smoke out of the pack. Laughing, I said, "about six." He let out a long groan and shook his head, knocking out the fog. "Damn you, getting up so early. That's ridiculous. I mean, why?"

I laughed, shaking my head. "Can't help it. I've got things to do. Besides, once I wake up, I'm not going back down."

"Yep, I know how you operate, brother. Just giving you shit. You got coffee?"

"Ready to go. You know where it's at." I stepped outside and climbed to the flybridge to sip coffee and watch the sun come up over the seashore. The air was cool, and it was early enough that the bridge noise wasn't too bad. Another hour and it would be a constant thump, thump, thump when the traffic picked up. Everett made his way up one handed, the other grasping the coffee cup, a cigarette hanging off his bottom lip. The glaze in his eyes told me he had probably spiked the coffee with some rum and amaretto.

"Well, what the hell did you do last night?" I laughed.

"I worked at Lost dummy."

"Aw no shit, well I was gonna stop by, but I got a couple beers in after work and then I made a couple of stops on the Key and you know how that goes." He sipped his coffee and took a drag on the cigarette, blowing out a cloud. "I started early, so I had to go down early. I walked down here about 9:00 and crashed out." He continued with his smoke, alternating between the coffee.

"Well, it was a busy night at the bar. That crazy dude who tried to kill me was there when I showed up, but he left right after I got there."

"What the hell is that guy's problem?" He said, sitting up in his seat, the cigarette dangling from his lips.

"I had a deputy hanging around, so I wasn't too worried."

He kicked his feet up on the railing. "But hell, what's that dude doing, you know?"

"He was hanging out with Commissioner Castle's assistant," I said. "I get this feeling that he's not a friendly; there's something about him. I also think he's got a buddy at FDLE who may feed him info on me."

He stopped and planted his feet; the smoke rising from one hand, his coffee in the other. "What? Did he tell you that?"

"No, but I got some info from another officer."

"Wait, what's the story with the investigator chick? Did she call?" he asked.

"We've been talking, but I think we're both a little reserved. Besides, I need to focus on this meeting. I gotta get up and talk in front of these guys. I'll put something together, but these elected officials have already made up their minds by the time they hear the development request. It's basically what I've been doing with Castle. I gotta remember that as much as I've been doing, they have been doing all that too, and probably more. It all boils down to money. If the developers push the bed tax revenues and the jobs, and increased tourism to the area, then that's about all they need to do. It's easy to get past all the issues I bring up when there's so much to gain economically by voting yes. But we lose so much more if the development moves forward."

He shifted in his seat to get a better look at a flock of waterfowl out on the bay. "Hey, you're preaching to the choir here, buddy. Plus, we need no more people on our fishing spots."

I shook my head. "Hell, I know I'm really practicing for the meeting. I'm sure it will be different then. Like I said, they probably already made their decision, but I have to get up there or it won't be on the record." He laughed. "Better you than me man, those politicians are crazy."

I sipped the last of my coffee, and Everett lit another cigarette. A barge fought the outgoing tide as it pushed through the no-wake zone. In a couple of hours, boats would load the canal, running in either direction with blasting music.

CHAPTER FIFTEEN

The morning had a low glow to the east and a gentle rocking from the Joe Cain pushing through the canal. After Everett left, I completed the coffee ritual and sat down at the chart table to go over the morning news, check emails and polish the presentation I had been preparing for the meeting. Following an attempt at a sad story, it was better to stick to the facts and figures. The meeting would be packed. I needed to be quick, or the natives would get restless. I would deal with some of that anyway, since I was running off jobs for some of these people. There would be some backlash and someone to speak for the project as well. I was expecting someone from the development firm to be there.

I got the presentation cleaned up and went over it a few times, set it aside, and moved on. Outside, the ripples and eddies at the pilings showed the tide was coming in. There would be some reds working the shallows in the lagoon. I grabbed my gear and fired up the skiff idling along on the tide, letting it take me into the channel. After following the edge of the grass beds, I pushed into the bayou off the lagoon. There was a great blue heron on the bed I was heading for, so I killed the motor and trimmed up. I climbed onto the poling platform and pushed toward the beds I planned to fish. The heron's focus was on the prey. The neck strung in a coiled S shape, a sharp beak poised for attack. From the poling platform, I could see the chain-link fence and the property that developers planned to raze. Out on the Gulf, towers of brilliant white and gold thunderheads rose against the backdrop of a blue sky; the smell of a summer rain pushed in. The picture was what I would convey to the commission tonight at the meeting. Stressing the importance of the place and the possibility of perpetual conservation for the property as opposed to perpetual devastation. I stood there leaning on the pole and considering the alternatives to what this place faced. A slow, painful death unrecognizable to most except the longest tenured residents, the ones who had witnessed the place before the high-rises, strip malls, new bridges, roads and souvenir shops took over. This place was in a slow decline and if I lost this battle, it would be one more nail in the coffin of The Lost Republic.

After an hour of fishing the bayous and grass flats of the lagoon, I perched on the tower of my skiff, leaned on the push pole, and scanned the southern horizon as the thunderheads reached from the blue water of the Gulf to the sky.

The hum of a barge in the distance brought me back from my daydream. I poled the skiff through the sea grasses and pushed a school of mullet out of the channel. When I hit deeper water, I cranked the motor and idled over to the channel, then followed the canal to Lost. Early morning on the canal is finest before heavy boat traffic, loud music, jet skis and the heat of the day set in. I passed under the bridge where Raymond, the deckhand, was loading ice on to a large red commercial vessel. I waved, and he waved back. One of the transient slips was open, so I eased in and tied off.

The dock master, Reggie, was sitting at the bar drinking coffee and running through the day's charters, a cigarette burning beside him. I grabbed a cup of coffee and took the stool next to him.

"Hey man, are you just getting in?" he asked.

"Yep."

He grinned. "Did you do any good out there?"

"I snagged a couple of decent ones, nothing spectacular," I said.

He shook his head, an exaggerated grin on his face. "Man, you know how to find 'em."

A couple of servers walked in and began prepping for the day shift. Britt emerged from the kitchen with an arm full of fruit and gave me a grin. Her hair was a salty sun bleached brown and blonde in a bun pulled up on top of her head. She wore a red tank top and her shoulders were dark brown from the sun, a bikini string trailing down the back of her neck.

"What's up, man? Have you been out today already?"

"Yep, trying to clear the head. Go to church, whatever you want to call it."

She focused her attention on a mango and pineapple. "Nice. It was a perfect morning for it. I paddled out and caught some decent surf about sunrise. The wind was offshore, and it was nice and clean, fun little barrels."

"Good way to start your day, huh?"

She stopped munching on the fruit for a moment. "Hey, don't you have that meeting tonight?"

"Yep, it's why I'm not working tonight," I said.

"Got it. Well, I hope that goes in your favor without too much grief."

I smiled and said to myself, me too.

The bar phone rang, and she answered it. After a brief exchange, she reached out her hand and passed me the phone; the expression gone on her face. "Who is it?" I asked. She shook her head, "not sure? They asked for you."

I answered and the voice on the other end said, "How's that pineapple?"

I stood up. "What?" I replied. "I'm coming for you." Followed by a low laugh.

"What? Who is this?" I demanded. The voice was low and as I held the phone, my palms became sweaty and my grip tightened. "Who is this?" I yelled again, facing the canal, the only place he could watch us. There was a low grunt and a laugh, then a click. Nothing more.

Britt's face was pale, and her jaw tight. "Who the hell was that?" she asked. I stood there, phone in my hand, scanning for movement.

"Who the hell was that?" she asked again.

"Don't know. Could be our pal from the other night, could be some local contractor who wants to work on the towers project. That's my best guess. They have my cell number, too."

Her eyes widened, "What the hell! Have you called the cops?"

"What am I going to tell them? Some guy is calling me making threats? What can they do?"

She continued, "At least they would know, what if something happens to you?" She may be right I thought, then answered. "Maybe I'll mention it to Hutch later."

"Thank you," she said, picking at the fruit on the bar.

After the cup of coffee and the unwanted phone call, I went back to the Origin. I retied the lines and positioned the fenders according to the outgoing tide. After that, I rinsed the salt off the decks of the skiff and the Origin. I knew I was busying myself to avoid preparing for the meeting. There would be members of the community speaking for and against the project, and the developers would be there to answer questions.

I would have some support from the community. The local fishermen would stand up there and talk about how "the place ain't like it used to be and letting these boys do this will make the place uglier. Bringing more people to the area, making it harder to get around and harder to buy groceries and longer lines at the store, but hell, y'all are gonna do it anyway, don't matter what I think."

The developer or their representative would boast about how great it would be. They had so many already pre-sold it would only make the island better with more jobs and more tax revenue. I knew there was a high likelihood that I would be alone with real opposition they might listen to.

I had been in a similar position before, but this time was different. Something else is coming, not the meeting, but I felt a foreboding. I had to get out of my head.

I packed a few things up for the night, did one last check before I left. The drive into town was uneventful. I rode down old Gulf beach highway watching shelf clouds roll in from the Gulf while the wind pushed at my back. The smell of fresh rain followed me. Trigger rode shotgun, front paws crossed with his head resting on them, his eyes upward to the dark clouds. I turned up the music and thought about what my dad might do were he alive now. There was not much that would have stopped him from pushing this development to the edge with petitions and injunctions until there was nothing left. In the old days, he and Dan might even have done some midnight mission after it had gotten started, sabotaging their equipment or sending some bogus claim to one of the regulatory agencies. I didn't expect to have to do this.

My phone buzzed in my lap. Analee checking in. It was a brief text that read, "call me". I waited until I got to the East Hill house.

A few minutes later, I walked into the backyard and kicked open the doors to let some air in the house. The rain had moved out over the barrier islands and the north wind kept a constant breeze rustling the palm trees. I settled into the hammock next to the pool and dialed her number. She answered on the first ring.

"Hello."

"Hey, I got your message. What's going on?" I said.

"Well, I'm glad you called. I was wondering," she said, sounding worried.

"I know. I've been working a lot lately, and I've been trying to prepare for this meeting later tonight," I said, the weight in my voice making it clear I had been stressing about it.

"That's tonight?" she said, sounding surprised. "Wow, it came up pretty quick, huh?"

"Doesn't feel that way to me. I've been preparing for a while now."

"Oh, ok, so you probably don't want any company do you?" she asked. Then continued. "I know you didn't really ask me to follow up, but I can't help thinking about how all this is connected to your case. I came across some information you might want to know. Do you have time to get together before your meeting?"

"Well, I was going to go for a quick run and then take a dip in the pool before the meeting. Do you feel like a run? I could use a partner," I said.

She fumbled with her words. "Sure, I mean no, I'm not busy."

"Ok well, let's meet in the middle at the park on 15th and Lakeview, then we can run and end up back here and take a dip," I said.

"Ok sure, I'll see you there in what about fifteen minutes?"

"Sounds good," I replied.

I snaked through the neighborhood and as I got to the park, I could see her standing next to the central light post in the park, waiting. I reached the center and slowed, and she fell right in at my pace. We headed towards the bayou and picked up the pace.

"I thought we'd head toward the water. Glad you had some time."

She smiled. "I made time."

We took one of the many streets lined with centurion live oak trees and I tried to match her pace so I could even out my breathing. I needed some distraction from the meeting tonight and thought a little cardio might help me out.

A smile came over her face. "It's good to see you".

"So, what did you want to tell me?" I asked.

Between her rhythmic breaths, she said, "After we talked the other night, I checked our system to see who the floater might be connected to. We have access to a database that shows links and known associates. It's like a cluster model with connections. It can even tell us history about each of those individuals. Your guy didn't have much, but when I searched for the developer, the system showed that she's connected to a bunch of people here and none of them is anyone you want to be associated with. She's also tied to people in Mexico and Texas and some of those guys are heavy hitters, business executives, bankers, that kind of thing."

I kept my pace and said, "Ok well, I appreciate you doing that and unfortunately it confirms what I've heard. I shouldn't be involved but, it's really too late now."

Huffing, she said, "Does this change anything for you? Are you still going to do this?"

"I can't back off now, I'm in it too far," I said.

By this time, we were about two miles into it and I could tell we were both hitting our strides. I cut down by the bayou and we got a slight breeze from the bay. I could hear her rhythmic breathing and realized mine was matching hers as we ran at an even pace.

We hit a big hill, and she said, "well, I guess you've been busy with lots of things. Work has consumed me."

She added, "I had to go over your case again with the Special Agent at FDLE."

"The same one who arrested me?"

"Yep, that's the one," she said.

I felt a little anxiety creep up, so I picked up the pace. "He's not letting up, even though I gave him all the info he needed multiple times." She said.

She started in on the explanation. "By this time, you already know the guy got choked out in a bathtub. Well, there was soap in his lungs, which means he drowned in a tub and then got dumped out there for someone to find."

My eyes got bigger, and she could tell it was news to me.

"Oh no, did he forget to mention that to you? He told me he was being up front with you and has all but ruled you out as a suspect." She cursed an audible groan. "Ah dammit, I can't believe I did that," she said.

I smiled. "If he ruled me out, he sure is persistent."

Her brow wrinkled. "Why? What are you talking about?"

"He's been on me. Last time he showed up at the marina unannounced and started asking me the same questions he had before, but then comes up with something new each time. I feel like he's putting together some fabrication to pin the charges on me."

"Wait, when was this?" she asked.

"Yesterday, he didn't even call. He showed up to see my reaction."

Puzzled, she said, "That's funny. By then, I had already given him that information." I smiled to myself.

"Ok, so I have to ask, did the two of you ever date or anything?"

She said, "Hell no! He has been after me for a long time, but I'm not interested. He even shows up to places where he knows I'll be and tries to work his way into my friends. We've had words before and he's persistent, but I'm very clear to him."

Her eyes feigned worry, and she said, "You can believe me. I want nothing to do with this guy. Ok."

"Hey, it's none of my business." I said. "Think about it. If the whole boyfriend in prison didn't scare me away, then this surely won't be a problem."

She stopped and put her hands on her hips. "There is no boyfriend in prison, only an ex-boyfriend who I might visit sometimes."

"Ok, I understand," she seemed placated and started picking up her pace. "Ok, glad we got that settled."

I realized we were only a couple of blocks from my place. "You wanna wrap it up and head over to my place?"

She wiped the sweat off her brow. "Sure, I need some water," she said, panting as we rounded the corner of Gonzales.

I noticed no one was home at the main house when we came through the gate. Trigger was lounging next to the pool and bypassed me completely for her attention. I grabbed a couple of waters from the fridge and collapsed in the hammock.

She went for the chaise and kicked back both legs, drenched in sweat and red faced. I looked at her and then at the pool. She could tell what I was thinking.

Behind her grin, she said, "No way."

I never broke eye contact and shed my shirt, socks and shoes and finally my shorts, leaving only my stretch shorts on before I dove in. The water was perfect after the run, and I swam to the side and shot her a smile. She had a huge grin on her face and shook her head. "No, nope, I don't have my bathing suit." Her smile seemed to get bigger. She took a sip of water and said, "I'm not getting in, even though it would be so nice after that run! Dammit."

"Hey, I'm not asking you to get in, but it sure is nice in here." She turned the water bottle up and drank down the last bit.

The smile returned, and she stood up, kicking off her shoes, then peeling the socks away. She took off the shirt, exposing a bright blue sports bra with straps crossing in the back. Then she shed the shorts, revealing a pair of tight black cheeky briefs. She took one hop and jumped right in with a quick giggle and a shout.

She surfaced and said, "Well, I did it!" I swam over to her and pulled her close. I leaned in for a kiss and she met me halfway.

"Well, I'd say this was a definite distraction." As I laughed, she smiled, and we kissed again.

She pushed away from me and kicked around the pool on her back. We ended up on opposite ends of the pool, treading water, knowing what was on each other's mind.

I made the first move towards her, and she stayed put.

"What are you doing?" she said, eyeing me with a smirk. I reached my arm around her and wrapped the other around her legs, scooping her up. She never made a sound until I lay her on the chaise lounge in front of my bungalow. We had a heated exchange for a few minutes before she stopped.

"I have to stop. I'm not ready." She hesitated, fighting tears. "I hope you can understand." The water streamed down her face.

"I get it. If you don't tell me, then I don't know. It's no problem at all."

"I don't want you to feel pressured into anything. I never want you to feel like that with me, ok? Everything is ok, right?"

She returned a teary, wet smile. "Right."

"Ok, let's dry off and maybe I can get dressed for this meeting. I'll take you by your house on my way downtown if that's ok?"

"Sure," she said.

"Ok, I'll be really quick, and we'll get you home, ok?" She smiled.

I couldn't tell if she was really ok or if I had done something wrong. I was missing something. Regardless of the reason, I shifted my focus, realizing I had an hour to get downtown and in place for the Commission meeting.

I showered and tried to look presentable, since I would stand in front of the County Commission. I got all my notes together. Analee was still lounging on the chaise. I walked out and said, "you ready?" She nodded with a smile, and we loaded up. Before I pulled out, I glanced in both directions, still keenly aware that I was being stalked by a lunatic who had attempted to attack me more than once. There was no sign of any cars, much less the distinct outline of Steve's sled of a car.

When we got there, she grabbed my hand and said, what are you doing after the meeting?

"I don't know yet. It depends how things go." I replied.

"Ok, would you mind if I came to the meeting?" She asked.

I hesitated. "I wouldn't mind at all, but is it possible for you to come in a little late so I'm done with what I have to say? If you're there, watching, it may throw me off. I need to be focused. I'm going to have a hard enough time getting that image of you jumping into the pool out of my head."

Laughing, she said, "Ok, I'll see you there, later."

"Alright." She leaned in for a kiss and I wrapped one arm around her, pulling her close.

CHAPTER SIXTEEN

I parked in the County parking garage and grabbed my notes. By the time I reached the door, I realized I had a pistol, and a blade tucked into my belt, so I turned around and shoved both under the driver's side seat in the lockbox. I felt naked walking back to the door with no weapon. I went in through the usual security measures, reminding myself that not only was I not armed, but no one in the chambers would be. As I gathered my things from security, I noticed Debo Robicheaux standing in the lobby. He was a Cajun transplant from south Louisiana. His tall, heavier frame and scruffy beard complemented the scratch in his voice that comes from years of smoking. He wore a button-down shirt under his jacket and a pair of jeans over his boots. Debo worked for a local land conservancy and nodded in my direction.

"Hey brother, how are you doing?"

"Alright." I said.

"You in for the Emerald Oasis Towers decision tonight?" I asked.

"Yeah man, I've been following what you're doing and I'm trying to convince my board to put the money together to make an offer on the property, even if it ain't for sale. Who knows?" He said, laughing, his belly shaking as he straightened his jacket.

"You never know. It may be more attractive after the meeting tonight."

"Damn man, I wish you would have reached out sooner. That would have helped my case."

"I know," he said, "but it's not over yet. We're still a long way off from funding, anyway." He fished out his smokes from his front pocket.

"Gotcha, maybe we can have another conversation after the meeting, huh?"

He grinned and popped a cigarette in his mouth, making for the door. "Maybe so my man. Good luck. I know you'll be up there eventually, right?"

"That's right." I said.

I found a seat near the podium and made sure they had my presentation ready. The room was filling up and there would be a decent crowd tonight. Commissioner Castle's assistant was in the front row with a couple of other county staffers. A local attorney who represents the developers sat in the back corner with a few others. He mumbled something to the others, who turned my way. There were a couple of guys in suits with Liona. As they got back to their conversation, Steve walked in and sat in the row right behind them. Liona spoke to him, and he glared at me. The room was becoming more hostile by the minute. Commissioners were filing in, and the press table was full.

There were various items before the Emerald Oasis Towers public hearing and a few that were interesting, but mostly county business and discussion. I could feel the eyes on me as the meeting wore on. The public hearings were coming up on the agenda and would draw some comments. I expected there would be someone from the crew in the back row. A few comments from the local fishermen and me at a conservation moment. It would need to be brief, but I could cover the basics and then let them make their decision.

The room had filled up since the meeting began, so it was possible there would be more comments. I stayed focused, ignoring the number of people in the room. Hearings for a couple of their minor developments came up and passed without a hitch. Emerald Oasis Towers was read aloud. The chairman asked if there was a representative for the project in the audience. One suit from the back row headed for the podium. He was tall and swollen in the face and carried a folder of papers with a set of rolled plans.

The chairman said, "Thank you sir, please state your name, affiliation and who you represent for the record."

"Yes, sir. My name is Joe Belfonte, and I represent the developers' group. I would be happy to answer questions you might have about the project."

Commissioner Castle tapped his mic to speak. "Thank you for coming in and being present tonight. It makes our jobs a lot easier, so we appreciate that. He smiled as he repositioned the microphone. Over the last few weeks, I've familiarized myself with the project. There are some unanswered questions regarding the wildlife on the property and, excuse me for the lack of a better term, for the environment on the property. I've been on site and I have witnessed some distinct areas that may only exist here. I'm also impressed with the wildlife on site and how they are thriving so close to civilization. So, those are statements. My question is: how will the design of the project minimize affects to these unique habitats and the local wildlife?"

From my seat, I could see the corner of Mr. Belafonte's mouth turn up into a smile. "Commissioner, I appreciate your question. Please know that we have done all we can do to minimize impacts on the environment and the current residents." He chuckled and got some slight reaction from the audience as he continued. "We have secured all the permits from the regulatory agencies to ensure there is minimal impact to wildlife on the property. It's all documented in the file if you would like to see it."

"Thank you, sir," Commissioner Lee chimed in. "Can you please elaborate on the tax incentives requested?"

"Yes, the owners are requesting no property taxes for twenty-five years and only a ten percent assessment for another 25 years. This is considering one hundred jobs created and the long-term investment the project represents. The County will still get the one percent bed tax for each night of any rental and the additional revenue from the sales tax the rentals will generate. My client and I believe this property tax exemption is a reasonable request given all the other benefits the project will generate."

Another Commissioner tapped the mic.

"Regardless of the other benefits, fifty years is a long time to give on any property tax break."

A couple of others echoed the same.

I could see Belafonte get a little fidgety, fumbling to plan a response.

He straightened his papers and corrected his posture. "Commissioners, I will agree that fifty years is a long time. I would also point again to the bed tax numbers that will be significant and will offset the tax exemptions. At capacity on a night at peak season, bed tax for each tower would yield approximately $10,000 dollars. That is a best-case scenario and reserved, as I mentioned, for the peak season. However, we expect this property to be at capacity regularly." I could see all the commissioners writing that number in their notes. Belafonte stood waiting for the next question from the board.

The chairman chimed in, "The board has no further questions, but please stay close as some of the other public comments may yield some additional questions. Thank you, Mr. Belafonte."

"Would anyone like to speak?" the chairman asked.

I was surprised to see a line forming at the podium. There were some familiar faces, local fisherman, guides, other people opposed to the project. Their objections were all similar and on par with their occupations. The guides focused on impacts to the sea grasses and aquatic habitat while the business owners would like to see the increased business traffic but also still had hesitation about another high-rise development without the infrastructure to handle it. It was another sticking point for the commission to consider. How do you allow hundreds more rooms on the beach without upgrading the roads and utilities? I took the last spot in line. I thought it appropriate to close with my presentation and have Mr. Belafonte answer questions after I spoke. The commission would discuss and then vote.

The room fanned out like an amphitheater. Ceilings were high and television monitors hung on the front wall. I positioned myself at the podium, facing the commissioners, my back to the crowd.

"Thank you for allowing me the time to speak tonight. I know that many of you rarely visit the Key since your districts are on the other end of the county, so I want to provide you with a snapshot of the natural environment where this development is proposed and explain why it can't happen, not in the way it is proposed. I started in on the overall environment, and as I spoke, I noticed some of them shifting in their seats. One Commissioner picked up his phone and checked out. I raised my voice louder and said, "Yes, this project means increased tax revenue for the county which trickles down to the residents, but it also affects our quality of life. We call this place home and watching another theme park on the beach that ultimately causes us to alter our way of life is not something that the residents can get behind. We understand that progress is inevitable," I paused, " but what we are asking is that it's done smartly to lessen the impacts on the environment, the locals, and the impacts on the infrastructure." I was careful to raise my voice louder when I hit each of these points, similar to a preacher in a sermon. As I did, I caught some reassuring comments from the audience. "Yeah and that's right," came from the back rows.

"Several residents here have spoken and everything is on the record now for you to consider. So, I ask that you make your decision not on the glaring monetary benefits of this project but on what's in your heart; would you want something like this in your backyard?" I noticed the chairman check his stopwatch and give me the wrap up signal. I returned his motion with a nod and said, "That is all I have tonight. Thank you for your time."

Behind me, a group of residents stood and applauded; it got louder and louder and the chairman banged the gavel down, yelling, "Order, order, please settle down." I took my seat and waited as he asked for any other comments. There was no one else. The chairman spoke up and thanked the public for being there. "Since we have no other comments, I would entertain a motion to approve the project as submitted." One other chimed in with the motion, and another followed. As they voted one by one in favor of the development, I tried to make eye contact with each of them. None returned my gaze.

It left a sense of relief but also of disappointment. The project had passed with a favorable vote.

The line from the Big Lebowski rang through my head as I walked out; "Sometimes you eat the bear and sometimes, well, the bear, he eats you." I had been eaten. I stepped into the lobby and Debo was standing there.

"Tough one, eh, man?" he said.

"Yeah, I know, it's done, but you know I tried."

"They're still a long way off from getting started, so there may be some other way to stop it."

I felt a hand on my shoulder and Elena said, "ok, so we keep going. We don't give up." She gave me a hug and then turned towards the exit where the mayor was talking on the phone. He put the phone down for a brief second, gave a nod and a smile. She said, "you did great in there. Thank you for what you did."

Debo stepped in, "Hey there, cher, you look dangerous tonight," he said in his grisly Cajun accent, the emphasis on dangerous.

She smiled, "Thank you Debo, I'm headed to another event with the mayor shortly." She laid her hand on my shoulder again. "I'll see you later this week." Then she turned and joined the mayor outside. Debo shook his head. "Shoo man, she is gorgeous."

His eyes shifted behind me, and I knew the development team was filing out.

"I'll keep working," I said.

"So will I, brother."

"Ok, let me know what your board's decision is. We could use that funding. "

"You got it," he replied.

I turned around and there was Liona, showing off the plastic smile. She held out her hand, and I said, "You'll excuse I me if I don't shake hands. I'm a little frustrated with the outcome of tonight's meeting."

"Yes, I understand. I wanted to commend you for what you did in there." She added, "You did your homework."

I couldn't muster the energy to speak, much less agree with her.

"The presentation was great and I have to say I'm convinced." Her crew stood by while she continued. "I think there is room for someone like you on our team. Would you be interested in coming to work for us?"

I stood there, shocked and furious, my palms sweating and my temperature steadily rising, but I kept my composure.

The others with her stood there, confused.

She knew I wouldn't give up on the fight. She must have thought buying me would be an easier option.

I smiled and focused my attention on the rest of the crew.

"I guess I would have to work with these guys, huh? No thanks, I have a job. If you'll excuse me."

I walked out and found Analee standing there. She was wearing a pair of jeans, a black t-shirt, her tattoos peeking out at the waistline and on her biceps. Her long blonde hair was up in a ponytail and her dark-rimmed glasses emphasized her blue eyes. She greeted me with a hug, and we walked toward the parking garage.

"How are you?"

"Ah, I'm alright," I replied.

"I heard everything over the broadcast in the lobby. So many people are against it and only a few are for it."

"I know, but most everyone that spoke against it didn't have valid arguments. In the end, the commission weighs what they have, and that's how they make their decision," I said.

On the way to the car, I scanned the garage to be sure we weren't being followed.

"Where did you park?" I asked.

"I'm over here on Palafox."

"Ok," I said.

She stopped me. "What's your plan now?"

"I don't know. I'll see if there's another way to stop the project. It's not over until they bulldoze the land."

She shook her head. "No, I meant tonight. What do you want to do? You wanna get some food or what?"

I nodded yes, realizing I hadn't eaten all day. "Sure, I haven't eaten in hours, so I should get something."

"Ok, let's walk down to Dharma and grab some sushi." She replied.

After we ate, I still felt defeated. But the walk helped get my mind off the situation. I hoped the win got them off my back for a little while.

As we strolled through DeLuna Square past Old Christ Church and through the historic district, I thought, this is what I needed, some air and a beautiful woman on my arm.

She smiled, pulled me close, and kissed me. The scene of her jumping into the pool after the run flashed across my mind. I returned the kiss and leaned in for a hug, burying my nose in her ponytail; her scent put me in another place.

I felt the air from the bay blow in and I wrapped my arms around her tighter. Her body was taut and lean, but soft in all the right places. I lifted her up and felt her toes come off the ground as she held on tighter.

"Are you going out to the Key or are you staying in town?"

"Not sure. I'm not excited about driving right now, so I'm thinking a shorter route is the best."

"Ok, maybe I can meet you at your house?"

"Sure," I replied.

Then, from the shadows, two figures emerged in one of the old alleyways.

One of them was smoking a cigar, a halo of smoke around his head. The other was crunching on pistachios, a trail of shells following him as he came from the shadows. It was clear they had been watching us since the meeting.

"Hey, nice try man, too bad things didn't go your way. You should have taken the offer from the nice lady."

The other one chimed in, "Yeah man, she treats us pretty good."

I felt Analee tighten her grasp on my arm. It was the two goons that had been after me since the day this began. They stood out in their black suits and sunglasses, gold jewelry glinting as they moved through the glow of the old town streetlights. They circled us and then split up, surrounding us as I backed up to keep Analee behind me. I found a defensible position with a fence to our back and said, " I thought I would see you two again, but I didn't think it would be tonight. What do you want?" But I knew the answer. They were here to finish the job they started the first time we met when they cracked my ribs and blacked my eye. It would be worse now if they got the drop on me. But this time there was more at stake; there was a woman involved, and I wasn't sure what they would do if I went down. I kicked myself for not grabbing my pistol and clinch pick from the truck after the meeting, my mind too consumed by the way it turned out.

The larger of the two smoking the cigar took one last drag and then dropped it on the sidewalk. He moved in closer and I pushed Analee flat against the fence behind me as I stepped in to meet him, his fist coming in a wide circular arc towards my head. In an instant, I was inside the punch and came up with a close uppercut to the gut and a head butt to the orbital, instantly drawing blood. I grabbed his arm and threw him into his partner, crashing them both to the ground. We backed to the fence again, and I yelled, "Run, go call the cops."

Analee didn't budge. "No way, I'm not leaving you here."

The two goons were up in an instant, more pissed off, their shirts untucked now as they pulled their sleeves up. This time, they came from both sides. One caught me in the ribs with a tight hook punch, the searing pain a reminder that this had worked before. The other grabbed my arm and held it down as he punched me right in the face, his right foot kicking Analee to the ground. I was taking a pounding and knew I had to stay upright, but as they worked me over, I got the feeling of a warm trickle of blood running into my right eye. My ribs were taking a beating, and I had no breath left in me. I felt my legs give out.

I heard a string of obscenities from some other language pouring out of them and as I felt myself go weak, one of them stopped abruptly and sank into the sidewalk, slowly holding his crotch. Analee stood behind him, adjusting her position in case another groin kick was necessary.

The other thug continued his pounding, unaware of his partner's condition. After a couple more kicks from my assailant, he realized his partner was lying on the ground. For a moment, his attention went to his partner, and I rolled to my side, braced myself with my right elbow and kicked for his knee, buckling it as an audible crack sounded. He let out a roar, and both hands went to his knee, grasping the now misshapen appendage. He fell on his back and rolled to his side, joining his partner.

Analee helped me to my feet and together, we hobbled down the old cobblestone street. We made it to Seville Quarter, where an officer was standing out front on duty. She explained the situation as I stood there bleeding and within minutes, an ambulance arrived.

I refused medical treatment when asked. It was clear by the gash on my head they had probably given me a concussion. The pain reawakened in my ribs and was more intense than before. I was fairly confident I didn't have any ribs poking into my lungs. I stood up straight and, after Analee explained everything to the officers; we walked the two blocks back to the parking garage.

She said, "you know you're coming to my house right, not up for discussion. I'll patch you up and take care of you."

Somehow, I managed a smile. "I will not argue with you. I can't handle hospitals."

"I got you. Let's get you in my car."

I winced as I folded up into her little sports car. I lay there for a moment, resting my head on the window. Then I remembered my dog and said, "Hey, we'll need to go by and get Trigger. He's at the house."

"No problem. I'll swing by." She said.

She drove through downtown. The roads were wet with heavy air from the fog moving in. The route took us north under the overpass by the railroad tracks. Blount Street shot right into the neighborhood and we stopped at my place to grab Trigger. He was lounging under the stoop in front of the

French doors, dozing under the pool lights that were dancing along the palms and walls in the courtyard. It was a quick stop, and as we headed towards her car, I caught myself scanning the street again.

I knew they wouldn't let me off that easily. In the back of my mind, I hoped we would all get a night off from all this. Wishful thinking, I guess.

It was a short drive to her house. The streetlights cast an orange haze over the neighborhood as we passed under the old live oaks. When we arrived, the house was quiet and dark. The screen door creaked as I opened it, and it rapped the frame behind us as we walked in. Trigger trotted in and took his spot on the couch.

Analee helped me to the couch and made sure I got comfortable. Within the minute, she set a drink next to me on the table and bound up the stairs. I took a sip of the rum and said to Trigger. "Hell of a night, buddy." He returned a smile and scratched his face with his hind leg.

A moment later, she was back at the coffee table in front of me, a large bin labeled "first aid" in her hands. She settled down on her knees, grabbed a package from the bin and cracked it on the table. "Ice pack," she said, "hold it on your ribs." Reluctantly, I pressed it to the area where it hurt the most. She retrieved a bottle of antiseptic and some gauze and cleaned up the gash on my head, working through the bandages and butterflies for something to secure the cut with. "It looks a lot worse with all this dried blood on it. Does that hurt?" She asked, watching me wince as she wiped the crust away.

"No, it's fine," I said, pressing harder on the ice pack.

"You know they could have done all this at the hospital?"

"I know," I said, "but I can't stand hospitals. It's never a positive experience."

"Whatever you say."

She added, "Close call tonight. I assume you know those guys?"

"Unfortunately, yes. Maybe this will be the last time I see them, but I'm not betting on it."

"So, who are they?" she asked.

"They work for the developer of this project I'm fighting. They've come after me a couple times before and I've been lucky. This time we got lucky again, and you didn't get hurt. Are you bruised or anything from that kick?"

She laughed. "Not really, it wasn't the kick that bothered me, it was the concrete curb I landed on, my butt is gonna have a bruise. But other than that, I'm fine."

"Ok," I said, "I'll patch you up next then." I smiled.

"Ha, hilarious."

"You're taking some downtime when I'm done. I'm afraid you may have a concussion."

"Nah, I'm good. I've had one before and this doesn't feel like that."

"Ok Doctor." A moment later, she had a small flashlight and shined it in my eyes. "Ok, so your pupils are good. How do you feel?"

"Fine," I said, "just sore."

She took the ice pack from me and grabbed an ace bandage. "Let me get that out of the way." She grabbed my shirt, and I groaned as I lifted my arms while she peeled the shirt off. A moment later, she wrapped the ice pack around my ribs and pushed me towards the stairs. "Where are we going?," I asked.

"I'm putting you in my bed." No arguments here, I thought. I settled in and she made sure my drink and phone were nearby.

"I'm grabbing a shower real quick. Try to relax." She disappeared into the bathroom and after another sip of my drink, I shut my eyes.

The tension between us was apparent, and we both recognized the attraction. Part of me wanted to fight it, but a voice in my head kept telling me it was time to move on. This time it was different and worth letting my guard down. I'm not sure if it was the rum or the exhaustion, but I drifted off to sleep within a few moments.

The next morning, the sound of Trigger's paws on the hardwood floors woke me. I felt the soreness that had set in overnight. Once I made it downstairs, I let Trigger out the back door and made a pot of coffee. The sky was still dark with fog, and I didn't expect her to get up anytime soon. I walked over to the bookshelf and noticed a copy of Wind and Sand and Stars, an airman's account of flying Africa and the Americas during the early days of aviation. I grabbed my coffee and the book and settled in to the chair at the front window, opening the blinds to get some visibility.

An hour later, I could hear her stirring and after, heading downstairs.

"Good morning, coffee is ready," I said.

"Thanks," she yawned as she spoke.

"I assume by the snoring you slept good, huh?"

"Like a rock," was her response.

I stood and approached her for a hug. She nestled her head into my chest and her hair right into my face.

We kissed, and in a sleepy smile she said, "it was nice sleeping next to you all night. How do you feel?"

"Sore," I replied. "I slept ok, though. I knew Trigger was on guard duty all night." She smiled.

"Are you hungry? I have some eggs and bacon in the fridge."

"Breakfast sounds great."

After breakfast and a ride to my truck, Trigger and I headed back to the Key after a brief stop at the bungalow in East Hill. The fog was still lifting in some areas while thicker along old Gulf Beach highway over the lagoon. I caught glimpses of the water and a ghostly barge, the barrier island appearing to the south as I drove. I needed to get some time on the water before my shift at Lost tonight. As I approached the state park, a convoy of black SUVs running tightly together and a familiar black German sports car following closely behind cut through the fog.

The convoy veered off Gulf Beach highway and headed north. I hesitated and then followed at a safe distance, my old truck struggling to keep up with their V8s. They stayed on the main roads and after several minutes were approaching Interstate 10, but instead of getting on the interstate, they took a service road north of the ramp. I stayed on them with several cars between us. The service road ran parallel to the main interstate corridor. It was dotted with industrial warehouses nestled in among large stands of pines. I passed one larger warehouse and saw the German sports car sticking out of the rear parking lot gate. I dropped gears and pulled into the next entrance to an empty warehouse. There was no activity at this building and the fence was closed and secure. I parked, press checked my pistol and grabbed my pair of Steiner binoculars I kept in the truck for bird watching.

Between the warehouses there was a large stand of pines growing through the red clay and I skirted through them, careful to move slowly as I emerged on the edge of the next fence. I came out in a clump of longleaf pines, bushy and perfect cover. I was on a large berm overlooking the rear parking lot of the warehouse. There was a semi-truck backed up to one bay, and the convoy had pulled around back and parked in a single file with Elena in the rear. I watched through the Steiners as she exited and joined the usual suspects in a circle, Liona in the middle doing all the talking, the goons shuffling around behind her.

I was too far out to hear what they were saying, but there were some hand gestures towards Elena and the semi-truck. I watched as they filed into the back door of the building; the goons bringing up the rear, the one with the limp standing at the back door. He lit up a smoke and found a suitable place to lean.

Damn, not much to go on here. What was Elena doing here, anyway? I considered it for a moment, but couldn't come up with a good excuse for her. I kept to the cover of the pines for a while and waited, hoping to catch more of the operation, whatever it might be. Half an hour had passed, and I was getting ready to leave when the back door opened; Elena came walking out alone. The goon guarding the back door said something to her, and she raised her voice briefly in reply, not taking the time to look his way. She jumped in her car and sped away. A few moments later, the rest of the entourage came out and left as well, the large chain-link gate closing behind them.

I stayed under cover of the pines, considering checking out the warehouse. The gate closed and a blinking red light came on, then another in each corner of the fence. There were cameras with motion detectors I hadn't noticed before. Top security for a warehouse yard, I thought.

All thoughts of entering the compound and checking the warehouse had been dashed. I backed out through the pines, keeping low, and made my way to the truck. What had I witnessed? Was Elena working for Liona? It could have been some business deal, but why would they be working together?

CHAPTER SEVENTEEN

The fog was still heavy on the lagoon as I crested the bridge. At the marina, everything was wet, as if rain had fallen. The water lay like a blanket over the Origin and the skiff. There were a couple of footprints from a heron stopping over and stalking a meal in the early hours. I gave the Origin a once over, making sure the lines were secure, and grabbed an 8-weight rod and reel setup. The tide had come in about an hour earlier. The water was still calm and glassy, and the fog would hold it longer if there was no wind. I checked the skiff out and fired up the outboard. Trigger was on the bow, alert to what might be outside the periphery of the fog.

As we idled out toward the flats off the state park, the island where I found the floater emerged from the fog. Black needlerush fringed the shoreline, and the crown of a pine tree shone through the fog beyond. After the past evening's events, everything was a dream.

I couldn't fathom how the objection to a major development project had made me a suspect in a homicide and resulted in so many attempts on my life. In the middle of all this, two women had entered my life unexpectedly.

It was clear one of these women was different. I had felt nothing like this before and each time we were together, another thought of the possibility of this working out crept in to my head. The other was feeling too calculated. Now, with this new information that she somehow had a connection to this developer, I was suspicious that she was trying to distract me from what was really going on with the development.

The near constant boat traffic beat the grass flats on the south in the lagoon, but in the early mornings at high tide, they were calm. Today, there was no wind, and the tide was at its peak. I approached the eastern most beds at the mouth of the small bayou that drained the wetlands in the park. I could see some nervous water as I approached. The tannins in the bayou gave the tea-colored water an even darker shade as it merged with the brackish water of the lagoon, mixing with a visible contrast, resembling a sloppy cursive dance of light over the sandy bottom. I clocked the bow and rousted Trigger from his perch. There was a dark spot moving on the far side of the bayou. The water was so calm I decided for the long cast and the jerking retrieve across the mouth of the bayou. I cast, with a reaching double haul, and skirted the needlerush along the shoreline. I gave the fly a minute to sink and started stripping the line back in a jerking motion—jerk, pause, jerk, pause, jerk pause. Water moved over the seagrass as I continued the strip.

No hits. I cast again, this time even longer and with the same motion on the retrieve. I was near the end of the beds and I saw the fish move. It hit hard, and I saw the yellow mouth come up and swallow the fly. The drag on the reel began to click, and I strip-set the hook. The trout paused and headed back into the bayou. I held the tip of the rod high and let him run, the reel whining as he went. I noticed the line running straight for the pilings on the walking bridge and feathered the reel to slow it down. As I fought, I said to myself, "Right on time."

The trout pulled harder as a last effort faded and a minute later; he was next to the skiff. I spent the next couple of hours poling east along the shoreline, fishing the edges of the docks east of the park. I landed a couple more fish, all while threading through heavy patches of fog that dissipated as the morning wore on.

By the time I made it back to the Origin, it was lunchtime. I hadn't seen Everett since the day before. He was working on securing another transport job, this time from the east coast of Florida back over to Mobile Bay. I assumed he had been on good terms with his lady, so it may be another day or two before he comes by the marina.

I tied the skiff off to the Origin. The fog was still holding overhead and out over open water. I could see the towering concrete monoliths on the Gulf with sections of the structures showing through the fog, the rest rising shadows. The bridge traffic thumped with a regularity that said the fog didn't deter too many people from the beach, which bode well for my upcoming shift. I washed down the skiff and the Origin for good measure and then took a rinse off at the dock shower. The scent of fried fish crept over the dock and the instant it hit Trigger, his nose perked up and floated in the air as if some imaginary treat dangled in front of his face. At that moment, I realized how hungry I was. I needed a good meal before I set out across the canal to go to work. The restaurant above the marina was easy.

The restaurant reminded me of a place down in the Middle Keys. A regular stop in the skiff on fishing trips. It was a marina with a bar and grill upstairs situated right on Boot Key Harbor. It was open-air all the way around, surrounded by mangroves and bridges, boats, and the trade winds blowing across the emerald waters of the Keys. The towers of Radio Free America to the south broadcasting American news to the good people of Cuba. The setting here was similar, a marina with a second-floor open-air establishment and a superb view of the Intracoastal, lagoon, and barrier island with the Gulf beyond. No freedom radio, but not a terrible alternative.

Trigger stayed put on the dock, and I headed upstairs to grab a bite. Fog and humidity had left the stairs wet, and the windows covered in a thick layer of condensation. The tourists had filled up most of the tables, so I grabbed a seat at the bar. The bartender was mixing Bloody Marys and Screwdrivers for the customers. His name was Jonathon, and he was in his sixties with a large mustache that turned up at the ends, heavier set, with shorts and boat shoes as a standard uniform. I had met him before; a career type with a place nearby and a story to tell about the many other places he had worked. This place had a hard time keeping staff, so it was good to see he had survived the off season. They would shut down for a month in the winter and then pick back up as the weather got warmer and business picked up. It was a familiar cycle in the area and The Lost Republic was not a business that had to keep to this seasonal schedule. Our business is established, loyal, and local.

The bartender made his way over with a handful of menus and tossed a coaster in front of me. I beat him to the intro, ordered my meal, and picked up my book. My phone buzzed. The screen read "Agent Crowson." I considered answering for a moment, then flipped it over.

A couple of stools over, another customer sat down. It was Hen, the guy who had found Lost and might stay.

"Hey man, what are you doing in here?" I asked.

He laughed and said, "well I've been wanting to try this place out since I see it every time I cross the bridge to the Key. What are you doing here?"

I took another drink and said, "well, I keep my boat here and came up for something to eat before I go in for my shift at Lost."

"Ok cool. Which boat is yours?"

"The one in the far west slip." I motioned with my hand in that direction and added, "it has a smaller boat tied to it."

He got up to look out the window and said, "Ok cool. Do you fish or just cruise?"

"Both," I replied. "I use the small one to fish inshore, mostly."

About that time, the bartender dropped my meal. I chewed up a couple of ibuprofen and went to work on the sandwich.

"Wow, you must have one hell of a headache?" he asked.

"Nah, sore is all. Had a rough night last night."

He laughed. "I get it, man." He stopped for a moment, finished his beer and said, "well I came in to grab a beer and check this place out. I'll let you eat in peace."

He reached up and gave me a salute with his two fingers and left some cash on the bar.

The bartender was across the island of liquor bottles, working with his customers.

His voice carried over the sound of the music and other voices in the bar.

"Yeah, there's going to be a big time new development right over there pretty soon."

"Should be nice if y'all are in the market to buy. I hear there's going to be a few new towers and a bunch of pools, a couple of bars and, of course, you'll have a big marina, so you've got access to the Gulf and the lagoon. Should be pretty nice."

The customers were listening wide-eyed and giving each other the elbow as he listed off the amenities.

I thought to myself, this guy should go sell some condo units over there. They'd love to know he was marketing their units before they even broke ground.

A breeze heavy with fog pushed in through the panoramic windows and I could feel the condensation on my skin. I checked my phone; one call and a voicemail from Agent Crowson and another call from Analee, followed by a text, "checking on you, still sore?"

"You know it," I thought as my left hand checked the tape on my ribs.

I paid the career bartender working on his real estate venture and over tipped, as was the custom among industry natives.

The persistent fog still obscured the bay over the water, enveloping the restaurant and marina. A boat was gassing up as I walked to the lone cruiser at the far end of the dock. Beyond, I could see the bridge pilings and the navigational markers, but only indiscernible objects poking through the fog. The sun was overhead but still shrouded by the fog. Back on the Origin, I made a cup of Cuban coffee and sat down at the chart table to check the voicemail. "Mr. Gonzalez, this is Special Agent Crowson at FDLE. Word is you got into some confrontation last night with a couple of thugs and you got banged up pretty bad. No police report, though. Anyway, hopefully you're alright. I'm calling because I have some information that you may be interested in. Call me when you're available."

Word had somehow gotten out about the fight. What new information could he have that he was willing to share?

When it was about time to head toward Lost, I changed clothes and packed up my nightly gear bag and tucked the

Glock in to my waistband. I called Agent Crowson back on the number he left, but the call went right to voicemail. If it was really important, he would call me back. When I got to Lost, my usual slip at the east end of the marina was open. As we coasted in, Trigger bounded up on the dock and took an inventory of his territory.

Raymond, the dockhand, was working next door at the fish market. As I tied up, he straightened up and said, "I'll be over to see you in a few minutes. Man, I'm ready for a drink."

"I'll have it waiting in your spot," I replied. I smiled and asked, "Long day?"

"You wouldn't believe it if I told ya," he said.

I shook my head and made for the bar.

I received the nod from a few regulars at the bar and then Britt rounded the corner, grinning ear to ear.

She dropped food in front of a couple of customers and returned to the register.

"Hey, what's happening, man?"

"You good?" she asked, seeming to know the answer.

"Yeah, I'm good, a little sore is all. How's the day been?"

She replied, "Ahh, pretty easy. Steady and easy. I guess the fog kept people from getting too far from home, so it's been locals stopping in, but we've been going strong since we opened."

"You should be all prepped up, though."

"Ok, I'll be back in a few after I look over some numbers." I was hoping to avoid questions about the fight I was in the night before.

I scanned the tables in the main dining area before I went in the back and checked the parking lot.

A good start to the shift; so far, no threat of the maniac. I felt my phone vibrate in my pocket. A quick glance revealed a "thinking of you" message from Analee. Unsure of how to respond, I let it go. Part of me was still not sure what to think about her split from her ex. I couldn't help but wonder if I was the reason or if there was more to it. Nor did I want to be the reason that she ended things with him. It was a lot to hang on me.

A few minutes later, I relieved Britt at the bar, and she grabbed a seat next to the well and cracked a beer. Within an hour, Raymond was sitting next to her. I poured his requisite double tall vodka water with a lime and observed as he updated Britt on his day, working the docks at the fish market next door. As he spoke, he would get animated and throw his hands up, a "Can you believe it?" on his face. Britt ordered another beer and Raymond another drink. That was his limit after work, as he still had to row his boat back down the canal to his house. It becomes all that more challenging standing up rowing a boat against the tide after a couple of doubles. He says the water helps even him out. I've never questioned that, since he always makes it to work and back home each day, regardless of the state he's in.

He stopped his story and waved me over. As I approached, he leaned in and said, "hey man, I wanted to let you know some guy was over at the docks earlier today asking about you. Maybe a cop, an older cop. He had the look, though." Raymond emphasized the word "look," and nodded like there was some secret message there.

"Ok so give me some details, man?" I asked.

"Like a cop, man, like I said. He had a funny accent and kept checking out your boat. I was loading up some ice, and I stopped him. He didn't say much, but he was sketchy, asked if you worked over here."

Britt killed the beer.

"Sounds like you better watch your back, Ace Gonzalez."

"Thanks for the info, Raymond. Drinks on me tonight."

He smiled and slurped the last of his cocktail down.

Britt said, "Hit me when you get off if you wanna grab a drink and catch up. And watch your back dude!" she said. "I may come back and check on you anyway after that story."

She followed Raymond out to the dock with her beer, then watched him board his row boat to head home.

In the parking lot, Hutch was standing next to his cruiser. I hoped he would be a deterrent for any retaliation from the public meeting.

The shift was uneventful, with a steady stream of people rolling in by boat, car and bike, drinking, laughing and enjoying themselves. The fog never seemed to lift. It stayed off of the docks and the parking lot but shrouded the place in some alternate universe. People would come and go, leaving by boat and breaking the barrier through the fog, while others would pull out of the parking lot, crunching the oyster shells and gravel and disappear.

The balladeer on stage continued into the night. The lyrics turned progressively more offensive until it was time to wrap it up. At the end of the night, I watched Hutch the Deputy leave, and I secured the place as usual while the servers wrapped up their side work.

I keep the doors locked when counting money at the end of the night. When I'm working, I'm the security for the place and precautions like this ensure there are no incidents.

After I had run the numbers, I locked up the night's take in the safe, then sat at the bar with Trigger and poured a couple of fingers of Flor de Cana. It had been a long couple of days and this shift was a welcome way to finish out.

Then the phone behind the bar rang. Trigger sat up from his spot on the floor. I reached over and answered it, "Lost, we're closed." It was silent on the other end, but as I listened, I could hear breathing. Then a low voice came through.

"You need to back off this thing. It's over now and it's going to happen no matter what you do." The hair on my neck stood up, and a chill ran down my back. This was an unfamiliar voice, making threats from a distance. "If you keep pushing, you're going to get more than bargained for." The voice remained silent for a couple of heartbeats, then with a laugh, "How's that drink going down?".

I said, "Who is this? Where are you?" I was mentally checking all the doors in the place to be sure I locked up.

"Don't worry about me, you mind your own business and you'll be ok. But if you keep sticking your nose in other people's business, you're going to get it broken!" Then there was the dial tone.

"Hello? Hello?" I set the phone back on the receiver. This guy was close enough to see me; too bad we didn't have caller id. I checked all the doors and peered outside into the darkness. The only lights were from the marinas along the canal.

Rattling of dishes and a couple of remaining staff from the kitchen overtook JJ Grey on the speakers as he sang of old Florida and how his grandfather would lay down and die if he could see it now. The line from the song seemed appropriate given the last few days. Trigger stirred, and the last of the kitchen crew left out the back. I made one last pass through to be sure all was clean and secure and headed for the dock.

The marina was quiet, and the fog was thick. The outgoing tide pushed the skiff up against the pilings. I watched the eddies in the current swirl out into the darkness of the canal and disappear into the fog. After firing the motor, I let it run for a minute. I had to slide the skiff back out into the canal and then right the bow to head towards the marina. The current was so strong I didn't need to use the throttle. I steered us through the bridge pass lights and eased on in with Trigger on his perch, straining to sniff out the fog in front of us. As we approached, I looped the bowline over the cleat on the end of the dock and the stern swung around with the current. I left the skiff in this position so that it would better take the outgoing tide which would continue through the night. The windows in the salon had streaks of water trailing down through the condensation to the deck. The amber light from the marina dock light cast a glow over the rear deck and into the salon. Trigger paced the dock, his nose still upturned to some unknown scent. I noticed an interruption in the condensation on the stairs to the flybridge.

As I looked up, the dark figure hit me. I went down hard against the deck. It was a flash, but for an instant I saw a man come out over the stairs and drop on top of me.

I woke up to the hum of the motor running and a slight rock as I opened my eyes. I was laying in the stern of the Origin. It was dark except for the pilot lights at the helm of the cabin and the running lights. There was a man at the helm and as I tried to move, I realized my hands were bound at the wrists in front of me. To my left there was a five-gallon bucket with rocks and bricks sticking out glued together by concrete, a large metal wire loop sticking out of the top. A Danforth anchor lay next to it. The sound of the motor increased, and the chop grew, spraying over the gunnels as the man at the helm brought the

Origin up on the plane. I lay there, rolling my wrists, trying to loosen the ties with little progress. I focused my attention on the man at the helm. He wore dark clothing with a hooded sweatshirt and his face seemed to stay shrouded in the shadows.

The glow of the screens and gauges cast a blue light over his face and I thought for a moment I recognized him. I stayed focused on him as I worked at the ties on my wrists. Then I saw his head turn, and I went limp. I closed my eyes as he moved towards the bucket beside me. I felt a rope threaded through my wrists and a tug as he cinched down a knot. A wave of reality came over me and hit me like a flash of light behind my eyelids, and I knew he was planning to drop me overboard to the bottom of the Gulf. If he went out far enough, nobody would ever find me. I felt the Origin take some wake and the hum of another barge carried over the lagoon.

"Wake up," he said stoutly and kicked me in the ribs.

I coughed and rolled, the pain of my bruised ribs screaming at me. I knew the voice but couldn't place it. He pushed me over with the heel of this boot. I detected a smile behind the darkness, and he pulled the hood from his head. It was a momentary search to recognize the face, but I knew the commissioner's assistant as he smiled down at me. "It's time to decide if it was all worth it," he said.

I was trying to make sense of it when he said, "I thought I had everything figured out and then you wouldn't go away. Apparently, you're still a threat, or at least that's what some important people think, and they're the only ones that matter in this whole thing."

"What the hell are you talking about?" I asked.

"You got in the way, man."

"What? Why are you doing this? Who are you working for?"

He played with the bopper, a weighted wooden club I use for dispatching fish, rapping it against his leg as he spoke.

"Me? No one. Hell, I'm working for me, man. I got an opportunity here and I'm trying to capitalize on it. You got in the way."

"What are you talking about?"

He smiled and laughed. "I got in good with the developers, and they were expecting some push back from the locals. I found out later that it was you."

"They offered me a primo Gulf front condo if I could cut you out of the picture."

At that moment, he confirmed all of my suspicions about the developers.

"They knew nothing about this?" I asked.

"No man. I'm a resourceful guy. You were collateral damage, like that guy you found in the lagoon."

"What?" I yelled as I struggled through the pain in my head and my ribs.

He continued, "I thought a murder charge or at least some attention for one would be enough to get you out of the picture. I had to drag his ass around that night. After he passed out, I threw him in the tub and held him under. He struggled but wouldn't conk out, you know."

I felt sick. No, I didn't know. I thought.

"I dumped him at the marina. The tide played hell with him and he ended up where you found him. He was supposed to be found right next to your boat."

"Jesus, man, you are one messed up individual," I said.

He stepped back and punted me in the ribs. I felt something give and rolled over, gasping for breath, coughing as I tried to refill my lungs.

He straightened up and said, "There's not much out there for a guy coming back from overseas. Those Gulf front condos go for a mil. There wasn't anything you could do to stop me. I know it sounds crazy. The pay at the county is crap, and a big payday like that would be huge for me."

It was hard to hide the disgust on my face. "And I got in the way?" I asked.

He smiled, "You need to be out of the way by tonight is what I was told, something about a big exchange and you can't be around to screw it up."

"What exchange? What does that mean?"

In my mind, it could only mean one thing: another shipment at the warehouse and this time, big enough to need me out of the way.

He continued, "It means you've been poking around a little too much and it's gonna get you killed."

"Another mission," I said, waiting for his response. He looked down at me and I caught the flash of the lighthouse across his face, the marker lights of the pass blinking at intervals.

"Don't worry about it. You'll never know what hit you."

He leaned down and snapped his wrist; the bopper bouncing off my head as I rolled with the wake into a watery sleep.

I woke to the sound of the motor and Trigger's muffled barking from the front v berth cabin. The beam from the lighthouse flashed again, and I knew I had only been out for a short time. My head pounded, and I rolled to take the pressure off of my temple. My captor had settled in at the helm, the bopper in the cupholder beside him. I tried to gather my thoughts, but the knot on my head and Trigger's constant barking made it difficult to concentrate. Once I pulled in some deep breaths and gathered my thoughts, I put everything together. He was headed out of the pass and then out to the Gulf. I had to think quickly.

I took inventory of what I had on board I could use. A dock line, cooler, tackle box and there in the gunnel, my bait knife next to the cutting board. That was my salvation; I had to get it. The ropes were tied too tight. If I wanted to get to the knife, I would have to move the concrete bucket and anchor, making no noise. I waited and moved it as the Origin hit another wake. I put my shoulder into it and an inch or two each time. Finally, it was against the stern now. I had enough rope to reach for the knife. It was a large kitchen knife, white handle with a long blade still stained with fish blood. I got up on my knees and wrapped a couple of fingers around it, then snaked it out and onto the deck. It skid with the wake and slid right under me. I hunched over it as I lay there in case he came back to check on me. As I fought dizzy spells, I wedged it against the deck and one forearm and went into short sawing motions, cutting through the strands of the rope a little at a time. My head throbbed and as I cut, it seemed to take hours, but I knew only minutes had passed. As I struggled, the nylon of the rope cut into my wrists, drawing blood and turning them to purple and red bracelets. The rope finally gave way. During all the cutting, he had not moved from the helm, confident in the last crack of my head he had delivered. I stayed in my hunched position, covering my wrists and trying to shield the knife from view. I rolled over and got my feet under me. My legs were shaky from the multiple blows to the head and we took some wake as we entered the narrows at the pass. I kept the knife in one hand and steadied myself with the other. Struggling to stay upright, my head was floating with the wake of the Origin. I thought about at the concrete bucket and its purpose. If he got the drop on me, he would use it for sure. I squatted down, wrapped my arms around it, lifted with my legs and caught the lip of the gunnel. The bucket teetered and then dropped over the side with a *ker-clunk*. My captor stopped and his head snapped in my direction. His hand reached for something at the helm, and he found the throttle and pulled it back to neutral. I stood upright, the knife in my hand tucked behind my back, my free hand holding my ribs. He reached in the cup holder by the helm and grabbed the club. I stepped to the side and showed him the blade in my hand. A smile came over his face as he sidestepped and shook the club, testing the weight and balance as he plotted.

I knew there was only one outcome here. We had to fight it out and I would let him make the first move. We had only a small arena here on deck, and I knew that one good blow from the club would stop me from where I stood. He eyed the blade in my hand and swung the club around again, demonstrating the heft. As the boat drifted in, the current moving through the pass, we stared each other down. It was dark and the glow from the buoy cast a red light over us. A wave rolled in from the Gulf and lifted the bow, sending the Origin into a roll that tossed him in my direction. I felt my body tense up, anticipating the oncoming attack. He rode the toss and lunged towards me with the club. In a split second, our eyes met, and I felt a spark in my core. I made myself small and drove forward into his midsection. Everything seemed to slow down; the lights, the sounds and the deck moved in half time as we inched closer to impact. My left arm came up to block the club and my right swept out into a circular arc, the blade of the knife crossing into his side. We both stopped as we cracked heads, bringing stars to my already cloudy peripheral, then the club came down on my shoulder blade, saving a blow to my skull. The sting of the club buckled my knees, but I wrapped my left arm around his right and held my feet under me. As I wrapped his arm up, he dropped the club, and it rattled against the deck and danced toward the scuppers. I felt his left arm drop hard onto my right wrist. The knife came loose and sunk into the black water below.

I raised my hands into fists and got my feet under me as he struck my head. While he continued his assault, I retaliated by putting two punches up into his gut, as he forced me lower and rattled my head even more. I pushed my body forward and into an explosive double leg takedown. I bent my knees, thrust my shoulder and head into his gut, clipping his legs and lifting upwards. The force of the thrust sent him into the air and over the edge of the gunnel. He tumbled into the black water with a splash. I sat there for a moment, waiting for him to surface. I watched and waited for what seemed like minutes. A few feet away in the darkness, I could hear him surface, coughing and choking. He yelled, choking through the salt water, "Help!", struggling to stay afloat. I couldn't let him go, not after the reality of what he told me about the murder and how he planned to kill me as well. On the deck was a dock line tied off to the starboard cleat. I grabbed the end, wrapped it around my wrist as I went in after him, taking in one long breath as I hit the water.

The tide pulled us away from the Origin. In the darkness, I followed the sound of his struggle and found his legs and an arm flailing in the water. I sunk down and grabbed both of his legs, holding him down as far as I could get. There was no chance of him getting his breath as my entire body went limp except for my arms. My hands climbed up his body as he tried to swim to the surface. I felt his hands searching for my face and he kicked both legs to free himself from my grasp. My grasp loosened, and I climbed up his back to his neck, reaching my right arm around his throat. I settled my right hand onto my left bicep and set my left hand on the back of his head. It was one quick motion, and I had it locked in. As his hands found my head, he reached to shove his fingers into my eyes, but I buried my face into the back of his neck.

I knew I had made a mistake going in after him, but I had no choice but to continue now. He was the key to proving my innocence. As I hover there suspended in the dark water of the pass, I considered my decision to go in. The pass is a favorite hunting ground of the bull shark, and after the knife wound, we were as good as chum.

He continued to struggle as I tightened my hold and settled in, calling on my breathing exercises from my days of lifeguarding and free diving.

At a certain point, the oxygen content depletes and a last-ditch effort, a survival mechanism, kicks in. The brain before succumbing to the loss of oxygen rallies for one last time. The attempted eye gouge and hair grab was his last effort. After he stopped struggling, I held for a few seconds. Then, the lifesaving mechanism kicked in. I had to revive him, but first I had to get him back on the boat. I released the lock, wrenched my free arm under his arm and across his chest and surfaced. Two big kicks towards the Origin got me moving. I made it to the stern and flipped the ladder down off the swim platform. I held his hands on the platform as I climbed out of the water, using my other hand for the ladder. Trigger's muffled bark continued. I got my breath steady and pulled him out with both arms onto the deck. As I rolled him on his back, I noticed his face had lost color. I positioned his head back and opened the airway. There was no time to call for help. I got in position and delivered two breaths and watched his chest rise and fall. After the breaths, I delivered a series of compressions and listened to the crunching sounds as I counted. I got into position to deliver another breath. His chest heaved, and I moved my head in time to avoid the brackish water that came up. I rolled him on his side and grabbed a dock line and secured his hands to his feet in separate knots with a slip knot in the middle. The knot would cinch down on itself if he struggled. It was perfect for an attempted murderer I had killed and brought back to life.

"Ahhhh, what the hell are you doing?" he asked.

"And why does my chest hurt? What did you do to me?" He yelled.

I was at the helm immediately, righting the Origin.

"Try to relax. You're hurt pretty badly, judging by the crunches your chest made when I was saving your life. Of course, that was after I drowned you." I opened the front hatch and Trigger came running out barking like a rabid coyote. He settled in, hovering over his head, teeth bared."Untie me," he said, while a red stain of blood grew beneath him on the deck.

I kicked the engine into gear, and said, "Hold on, boy."

CHAPTER EIGHTEEN

I made for the bridge over the canal to the mainland. By now they would be at the warehouse and If I wasn't too late, I could catch them in the middle of the exchange. I kept the old truck spun up, so I made it to the interstate in a matter of a few minutes. Sam the dockmaster agreed to watch Trigger, since he was not budging from his place as guard dog. On the way, I called Hutch, betting he was on duty. I let him know I was chasing another suspect, hoping to avoid a leaving the scene charge. The service road along the interstate where I had followed Liona and Elena the day before was dark and empty. It was quiet and the only light came from the interstate traffic and the glow from the warehouse units on the north side of the road. The gate was open to the warehouse. Like the day before, a semi-truck with its running lights sat in the loading dock. My truck fit right into the same turnoff past the warehouse. I grabbed my surefire flashlight, Glock 43, two spare magazines and my clinch pick to round out my defense strategy if I got close enough to need them. Inside the fence there was the usual entourage of SUVs and the same German sports car. No blinking red lights on the surveillance system. Through the pines, I scanned the fence for an access point. Below me was a washout covered in large rocks. There was a gap under the fence large enough for me to move through. I slid down the embankment and shuffled under the fence through the red clay and rocks.

Now what? I couldn't just walk in there. My heart thumped and my palms were caked with sweat and red clay. The back door was shut, and I couldn't see any guards outside this time. Between the door and me stood a large cooling unit and a ladder to the top; above that, a large air vent on the side of the warehouse used in the hotter months. It had a metal grate that slid into position, offering ventilation to the large warehouse. That was my access.

I kept cover and made for the ladder. In a matter of a few seconds, I was on the cooling unit and flat against the wall of the warehouse. The grate slid open with some coaxing and a large open warehouse came into view. The loading bay stood open, and someone had unloaded the truck. There was a large group of women, children, and only a few men gathered to one side of the warehouse, all seated on the ground. On the other side, there were stacks of large, heavy duty wooden crates and pallets. The thugs that had been trying to kill me and a couple more were standing around them, holding guns and keeping the people hemmed in. This explained the lack of security outside.

A moment later, Liona and a couple of other thugs came into view, with Elena following. They were having a discussion, but I couldn't hear what they were saying. I had seen enough to confirm that what the commissioner's assistant had said was true. This was a trafficking and shipping operation and these people had not chosen this situation. I picked up my phone to text Hutch and saw six missed calls, all from him and another unknown number. I sent him a text with my location and a brief explanation, ending in 'get here quick'.

I checked the grate one more time and as I stood, three large vans pulled into the parking lot. I dropped and flattened myself out against the top of the cooling unit. The drivers joined the others inside the building. Were they getting ready to move these people somewhere else? If they were being held against their will, I couldn't let that happen. My mind ran through some possibilities, and then it hit me. The gate. They were all behind the gate. If I could get it closed, they may be stuck here. If it worked, maybe the surveillance cameras would activate, catching everything on film.

I slid down the ladder and used the vans as cover. On the way to the gate, I wedged a wooden pallet under the door and bolstered it with an empty fifty-gallon drum. A large rusted chain lay on the drum. The gate was heavy and when I pushed, it didn't budge. It was on a track with wheels and they were not moving. At the end of the gate stood a box and a keypad. I ran for the keypad and popped the box below the pad. A jumble of wires and circuit boards stared back at me as I ripped the three largest wires from the bundle. I touched two together, and the wheels activated, but the gate tried to open further. I reversed the connection, and it moved the other direction, slowly closing the gap to the only exit they had. As soon as the gate reached me and closed, I pulled it tight and used the chain to jam the track and tie the gate off. As I stopped to admire my work, I realized I had trapped myself in the fence too. I checked the corners of the perimeter fence and the red lights were blinking. It was a matter of seconds before a bang on the door I had blocked. I ran back towards the cars and the way I had gotten in, but they had breached the back door. Two thugs muscled their way out and kicked the pallet and drum to the side. One still had the limp, but what most concerned me was the Kalashnikov rifles they held.

Diving behind an SUV, I held my position at the front wheel, trying to keep as much cover as I could in the parking lot. I only had one choice; go out the way I came in and that would be difficult with two guns on me as soon as I moved. My phone kept buzzing silently as I tried to control my breathing, slowing my breaths and preparing to run.

They moved towards the gate, assessing the situation they were now in. I saw an opportunity and made a run for it. Within seconds, a spray of automatic gunfire scattered at my feet. I put on the brakes and slid to a stop in a pile between the SUVs and vans, my hands over my head as if to avoid a beating. I assumed the hands up position but kept them lower in case I could draw my pistol. A moment later, Liona and the remaining crew came outside with Elena bringing up the rear.

I stared Liona down, then fixed my stare on Elena. Immediately, her face went slack, showing no emotion, avoiding eye contact. Liona spoke up, "Well, Mr. Gonzalez, you've given us the chance to finish you for good. You really should have taken my offer. Too bad I can't stay to watch, but your interruption has hastened my departure time. My associates here will deal with you."

She moved to the lead SUV and stepped into the back seat. I caught a look from Elena and she too went for her car, but never spoke. They pulled around to the gate, but it was clear my rig had done the job. The gate wasn't opening. One thug moved to inspect the gate, crunching on pistachios as he scanned the driveway and street for traffic. His partner, Limpy, kept his Kalashnikov trained on me. I was searching for an opportunity to make for the fence when Limpy turned to ask his cohort for something in Spanish. In a split second, I reached for my Glock and pulled for a high ready stance and fired off three rounds right into his lower torso. He folded in a split second and sprayed the passenger vans with lead as he went down. I ran for cover and behind me; a crash and scream, then the sound of metal on metal with more automatic weapon fire. It was Elena. Her car buried into the side of the warehouse, one of the other thugs folded into the metal and his rifle laying over the hood of her car, a smattering of bullet holes across the windshield.

Liona's SUV was backing up and preparing to ram the gate when the place lit up and three deputy cruisers came straight up the drive to the gate. The driver of the SUV just pulled back and parked while no one exited. They watched the deputies as they surrounded the gate and the building. I ran to Elena's car and opened the door. She was laying in the front seat and had taken a round to the upper chest. Blood was pouring out. I immediately grabbed my handkerchief from my back pocket and pressed it over the wound. The deputies were still trying to access the gate with no luck. "I need an ambulance!" I yelled. "Hurry! Call an ambulance!"

"Ace, is that you?" It was Hutch, standing at the gate.

"Yes, it's me, man. Get an ambulance here fast! And bring a trauma kit if you have one in your cruiser!"

Elena gave me a hollow stare. "I'm sorry Ace, this isn't what I wanted. I hoped you might move on after the meeting last night." Her face was turning pale, a stream of blood trickling from her mouth, and I knew if she didn't get attention soon, she wouldn't make it.

"Don't talk, there's help coming. Stay with me, ok? Stay with me."

Hutch had pulled the fencing back from the gate and had another deputy with him; they arrived with the trauma kit as she passed out. Her pulse, still strong but fading. They went to work and a few minutes later; the ambulance arrived. They took her out on a stretcher as two deputies pulled Liona and her henchmen out of the SUV. Hutch turned to me, his eyebrows raised, an expression like he wanted to speak but didn't have the words.

"I know, man, it's going to take some time." We moved to an area away from the commotion and I started with the story from the Origin.

"Alright, so I filled you in on the phone, but it was pretty quick since I had to move to get here. I had gotten off my shift at Lost. I took the skiff down the canal to the Origin and immediately, Trigger knew something was off. He was on the bow of the skiff, sniffing out the guy. I should have known. I rode the tide through the canal and the fog was so heavy I could barely see the boat. Maybe he couldn't see us coming, either. I tied the skiff off and boarded the Origin and within seconds, this guy was on me. He came off the flybridge and took me down. He had my fish club and came down on my head with it. I was out before I knew what hit me. Then I woke up next to a bucket full of concrete with a massive headache. Trigger was locked in the cabin and this guy was motoring across Big Lagoon towards the pass. He told me his entire plan. He was heading to the drop-off to sink me to the bottom. I cut myself free with a bait knife and we fought it out on the boat, then went overboard in the pass. He was going nuts struggling, then I got behind him and choked him out."

Hutch's eyes got wider. "You're shitting me, right? Underwater?"

"No man, it was all I had. I didn't want to keep fighting this guy in the water and risk drowning. I had the upper hand and I couldn't let it go. Once I knew he was done, I got him out and brought him back as quick as I could."

Hutch stared at me, shaking his head in disbelief. "I'm guessing he was pretty messed up when the medics got to him?" I asked.

"You got that right. They said he had some cracked ribs or something, maybe a knife wound too, and needed to go to the hospital. He also blamed it all on you but couldn't say what he was doing there," Hutch said.

I stopped, a look of confusion came across my face. "What? You didn't take him in?"

"No, he needed to go to the hospital, and you weren't there to confirm anything," said Hutch. I let out a deep breath. "So he walked?" I said.

"No, he didn't walk. I have deputies with him now." Hutch replied.

"Did you know this was happening?" I asked.

Hutch shook his head. "Not all this, but FDLE has been working with the department on a joint task force. They should be on their way now. This trafficking is getting big around here. It's not in the media much, so you don't hear about it. You know the Interstate 10 Corridor is one of the hottest trafficking routes in the country? It's a direct route from the border to the east coast. You're part of a huge bust here, man."

I shook my head, considering the cost. "Have you gotten any word on Elena yet from the medics?"

He checked at his phone, "not yet, but they just left man. I'll call when we get done here if I don't hear from them."

"So fill me in here. You found out about this from that guy on your boat?"

"He said something was going down tonight at one of her warehouses and I knew about this one. I went on a hunch and now here we are."

"Are you hurt or anything?"

"No, I came out ok, but I put a couple of rounds in that guy over there." We turned to see Limpy there in a pool of blood, the medics finishing up on him. He wasn't fortunate enough to leave in the ambulance.

Hutch's eyes focused on the gate the deputies had freed up and were now opening. "Your pal from FDLE is here. They're probably going to take over, so be prepared for some questioning."

"What, isn't this the county's jurisdiction?" I asked.

"It was until we found all these people. State and Feds take over after that since they came over state lines. We'll assist as needed, but it's their show now. You better get your story straight."

Special Agent Crowson spotted us from the gate and made a beeline for us. "What's the story Deputy?"

Hutch motioned towards me. "This individual here was in an altercation off-site. He learned of this situation during that altercation and called it in. During that time, his life was threatened, and he discharged his weapon. He can give you a report."

He focused on me. "I'll expect a full report as soon as possible. Don't plan on leaving anytime soon. Hutch, a word with you. Mr. Gonzalez, an investigator, will be here to take your statement in a moment. In the meantime, please stay put."

I watched as Hutch ran through my story with Special Agent Crowson. I wasn't worried about the local law enforcement but more so the State guys, especially this one who already held a grudge with me.

I watched crime scene move in and begin laying out the scene along with a swarm of officers interviewing the people from the warehouse and Liona with her associates. A few minutes later, another FDLE agent pulled me to the side, away from the scene, and began with the questions. I ran through the events leading up to my arrival and the details associated with how I came to know about this location. I also ran through the history I had with the developers and what this all meant. When the Agent was done, he reported back to the guy in charge. I noticed them looking my way several times, making notes and then examining my Glock now bagged up and tagged as evidence since I had used it to shoot and kill someone. Not going to see that again, I thought.

My attention shifted to the gate and two dark blue SUVs had pulled up. Each one held three people and one man emerged as the leader. The rest fanned out at the scene, and the leader went straight for the LEO in charge. The lead agent wore a hat and was younger, near my age, decked out in BDUs, a gun on his hip. I thought I recognized him, but once with law enforcement; he went into the building. I was having trouble keeping track of all the law enforcement agencies represented here. This guy was obviously higher up than the others since they jumped when he started asking questions. A few moments later, they all emerged from the warehouse and I moved closer to hear the discussion. The man in charge was doing all the talking.

"Officers, thank you for your cooperation in this investigation. We have been monitoring this operation from a distance for quite some time. What we have is a large-scale smuggling operation, not only in people but artifacts. This is black market stuff, usually sold on the dark web or in some upscale auction houses when it's clean enough to move. She buys these things and sells them, but of course, it's not totally legitimate, so we have been monitoring things from a revenue standpoint. She has been using this as a stopover point for merchandise and people. Now that we have her and the crew, I will secure a warrant for her home and any other properties we can find in her name. I suspect there is an extensive collection locally and more evidence on the trafficking as well. I will follow up with you as the investigation progresses." He stopped. "Can someone tell me who is responsible for this whole thing?"

All at once, the group shifted their gaze on me. I was a silhouette of a target waiting to be fired upon. Then I realized I knew the guy in charge. It was Hen. It took him a moment, but I could see the recognition in his eyes. He stepped over and reached out a hand. "Nice work sir, ordinarily this would have screwed things up big time, but you hit this at the right time. All the puzzle pieces fell into place." Through the crowd, I saw Hutch on his cell phone; his eyes caught mine, and I knew it wasn't good news. He motioned in my direction, and I excused myself from Hen and the other investigators.

"Hey, I got word from the medics. Elena didn't make it to the hospital." He paused. "She lost too much blood. They couldn't save her, major trauma." He paused again. "Those AKs do their jobs well. Sorry, man, I know you two were good friends."

I felt the air seep out of my lungs. A sick feeling grew, beside me her car smattered with bullet holes where a short time ago she was sitting. She had saved my life and, by doing so, had sacrificed hers. A sick feeling overtook me, and the acid in my gut began to bubble up. I stepped to the side and released what was there, splattering bile onto the asphalt and my shoes.

I wiped my face on my sleeve and straightened my hat. As I turned around, the head FDLE Agent was on my heels.

"Mr. Gonzalez, we need some more information from you. I'll need your license to carry the handgun you used in the incident and we need another detailed account of what happened and additional details on what led to the murder of Mrs. Elena Vasquez."

I felt dizziness creeping up on me again and reached out to steady myself on a nearby vehicle. "Can you give me a minute here?" I asked.

"The investigator is right over there. When you regain your composure, I expect you there and engaged. We'll be keeping the handgun as evidence." Agent Crowson walked into the warehouse, moving towards the other officers and the victims.

The dizziness lingered, but I finished with the questions and after what seemed like narrowly avoiding arrest by the State, I left. The eastern sky glowed as I crossed the grid of streets lined by oaks and palms in old Pensacola.

CHAPTER NINETEEN

I woke a few hours later to my phone ringing. It was Everett.

"Hey, what the hell went on last night, man? I heard there were cops everywhere, and you about killed somebody?"

I returned a scratchy reply, "Yep" and then realized I *had* killed someone.

"That's nuts, man. Where are you, anyway?" he asked.

"I'm in the hill trying to catch up on some sleep," I said.

"Well, get movin' son!" His southern drawl amped up a notch.

"Alright, alright," I said. "I'll meet you at the Origin. I'm sitting here with Trigger and Sam at the marina store right now." He replied.

I got to the marina an hour later, and the place looked like it did every other day. No commotion, no crowds, a few folks out tending to their boats and a couple shopping for a new cruiser. I stepped into the dockmaster's office and Everett was sitting there drinking coffee and keeping Sam, the dockmaster, from getting any work done. Trigger instantly jumped up, performed his cross paw stretch and nuzzled my leg. The brass ship's clock on the wall still read the wrong time.

"Well?" Said Everett.

"Well, what?" I said.

Everett walked over and slapped me on the shoulder and said. "I don't see any blood, so it couldn't have been too bad." I rubbed my temple where I was clubbed the night before.

"I got a couple of hours of sleep. Is there any coffee left?" I asked.

Sam laughed and Everett replied, "I made another pot a few minutes ago."

"Yeah, he drank all mine and felt bad, so he made another one," said Sam.

"And I knew he was coming in and would need a cup. Here, I made the whole thing for you," said Everett.

"Alright, you got your coffee now, so tell us the story,".

Where do I start? I thought. "I got in last night from Lost, which reminds me I need to tell Britt about all this and let her know I'm still alive and not locked up or dead."

Everett laughed.

"I already caught her up. She's been by this morning before her shift. But you should go see her pretty soon. Tell her yourself."

"Ok, good. I owe her a visit then," I said.

Everett and Sam both stared me down and finally, Everett said, "Come off it man, give us the story. What are you waiting on!"

I let out my breath and grabbed a stool.

"After my shift, I pulled the skiff up to the dock. The fog was thick, and the tide was running out, so guess I was quiet coming in."

"I didn't spook the guy until I was on the Origin. He came down from the flybridge and nailed me, then I was out. I was conscious long enough for him to tell me he was going to drop me to the bottom of the Gulf and probably Trigger too. Then he cracked me on the head and I was out again. I woke up tied up while we were motoring into the pass. This guy was at the helm of the Origin, running it like it was his boat. He must have thought I was out cold, so he wasn't really watching me."

"I found an old bait knife in the gunnel and cut myself free. We fought it out on the deck and he went overboard. I went in after him and all I remember in the water is that I got around behind him, tucked my head down and put a choke on him. He kept trying to punch me, but I was behind him and he couldn't reach me. I knew once I locked down, it was over."

"We struggled for a minute and I let the rest of my body go limp and heavy. He was pulling at my arms and trying to scratch my eyes, but nothing was working."

My eyes went still, and I slowly drifted back to that moment in my mind. "I could hear him screaming under the water."

Everett's face showed disbelief but also satisfaction.

Sam said, "Wait a minute, you killed this guy?"

After a moment, I replied, "I was fighting for my life, man. I knew I could revive him, anyway. Once he was done, I got to the ladder. I pulled him out and started CPR. It messed him up real good, but I brought him back. He barely got all the water out and I'm pretty sure I broke some bones, but I had no other choice. I tied him up on deck after that and got back to the marina as quick as I could."

"This shit is crazy, man. I've never heard of anyone drowning somebody, then bringing them back to life," Everett said.

Sam said. "We got some of the story from the FDLE guy this morning. He was checking a few things out around here."

"Was he alone?" I asked.

Sam took another sip of his coffee and said, "Yeah, he was looking around. He kind of made you out to be a bad guy and a little crazy."

"Ok, it sounds like this is the guy who's been trying to pin the floater on me. He's also pissed off that I've been hanging out with Analee. I think he knows the guy who's been after me too, so he's going to be back. If you see him, let me know."

"Will do," Said Sam.

Everett chimed in, "So, what happened next? Did you call the cops?"

"Of course. I made the call and let them know to send an ambulance. It's all a blur now."

I ran through the rest of the night for them, and then I got to the worst of it. "In the middle of it all, someone killed Elena." My gaze focused downward, trying not to replay that moment in my mind again. "She basically saved my life. I didn't know until the other night that she was involved. This whole thing has gotten way too crazy."

"I found out later that they didn't even arrest the guy who broke into the Origin and kidnapped me. Hutch said the guy's story turned it all around on me. Like I was the bad guy," I said.

Everett laughed and slapped his knee with a pack of cigarettes. "Man, that sounds like a crazy night, and after you worked over at Lost!"

"Yep, I'm spent. I need to go check out the Origin, though, and see what the cops left behind."

I walked out of the marina store and down the fuel dock, Everett and Trigger flanking me.

I noticed Sam giving me a side glance, not sure what to think of the situation or me now that he knew I had killed a man. I did a once over to be sure nothing was missing and Everett came aboard.

"How you feeling? And more important, what are you gonna do?"

I looked out over the lagoon, then further south to the Gulf. Flecks of seagrass and sargasso rode in on the tide, flooding the estuary and bayous grass flats and sloughs, triggering the bite for all the game fish in these waters.

"Well, I really want to go fishing, but I need to find out what happened to this guy."

"Hutch can tell me what they charged him with, if anything, and maybe I can get some more information on this detective. I thought after this public hearing was over I could focus on my trip, but that's probably not going to happen."

I've got to work at Lost later anyway, so I can't go too far.

"Maybe we can go out in the morning?" Everett said.

"I've got to make a few calls." I said.

"There are some leaders that need rigging over there on the chart table."

He smiled. "I'm gonna need a beer for that. I guess it's about that time," he said to no one in particular.

I glanced at the marine cote shotgun above the door. "They took my pistol."

Everett laughed and said, "yeah, that's what happens when you shoot somebody with it."

"I know. It'll probably stay locked in evidence for a while."

Everett stopped and said, "Wait a minute."

"You mean to tell me you had a gun the whole time you fought this guy on the boat, and you didn't draw?"

My forehead wrinkled as I considered what he was getting at. "I thought about it, but no, I never had time to get a shot off, anyway. The story would be a lot different right now if I had shot that guy. He wasn't drawing down on me with an AK like the other guy. Besides, I sized him up before and I knew I could handle him, especially when I got him in the water."

"That's ridiculous, man. There's plenty of justification for dropping a guy that trespassed on your boat and tried to kill you," He said.

"It sounds like it when you say it like that, but they didn't lock this guy up. It would have been a tough sell to the cops." I replied.

I was getting tired of pleading my case to my pal.

"I guess the county crew takes care of their own, huh?" He took a swig of his beer and shook his head.

"I guess, man, that is messed up, though."

I laughed and said, "We'll see what Hutch comes up with. Besides, I would have never gotten to the warehouse and made that connection if I had shot that guy here. No way I could leave that scene, right?"

Everett thought for a minute, "I guess not, but damn you got a crazy guy like that waiting for you on your boat to kill you and if that's not justification, I don't know what is."

I considered what he said. He was right, but it wasn't as clear as a thug holding an AK on me.

CHAPTER TWENTY

As the day wore on, a low layer of clouds descended on the bay and intermittent rain blanketed The Lost Republic in a slow drizzle. Fog had settled in on the Gulf and reached the into the estuary. That afternoon, the rain stopped, but the fog lingered, holding in pockets of the bayous obscuring the sky and the sunset.

Before we loaded up in the skiff, we checked all the lines on the Origin. Everett rode over to Lost with me to have a drink. I suspected he was monitoring things and watching out for any suspicious characters.

When we arrived, Britt had already checked out and left another bartender to handle shift change. Trigger posted up in his usual spot and I got in gear for the night. I hit the office to pull some things for the night and noticed most of the regulars at the bar and the surrounding tables. I knew I would tell the story several times throughout the night. Regardless, at least I'm safe and now more prepared for an encounter with another bad guy. A situation like that puts you on alert. It's like the awareness dial gets turned up a couple of notches.

After the shift and running through the story countless times, I sat down at the bar and began the closing duties. Locking down the place and counting the money was the bulk of the work after cleaning. A couple of servers and kitchen crew sat down with me and had their shift beers.

I was digging through my tip jar when Britt came rolling through the back door, a beer in her hand and sunglasses on. I could tell by her walk she had been out since her shift ended, making the rounds as well. She sat down beside me.

"Hey man, how was the night?" she said.

I shuffled the cash and finished counting a stack before I responded, "All good, no complaints. I'm not as exhausted as I expected after the late night I had."

She hesitated and then said, "Are you gonna tell me what happened?"

"It's kind of crazy story. This guy tried to kill me and may have done it if I hadn't escaped. He got the drop on me and I went down. He was planning to drop me to the bottom of the Gulf, watch me go down, but I freed myself and turned the tables." She shifted in her seat and took another swig from her beer, then let out a long breath. "Then I chased down a lead I got from him and ended up getting into an ugly situation with some nasty people." I paused again. "Then I shot someone and watched someone I've known for a long time die saving my life!" My voice slowly got louder as I recited the events again; this time it sounded more real in my head because I was telling the story to someone I cared about.

I could see her body stiffen up and her jaw tighten as I told the story.

"Dude, you act like it's all no big deal!" she said.

I threw up my hands in the air. "What are you talking about?" I asked.

"Someone tried to kill you and you act like it's nothing?" she replied, her sunglasses bouncing on her face.

The servers, sensing the tension, packed their things up and moved on out.

"Whoa, hey, I'm not excited about it, but I can't get all worked up about this. Most of these guys are still out there, and I don't even know how the rest of the situation unfolded. I'll go nuts if I worry about all of this."

"Right, I know that, but you don't seem to take any of this seriously! You walk around like it's all cool and there's nothing going on!"

"Hey, I know these guys are still out there, but I can't let that show up in my day-to-day life. If I was on edge all the time, I would drive myself crazy. I'm taking precautions and have people watching out for me. That's about all I can do."

"I think you need to do more. Get the cops out here to monitor things or work different shifts so they don't know your habits." She hesitated and then said, "Stay in town more often or something." Then she stopped, took another breath in and said, "I just know that if you got hurt or worse, I couldn't handle it and I guess I want you to take this as seriously as I do, that's all." A tear streamed down her cheek from under her glasses.

"Alright, I get it. I'll work on it and try to be more aware of my surroundings and people."

She got up and walked around the bar to grab another beer from the cooler. I saw her take the sunglasses off and wipe her eyes, then turn the bottle up. She put the glasses back on over her swollen eyes and wiped her nose with her sleeve.

As she opened another beer, there was a commotion from the back and then silence. Everett emerged from the kitchen. "Christ, it's like y'all are closed or something!? I had to come in the back way. The damn lights were off. Spilled my beer," he said as he drained what was left of his beer.

He met Britt and gave her a hug with one arm and grabbed a beer from the cooler with the other.

"I got some info on this dude that you hung out with last night and also who else is involved in this thing."

He assumed the bartender position leaning in towards me and continued to work on his beer, saying nothing. I looked at him, "well, come on with it."

"Well shit, I was waiting for you to ask. I thought for a minute you didn't give a damn that I got my finger on the pulse of The Lost Republic! Ha! It only took a little asking and lots of beers." He sat at the bar, pulled out a cigarette, and reached behind the bar for an ashtray, settling back into the barstool. With a click of his lucky green zippo and a puff of smoke, he was in storytelling mode.

"First, I took the beach cruiser to the boat ramp for sunset. There were a few locals there. Everybody was talking about your night. At first I listened and then they realized I was there and started asking me questions. I didn't tell them much and after a few minutes, they started in on what they knew."

"I got everything from a hitman to someone who was on the wrong boat drunk and you kicked their ass. They didn't know about the warehouse. I added some in but didn't get into details there. Then someone asked about Elena and I played dumb, but they knew she was involved somehow."

"That goes to show you that the coconut telegraph is alive and well here. Everybody repeats what they heard with a little extra added in to make it more interesting." He took another drag off his cigarette.

"One common theme is that you're an A1 badass, but nothing else that was accurate or helpful. Everybody knows to be on high alert. If this dude or anyone shady shows up, then we'll know pretty quick," he said.

"Hell, I guess I should be thankful you were out and about grilling the neighborhood about my night." I said.

He took a long drag of his smoke. "Damn right."

Once I had everything locked up at Lost, the three of us loaded up on the skiff with Trigger and headed down the canal to the Origin.

The Seabreeze Effect was in full force and the winds had turned offshore. Above us, the night sky was clear, and the air was cool with the north wind. The night birds and the bats beat their wings at the sky just above our heads as we idled down the canal with the tide.

I stayed silent and considered the fact that these friends of mine and others in the community had come together and would alert me to anything suspicious. As we came under the bridge, the familiar thump of a late night car welcomed us aboard.

The Origin was there, no sign of anything out of the ordinary. I suspected this would be the case. Anyone who wanted to do me harm would keep their distance for a while.

We eased up to the dock, and by this point, Everett was sitting on the cooler in his usual position, arms crossed, head down and a beer tucked in the crevice of his armpit.

Britt, a natural on the water, was on the bow with Trigger and tied everything off like a seasoned deckhand. I roused Everett, and he moved from his seat to the couch.

Britt shed her sunglasses and jacket.

"I'm going to crash if you're cool with that?" she asked.

"No problem. I'll pull the hammock across the salon. I'm going to shower and write a little before I go down."

A shower on a boat is not your typical shower. It begins with a shot of warm water, lather, and ends with another hit of warm water. Tonight I let the water flow. It scalded my shoulders and consumed the cramped head in a steam bath. I had two of my closest friends staying on my already cramped boat with me. It was clear they were concerned about the situation I had found myself in and I suspect they felt that staying by my side would be one of the few ways they might protect me should there be another attempt on my life. The trafficking syndicate I had exposed spanned much farther than The Lost Republic. Little to no emotion had come over me when I saw those people being held at gunpoint, herded to the waiting vans. It was something I had never considered or experienced. When I closed my eyes, the vision of the thug I had killed flashed across my mind's eye. It was the first time I had drawn my weapon to defend myself and I had killed a man. The last part I remember was his lifeless body, a pool of crimson, growing around him. I felt a weight on my chest. I struggled to take a breath, and I had to steady myself on the wall. Within seconds, the small space was closing in around me and my knees buckled. I ended up in a ball in a corner of the shower. I couldn't tell if I was crying or if the steam from the fading hot water was settling on my face. The fetal position was all I could manage while I struggled to breathe.

I came out of the fog as the water turned cold and I again struggled to get a breath.

After my shower, I sat at the chart table and laid my thoughts out on paper. Trigger was by my side on his back, his leg twitching and kicking as he dreamed. My other protectors here sleeping and, in their minds, a deterrent to another attempt on my life. I hoped I had not pulled them into the fray of all this and made them targets as well. It was hard to know, but it was comforting to know they had not been directly involved in anything. The boat rocked gently, and the hammock strung across the salon swayed with the motion. I closed my laptop and, with a pillow and blanket, settled in for the night.

The next morning, I woke to the familiar toss from the wake of a barge pushing down the canal. The sun was breaking the eastern horizon and a brilliant yellow light filled the sky in the east. In the west, dark lavender reflected in the canal. A long lanky heron flew from its perch on the bridge pilings and glided above the surface of the canal to its sunrise fishing spot on the shoreline. The wind was still offshore and would turn soon. Britt rolled over when she smelled the coffee and emerged from the v berth. She grabbed her gear, then stepped out on the stern and checked the wind, a smile forming as she listened for the sound of the surf breaking on the seashore.

"I'm gonna borrow your bike, ok? I'll bring it back later today. If the wind is still right when I get home, I'm going to paddle out," she said.

She jumped up and wrapped her arms around me and grabbed her bag. She already had her sunglasses on and her hair hung from a loose bun around her wrinkled shirt.

"I'll hit you later and see what you're up to," she said.

As she hit the dock, I said, "Ok, I've got coffee going?"

"Nah, I'll get some on the way."

Everett was up not long after that. He waited for a cup before he left to go check on his lady friend at home. I grabbed my cup of Bustelo, sat on the flybridge and watched as the Lost Republic woke up.

After my coffee, I took the skiff on a ride down the canal west through the grass beds and old river. There were a couple of large developments going in along the way, and I needed to see them and snap some pictures of another untouched sea-shore giving way to the bulldozers. I idled most of the way on the north side of the Key along the grass beds. The skiff drew enough water to hug the shoreline and stay inside the channel between the Key and Ono Island, known as Old River.

I watched the grass beds as flickers of metallic shimmer shot away from the bow of the skiff. These beds were home to countless baitfish that supported a lively population of red-fish, trout and flounder, and also made this area a relatively unknown fishing destination. I crossed over into the shallow channel between Ono Island and the seashore barrier island. Barrier islands are a special part of the coastline and are always in flux. They serve as a natural buffer for tropical storms and hurricanes. They take the initial brunt of the force of the storm and roll the sand and shoreline over onto themselves, effec-tively saving the structures on the mainland. There's evidence of this in the beach dune system and ridges that make up the barrier island systems. The kink in nature's plan is manmade development on these islands. Once hardened with these con-crete monoliths and parking lots, the islands stay static. This means that the developments take the force of the event and end up buried in sand or undermined from the wave and storm surge. They get into the habit of beach renourishment and re-ceive sand from a major dredging project pumped onto their beaches to restart the cycle. This cycle affects the seagrasses and the larger marine ecosystem by starving coastal areas of the transported sand and choking others with it. The islands cannot roll over and maintain the cycle, disrupting the natural rhythm of the system.

My skiff slid over the surface of the clear water and sand only a couple of feet below. The tide was outgoing, and I felt the pull as I entered the channel. I could see the skeleton like bones of the concrete foundations of towers rising from the Key to the south. In the last few years, development had increased as moratoriums expired and money moved in. In the past, many developments would begin and the machines would level the place for the concrete trucks. These projects would only last for a brief time before an investor ran out of money and scrap the whole thing. Most of the new breed of the developers had been taking a different approach. They finance the purchase of the land, then pre-sell the units until they made their money back. Each had a shortlist of financiers. These backers knew they could turn around the next day and resell the units for a twenty to thirty percent markup. It was a game they all played. I guessed the main backers of some of these projects could clear twenty million every time and never spend a dime of their money. It was a great business plan, and each time, they would plan the next one.

I brought the skiff to the mouth of the pass and faced into the current. I stayed close to the north side of Ono Island and traced the channel back towards the lagoon. There were schools of mullet in the shallows near the edge of the channel and dolphin working the school as they swam in tandem with my skiff. As the outgoing tide pushed out towards the pass, it carried seagrass and sea creatures with it. Water was clear over the sandy bottom and grass beds and shadows of fish moved below as I idled the skiff along. The sky had changed to pale blue overhead and white dreamsicle towards the east. The bridge was visible in the distance and the sisters' islands to the south of the channel. I followed the corridor into the no-wake zone and by the time I was tying up at the marina, my shirt was sticking to my back.

I noticed the familiar color scheme of a deputy's cruiser in the marina parking lot. Hutch was waiting at the marina when I tied off. Trigger sniffed him as we stepped on to the dock.

"Ace, how are you?" he said.

"I'm good man, took a cruise down to the pass and back. What are you doing here?" I asked.

"Well, I'm on patrol, but I wanted to stop by to see if you had any more issues."

I shook my head and said, "Nothing other than people asking lots of questions."

He laughed and tuned the dial down on his radio. "Nosy people can't be helped, right?"

"Not around here," I replied.

"I thought you'd like to know that your boy walked. The FDLE agent working the floater case is friends with this guy. I think they served overseas together. Anyway, he came in and made an official statement clearing this guy, said he was working with him but couldn't give details. This guy has some pull around the County but I can't understand why?" He paused for a moment as I stood there shaking my head.

He continued, "I was told that he's losing his job with the County, but no other details. The information you gave about what he told you could help us. I'm trying to decide how to use it."

I didn't know how to respond. On the Gulf, white thunderheads rose out of the water and reached into the sky. There was a slight breeze stirring the humid air, and beads of sweat rolled off his forehead. I felt sick to my stomach. If this guy could kill someone, then kidnap me, steal my boat and get away with it. It was going to take a huge screw up on his part to get arrested. My gaze shifted to Hutch. "I appreciate you coming out to check in. That guy tried to kill me man, so this is not making me feel better about things."

"I get it, man, and I would say you're approaching it right by carrying your own protection. We can't be there all the time."

I thought to myself, what protection? FDLE had confiscated my carry gun and now I was relegated to only a knife if things got up close and personal.

"I'm not sure if that's comforting or if it makes me feel worse," I replied.

"It wasn't supposed to do either," he said.

I nodded in understanding, with a little exhaustion.

"I know I sound like a broken record, but think about getting some real training after all this. There are some guys over in Orange Beach that are doing some things you could benefit from. Real world training. I think they train rescue teams or something. They have a private facility and range over there. I expect you have other enemies you haven't met yet. We found out that the guy you dropped the other night has ties to the cartels down in Mexico and South America. He had tats all over him. Someone is bound to come looking for him."

I waited for the joke, but it never came. "I'm serious man, I know they took your pistol, so think about getting another one."

The reality of what he had said sunk in. "You're probably right and now that my pistol is evidence, I'll need to go shopping. I still keep the shotgun on the Origin and my Glock 19 at the house. The 19 will do for now, but the 43 was so easy to carry."

I paused and shook my head. "It's hard to believe it all went down like this," I said. "I've been doing this for a while now and I've never been in this deep."

I considered the weight of the situation I was in. "I'm on this road, and I'm alone."

He returned a chuckle, then his faced turned serious.

His reply was, "We're all alone on this road, but we get to decide the path we take. Watch yourself, man."

I could hear the water rapping against the dock and the hulls of the boats in the marina. The smell of engine exhaust, the brine of the American sea washed over us as I considered what path I was on.

After Hutch left, I didn't feel any better. They were building a case against the guy that attacked me, but nothing was certain. I was considering moving my boat excursion departure date up to get out of the way of any other uninvited visitors. The idea of running away from this and hoping it was over when I returned didn't sit well with me. I knew I would have plenty of watchdogs here at Lost and I would get wind of any funny business if it occurred.

I washed the decks down on the Origin and completed the usual maintenance of the skiff as a distraction from all the events in my mind.

I went into Lost early that afternoon and grabbed a bite, watching the incoming tide. The bar was full when I began my shift and Jerry, the local talent, sang a song JJ Grey wrote about Florida, and how it's getting harder and harder to find. There was the usual band of regulars at the bar and a few tourists book ending them. I caught Britt up on the service and stocked the bar for the night.

She stopped to scratch Trigger on the head and said, "Hey, what if I take Trigger with me? I'm on the bike and cruising around the point until later."

I smiled. "I'm cool with it if he is."

She scratched his head again and said, "Come on boy, let's ride."

He followed by her side, and at the back door, he turned to me. I smiled and said, "Go ahead boy, I'll see you later." Then they rode into the sticky haze of the afternoon.

A few minutes later, Hen sat down. "Hey man, good to see you again," he said.

"Likewise," I said and, recalling his preference of beer, and set one down in front of him.

He grinned. "Excellent memory. So, how are you? Rough week, huh? Oh, and sorry to hear about your friend. I only got the story after you had checked out."

"Yeah, thanks." I shook my head. "I'm still not sure if it was worth it."

"Hey, I know it doesn't bring your friend back, but think of all those people that you saved by doing what you did. You made a big difference in their lives and all that might have come after."

Through everything that happened, I hadn't stopped to consider this. A collateral positive from the entire experience was that I had stopped some people from being forced against their will to work in modern slavery. "Yeah, I guess you're right. I sure didn't expect you to jump out of that SUV after everything that happened."

He laughed.

"Are you still thinking of moving here?" I asked.

"Yep, I'm still considering it. Where I live doesn't have much to do with my job since I travel a lot. I like it here and I believe you should enjoy the place you call home."

Smiling, I replied, "I'd have to agree with that. Have you been out on the water yet?"

He shook his head. "Not yet. I was thinking of going out on a fishing boat or charter or something, or maybe a sunset cruise, but I haven't booked anything yet."

I said, "Ok, well how about coming out with me on my boat? It's not much, but I know the water around here pretty well, and I may put you on some fish."

The grin returned. "Sounds great man. Are you in the charter business too?"

Shaking my head, I said, "No, I take friends out sometimes if I can manage it."

Jason chimed in from behind him, "Don't let him bullshit you. He's better than most of the guides around here."

I laughed and handed Jason another beer as he settled back in to the foosball table with big Dave.

Hen's gaze shifted back to me, a surprised and excited expression. "That would be great."

I said, "Tomorrow afternoon we've got an incoming tide. Conditions might be right for a decent inshore trip. Are you available early afternoon?"

He hesitated.

"I know you're working, but the tides dictate our schedule around here."

"I can knock off early, I guess."

"It would help your chances of getting on some fish," I said.

"I'll make it happen then," he replied.

"Great, I keep my boat across the canal at the marina. I'm all the way to the west end at the last slip. Get there around two and I'll have everything ready to go."

"Are you sure, man? This is way cool, but I don't want to put you out," he said.

"No way, man. I would be out anyway, and besides, I need a distraction. I'm sure I can put you on a decent fish."

"I like the sound of that." His grin returned as he took another pull off his beer.

The rest of the shift was busy and the regular customers all wanted information on what was going on and if I had any more brushes with death. Most had genuine concern but also wanted the gossip in the Lost Republic for the week. Hen moved on to "get ready for the fishing trip." The sunset was another spectacle and drew a large crowd, as it did on the weekends, and the docks were loaded with people. As the night rolled on, I had a strange feeling. The customers came and went and it was as if I was in a dream, floating through the motions I had so many times before.

After my shift, I was sitting at the bar having my usual nightcap while I ran numbers. The servers left for another bar and the clatter of dishes from the back told me there was only a dishwasher left.

As I took a sip of rum, a breeze hit me and I noticed one of the folding doors along the dock was open. I stepped off the barstool to secure the door, and as I did; I realized I was not alone.

In the corner of the bar, only a few feet from me, stood Cadillac Steve in the shadows. He was breathing hard and his face was red, swollen with booze. He was mumbling something about "settling this." I put both my hands up, palms facing him, as if I could push him off of me. "Hey man, back off!" I said. He continued mumbling, never acknowledging what I said.

I could smell the stale sweat on him from a few feet away. His knee, still wrapped from our initial confrontation. It hadn't hindered him from showing up tonight to close this chapter. My heart was pounding, and I knew if I started backing up, then I would only show him he was in control. I side stepped and kept the upright stance and drew him over to the dining area so the bar didn't limit me in movement. He followed and seemed to pump himself up to make the move. I assumed he would beat me senseless if he got his hands on me. I saw the fire in his eyes change and his shoulders drop. In a brief second, he lunged at me, arms outstretched, prepared to grab me. He was so big; I stepped to my left and dropped to one knee, driving forward under his right arm, then turned to face him as he passed me. I felt his arm skim the top of my head as he passed and busted through a table and chairs on the dining room floor. The dishwasher could give me no help, so I had to get to a phone without giving him the opportunity to get his hands on me. He kicked the chairs off and got back to his feet, while looking around the room trying to make his eyes focus, blood dripping from his face, mixing with the sweat he wiped from his brow with his sleeve.

"Stay still, you bastard, I'm gonna break your neck!" He grunted.

He continued to advance, and I got back with my hands in front position, one foot in front of the other, trying to keep a ready stance. He advanced again and this time; went lower with his arms. I saw my chance and took my left hand, balled my fist and chopped straight down on the arm closest to me. My right hand came down on the back of his neck and, pushing down hard, my legs sprawled out behind me to keep me from being knocked on my back.

He let out a grunt as the chop landed at the elbow joint and dropped his elbow to the ground, the rest of his body following with a guttural thud as he landed in a pile on the floor. He was at my feet and I stomped straight down with my heel in the kidney, a grunt coming from the pile of man on the ground. Then I stepped back, out of reach. He was slower to get up this time. He got his feet under him while holding his elbow, hanging low and swelling.

He yelled out, "You bastard, you broke my arm or something!"

He was doubled over, holding himself and pulsating red as he tried to regain his focus. I moved back into my stance and let him drive towards me again, this time with only one arm, the other tucked and useless against his side. I made the same side step, and this time spun around and slipped an arm over his shoulder and grabbed his chin, then pulled back with my right hand. In the same motion, my left came up and pulled the hair on his head back. The action of the pull back with his momentum forward stopped his head and his legs continued forward. He hit the ground, the air in his chest exiting at once as his head bounced off the concrete, making a hollow thump.

He lay still, his right leg tucked under his body and his left stretched straight out in front of him. He was clearly unconscious. As the pool of blood grew around his head, I nudged his injured elbow with my foot and there was no response. I went straight to the phone and dialed dispatch. In a few minutes, there were three cruisers and an ambulance in the parking lot. They located his car parked down the road under the bridge. Hutch pulled up after I had given my statement to the other deputies. He was relieved, shaking his head.

"This guy again? I know I keep saying this, but you really need to think about some training after this so you know how to handle yourself."

"Ok man, whatever you say." I was still trying to fathom how I had dropped this guy for the second time.

"Did this guy break-in here?" asked Hutch.

I motioned to the door by the dock. "I think he came in the side door or something. Best I can guess."

"You're good though, no injuries?"

"No, nothing," I replied.

He lifted his hat and scratched his head. "Ok, did he say why he was here?"

I shook my head. " Something about settling things. He was pretty set on pounding me."

"He still thinks you're the guy who killed his buddy, huh?" he asked.

"He's the only guy that's worried about it," I said.

Hutch said, "We still haven't found next of kin for the floater."

"What's the story with the assistant?" I asked.

"We're still working on the case. Have you had any more contact with him?"

I shook my head. "No, nothing. I think he's keeping his distance for now. He may have a hard time explaining why he's back around my boat or me after he tried to kill me."

"He should keep his distance, at least for a little while. In the meantime, I'll work my angle and see what turns out. The crew is finishing up. Your guy rode in an ambulance out of here, so you've got nothing to worry about except the blood to clean up."

"Great," I said.

"What do you think he was on?" Hutch asked.

"No telling, he's a drunk, but there may be some other chemical influence there." I stared at the puddle of blood on the floor.

"How the hell did I get here?" I asked no one in particular. He returned the smile but said nothing.

I had to wait another half hour for all the officers to leave. I cleaned the place up as best I could and locked up around 1:30. Back at the Origin, Britt and Trigger were both asleep. I shook off the headache that came after the adrenaline wore off and tried to fall asleep, but my mind kept spinning.

The man I sent to the hospital was now in the drunk tank and I would not miss the chance to press charges this time.

Would he back off for a while?

I believed news of the man who killed his friend would come to the forefront soon and he would redirect his attention to someone else.

Another time my life had been in danger recently. I knew I was on the right path.

This most recent storm was forcing me to weigh the consequences, and consider if the reward was worth the risk.

I hadn't decided yet.

CHAPTER TWENTY-ONE

The next day, Hen showed up at the Origin right on time. He was wearing a Lost Republic Ball cap, the requisite pastel button-down fishing shirt, board shorts and a pair of flops. He carried a soft cooler on a shoulder strap and had a big smile as he stopped and spoke to Sam. There was a light chop on the canal, and the palms and oaks across the water rattled in the breeze. The air was heavy with humidity and his shirt stuck to his chest where the strap of the cooler held fast.

"This is where you live, huh? Pretty nice. I never even thought of living on a boat here until I met you."

I laughed, and said, "It's a part-time gig when I'm working out here. I have a place in town."

He motioned at the boats in the canal and the marina, the bridge overhead. "Great setup, though, and right down the canal from the restaurant."

"It works out pretty good for me," I replied. "Go ahead, look around."

He dropped the cooler on the dock and Larry the Pelican moved in, hoping for an easy meal. Hen stepped back and looked over the Origin, then settled on the skiff.

"We'll take the skiff out. It's already gassed up and ready to go," I said.

"Cool, I brought the drinks." He said, motioning to the cooler.

"We'll wait a little while for the boat traffic to let off and then head out."

He reached in the cooler and grabbed a beer, popping the cap in one quick motion. "You want one?" He asked.

Smiling, I said, "No thanks. I'll start a little later after I get you on some fish."

His grin returned. "sounds good to me!"

I set about rigging a couple of leaders. "Still looking for a place to live?" I asked.

"Yeah, I am, but there's not much available around here. This setup gave me another idea, though."

"What? Living on a boat?" I asked.

"Yep, this looks pretty good and you're always on the water."

"It's nice, but not always great during hurricane season, and a boat gets pretty small real quick," I said.

"I guess you're right, not the best place to be in a storm," he said.

I loaded the last bit of tackle on the skiff and stepped aboard.

We headed west in the canal with the stream of other boats headed back to the dock. The bridge overhead thumped with traffic and a cluster of boats gathered at Lost as we passed. Water reflected the sun overhead, and the breeze kept the sweat off as we idled through the straights to the open water of the bay. The smell of brine and fried fish floated in the air.

"So, what's your story? I only know you through the few times I've caught you at Lost."

"Not much to tell," he said. "I've been working for the government since before I got out of school as an intern, then they offered me a full-time gig, so I took it. Grew up in Georgia, around Athens. I went to school in Tallahassee and that's where I got the Federal gig and stayed there. It's a home base since I travel so much. When I get back from working a case, I travel around the panhandle. I get out in the world now and then. I like to go down to the coast sometimes, but it's not the same as here. This place is different. It feels like another world here. It's tough to explain." He stopped and took a deep breath, held it and slowly let it out.

I knew the feeling well. "I hear you. It's real and you're right, it's different. It's also becoming more popular because of that. One day, you'll figure out what makes the place special," I replied.

He paused thoughtfully, trying to figure it out. "Why don't you tell me?"

"I can't," I said. "It's different for everyone. It may be a smell that triggers a memory. The beach and the open water. A person who reminds you of a long gone relative. You may never know, but that feeling won't go away. You'll always have that. That's how you know."

I stopped and watched him consider what I had said as I continued.

"I believe we all tell ourselves a story and that story helps us decide who we are. The place you live is part of who you are and your identity; it's all connected," I said.

I glanced ahead and a million dollar yacht pushed through the channel, ignoring the no-wake signs, blasting horrible music, the passengers gyrating with the beat.

He shook his head.

Smiling, I said, "That's one downside of all the people. You're guaranteed to disagree with someone's music." I smiled and turned up the reggae as we idled on past the sisters' islands and into the grass beds towards Old river.

When we pulled out of the channel and into the grass flats, I saw my chance.

"So, can you tell me about the investigation the other night? What happened and how did you get involved?" I asked.

He laughed. "Good question. I can tell you some, but not everything you probably want to know."

He continued, "We have been aware of Ms. Morales for a while now. I'm in town because of her. She's been bringing these people in, and then basically holding them hostage. What we didn't know is that they were being trafficked to other areas of the country. She was keeping some here to work in her hotels and condos. There are tax implications for all of those activities but," he hesitated, "do you remember all the crates and pallets in the warehouse? We checked all that out and found out she's trafficking stolen and historic relics."

I stopped what I was doing and faced him, to be sure he wasn't making that part up. His expression never changed.

He continued, "There's a market for that here, coming and going. Most move to New Orleans, but there is a small group of local buyers here as well. The warehouse was a stopover for both operations. We've served warrants for a couple of other warehouses in town but are still searching for another one that, based on our intel, should be full of artifacts. We don't know where it is. That's the big one. Either way, she's going away for a long time for the tax evasion charges. The attorneys can't make that go away."

I knew she was crooked, but man, I had no idea it would go this far. "Wow," I said. "All that here?"

"Yep, and you'd never know it, huh?"

I shook my head.

He continued, "We know she is the head of the snake here, but based on the financials we know where is at least one other player involved, likely in Mexico. We have a name, but we're still working on that lead. It's a matter of time, though."

We idled towards a thick grass bed and I killed the engine.

"I'm going to approach this assuming that you've never been fly-fishing before?"

"I've been before, but I'm not an expert." He replied.

"Ok, that's not a big deal. In fishing, I prefer this method, as it takes some skill and puts your mind to work while you're fishing."

I grabbed the 8-weight fly rod from the gunnel and stripped out some line. I went over the basic cadence and placement of the hands in relation to the rod and the target. After he understood the principles, in a few minutes he had the makings of a decent cast coming together.

I went over the double haul for distance and noticed he was white knuckling the cork handle and his cast was a little off.

"One correction, ease up on the grip. Everything else will work."

We spent the next hour pulling trout and reds out of the bay as the sun sank lower in the west. At sunset we were idling back down the canal, drinking a beer and talking about the fishing and what kind of boat he should get.

He was hooked, but my mind was in other places. My phone buzzed, and I checked it to see two missed calls from Analee. She hadn't called, save a couple of brief texts over the past couple of days.

I had been on edge all day. I woke with some cloud over my head and couldn't shake the impending feeling that something was coming and I wasn't clear about what that was. The sky behind us was a painting of some unnamed setting from another time. The water reflected the setting in a different tone, one with darkness and shades of black in the ripples of the wake we left behind the boat.

I docked the skiff and tied off while Hen unloaded the gear. He ran to his car and as he walked up the dock, Analee passed him, heading my direction. She wore black jeans and a gray shirt. A gold pendant hung from a long necklace, and her sunglasses sat propped on her head. Her hair was in a high ponytail and the clothes she wore emphasized her athletic figure. She was drinking a cup of coffee from the marina store.

"I need to tell you something," she said.

"Ok, what is it?" I asked.

"I told Chris I wouldn't be back. I went to see him, and he was asking me to do things for other inmates. He gave me two envelopes and asked me to open bank accounts and drop other money off at some businesses. At first I was hesitant, but I kept thinking that it might make things better for him inside, helping people out. I even went down to the bank, but I sat outside in my car." She moved closer to me as she spoke.

"I keep thinking about what this might be for and what it might mean for me, how I could get tied up in things and what if I get in trouble? It may not even be legal. I kept telling myself he wouldn't do anything to get me in trouble."

She took a deep breath and slowed herself down. "Another part of me wonders how he's doing in there. He may be in trouble, I don't know."

"I sat on it for two days thinking about it. Then I went back for a visit and gave everything back to him. I told him I couldn't do it anymore, he still has years left, and it's no way for me to live. I'm not in the best place, and I guess my loyalty is a fault."

"My mind tried to imagine what it would be like sitting and waiting for him all that time and then what our life would be like when he got out. I couldn't do it." I saw the beginnings of tears in her eyes. "All these what if scenarios flashed through my mind and I realized that it's not what's best for me."

I felt a warm sensation in my core and then nervousness, butterflies in my gut. Was this her way of committing to me? Or stepping away from her past?

She continued, "In the end, it was his actions that led him there. He was protecting me, but it was another choice that got him in there. I'm still beating myself up about it. Anyway, I needed to tell you face to face and let you know that I'm not doing it anymore. I came here because I couldn't sit at home alone and keep thinking about it. I needed to see you, too," she said, and leaned in, wrapping her arms around my waist as she rested her head on my chest.

"I'm glad you came. It's been a lot for you to deal with." I said. "You waiting for him to get out with no idea who he'll be after being in there for so long. He may be a different person after he sits in there. You would be too. And I think what you did is what's best for you."

"I also came here because I need you to know that I'm here because I want you. But sometimes I get a kind of hangover or something after I deal with something heavy and it takes some time."

"I understand, I'll be here," I said.

She splashed the coffee out into the canal and said, "I need a drink. Do you have anything on the boat?"

I smiled. "Sure, there's some rum in the galley. I'll make us a couple. A warning, though. I've been drinking beer and I smell like fish."

Without hesitation, she said, "I hadn't noticed."

"Great. I took a friend out fishing today."

About that time, Hen came back with another cooler full of ice. He introduced himself, and she smiled and shook his hand.

He had already gathered his things, and he seemed to get the message that she had moved in, so he excused himself.

She and I climbed up to the flybridge and settled in to watch the stars as the night sky came on. I could tell she was tense, and the rum helped loosen that up. She kicked her feet up and leaned back in the captain's chair. Then she turned to me and said,

"Do you ever wonder what your life was supposed to be like? I mean, what things could have happened had you made some choices a little differently? I've been thinking a lot about that lately. Choices, decisions and outcome of those actions. My life feels like it's been on hold for the past couple of years, waiting for things to change. I think maybe I realized that change had to come from me, deciding to move on, get past things, whatever it may be."

She added, "I think some people get held up waiting for something to happen to them, but they're wrong. Make things happen for yourself. Take action, right?" She looked over at me for acknowledgement. "Is this too heavy or philosophical for you?"

I shook my head and returned a smile.

"No, I get it and I think you're right," I said. "I also get why this is coming up. You made a pretty weighty decision that will change your life. I don't think anyone would take that lightly. For what it's worth, I think you made the right decision. Putting your life on hold for anyone doesn't make much sense." I hesitated for a moment, then said, "You lose every time."

She stared at me for a moment, then a breeze kicked up from the south and she looked up at the fading light in the lavender sky, and then her drink. She tipped it up, and in one gulp, finished it. I did the same.

We watched the night falling over the key and the bay and the stars, one by one, blinking in the heavens. The moon rose into a glowing beacon reflecting over the lagoon. In the east, the flashing of the lighthouse kept time, and a distant barge pushed toward the marina, the green and red running lights signaling the leading edge of the cargo. I broke the silence and announced, "I'm getting another drink. Do you want one?"

"Absolutely," she said.

She met me in the salon and pushed me back into the bar. Her eyes fixed on mine and the smell of rum and the day were on her. She leaned in for a kiss and I returned the advance, pushing her against the wall of the lounge and reaching my hand to the back of her waist.

She was trembling as she approached me. I felt the draw between us. The rum had only sparked the fire.

I woke with the first light in the east and made coffee.

I sat at the chart table and wrote for some time as the sky grew into blue light. The canal was still and a patch of red and hot magenta sky in the east reflected from clouds on the horizon. The mist had receded, but the air was still heavy with moisture.

My mind was consumed with thoughts on this waking morning in the Lost Republic. I had spent the night with a woman I had a serious interest in, but I couldn't help but feel it was more for her than us.

I sensed she had used the act to resolve her past relationship. She was now free from any ties that may have bound her to this other man whom she had loved. Myself, I still felt as if

I was in danger from these developers, which meant if we continued to build this relationship, she might be in danger as well.

I filled my cup and glanced into the berth at the silhouette of a round rump under the sheets and a twist of tousled blonde hair glowing from the waking day. The sheets continued to rise and fall with her periodic breathing.

The smell of strong coffee roused her from sleep and we watched the sun rise over the lagoon together. She was quiet, and I was unsure of her feelings as she departed. I felt some pull back as we split that morning and wondered what was next. After her confession the day before, I wasn't sure what would come. Had she done all of that for her and as a way to close a chapter in her life? Or maybe I was another beginning?

We had made no plans nor discussed another time to see one another. There was an unspoken draw between us, but neither one of us could decide if we were ready for more than what had occurred the night before.

Later that afternoon, Trigger and I loaded up and headed into town. On the way, I took old Gulf Beach highway. The fog had moved out, but low clouds and a light rain had fallen over the Lost Republic. As I drove past the sheriff substation, two deputies kicked up gravel, lights on and pulled out in front of me, racing towards town.

I continued on and slowed as I passed the entrance to the state park. In the distance, I could make out their tail lights rounding the bend as I crested the rise. I came to the bend where Liona's compound was situated and was greeted by a wall of flashing lights and traffic slowing. The gate to the property was open and several deputies gathered, one directing traffic. Trigger was now on his haunches, his snout sticking out the window.

"Hold steady, boy," I said as I patted him on the back. We pulled past the gate, my view distorted by the reflection of the rain and lights on the windows. As we passed, I could make out Hen beside his government SUV, surrounded by several other plainclothes officers with IRS in big letters across the back of their jackets.

I stopped and was hurried on by the deputies, directing traffic. I had a moment to think as the traffic stopped again. A moment of hesitation came over me and then I pulled over to the side of the road and stopped to think. What the hell was going on? Were they there for a bust? An arrest? I stopped the truck and began walking toward the gate, careful to stay behind the cruisers, to avoid the deputies directing traffic.

I made it to the gate and slipped in; as I did, Hen gave me a double take and held up one finger in a "just a moment" hand motion. I watched the action as it unfolded. Deputies and plainclothes officers were moving in and out of the house and the garage. There were several in the backyard as well, with flashlights and dogs tracking some unknown scent. A few officers carried out boxes and a computer. I was lost in all the activity when Hen slapped me on the shoulder. "Hey man, what are you doing here?"

"I'm not sure. What's going on?"

He looked around. "Wait a minute, were you just driving by or what?"

"Yeah, I was headed into town and saw the action," I said. "Did you arrest her or what? What happened?"

"No, we got here a little while ago. The judge released her yesterday on the stipulation that she wear a monitor. We noticed it did some funny stuff earlier, so we came to investigate and she was gone." He motioned to the dock. "If you notice, the Yacht is gone."

The massive cruiser that was usually docked there was missing. "What, she skipped out?" I asked.

"Yeah, she left sometime last night. She's well into international waters by now, but we've got a tracker on the boat." He held up an iPad with a blinking red dot plotted on a chart. It was offshore, near Texas. Hen spoke up, "See, I had a feeling she would run and since flying was out, it only made sense that she hop on the boat and get out of here. We're finishing up our search now and clearing any potential evidence out."

I stopped and stepped towards the dock. "So she skipped out huh?" talking to myself.

"Wait a minute, you knew she was going to leave?" I said, motioning to the dock and resting my hand on my head.

Hen's voice stayed steady the entire time. "It's like admitting guilt. The Federal prosecutor deemed her a flight risk, so they gave her bail on the condition she wore the monitor. I probably shouldn't tell you all this, but most of it's come out in the initial proceedings."

"We believe she's the local orchestrator of a large trafficking network, bringing migrants in from Mexico and Central America and forcing them to work while controlling their access to the outside world. Right now, because of the task force, we have leads on these operations in three areas across the Gulf Coast so far, and we'll probably find more as the investigation continues. The Lost Republic is also a hot spot for trafficking and until now, we thought the area was a pass through on the Interstate 10 corridor."

He continued, "Now we can expose these operations and slow the flow of trafficking in the area. And we have only scratched the surface of the smuggling operation related to the artifacts."

We've also gotten some information about the big boss in Mexico. His name is Roberto Mendez. He's actually Cuban but has been running the show from Piedras Negras to Mat-amoros for the last few years. He started as a small time coyote and worked his way up. Funny thing is that the first hit we got on him was back in the eighties. Guy actually came over to the states on the Mariel boat lift as a kid. He bounced around south Florida for a while and even down in the keys until about 10 years ago. He goes off the radar then, and a couple of years later he shows up in Mexico. All our intel says that he is the man in charge there now. At least for the southern part of the Texas border. The task force is working with Mexican author-ities now. My guess is that she's running to him and if that is the case, then maybe we get them both.

As my facial expression changed to one of disbelief but also more concern, he stopped and rapped me on the chest, bring-ing me back to reality. "Hey, I know it sounds heavy, and it is, but we're on this. We've got her now and anything we throw at her will stick. If, and I emphasize if, she gets away, she's on the wanted list with her man Mendez, which means there will be an alert if either of them ever tries to enter the country again."

He stopped and said, "hey, but consider this: it also means that the development is dead unless someone else tries to pick it back up, but I suspect it's going to be tied up in litigation for a good while."

"Ok, well, thanks for the update. It all is so unreal."

"I know, like a movie gone wrong, huh?" he said. "I've got to get back in here, though. Hey, hope everything went well last night. It looked like your lady friend needed to tell you something, so I took the hint and got out of there."

"Huh? Oh right, thanks man, it was fine." I said.

He reached up and grabbed my shoulder, righted me and said, "hey, this is no big deal. I'll catch up with you at Lost, ok? We can schedule our next fishing trip!"

I thought to myself, who is this guy? Then replied, "yeah, ok," as I turned to walk back to my truck. On the way into town, I considered the possibility of Liona making it to Mexico. I would surely have a target on my back then. The sound of rain on the windshield and the hum of the tires on the wet roads were a lullaby I didn't need. When we got home, Trigger and I settled into our poolside palace, and I opened the doors and windows to listen to the rain on the palms and oaks. I opened the closet safe and pulled out my Glock 19, checked the magazine, press checked the chamber and slid it under my pillow, a habit I didn't like.

The next morning I felt the need for some time on the water, so Trigger and I made it to the marina with the sunrise. I shot Dan a text and set off on the skiff towards the long, slender peninsula where Dan had his home. It was an area called Bear Point, settled 100 years ago; even longer ago by the Native Americans. This geographic feature had served as a refuge for the early Native Americans here as it came to a ridge and a high bluff. The bluff was anchored with centurion live oaks and hickory trees and longleaf pine. The natives chose this area because it had a constant breeze in the summer and gave easy access to the natural resources along the coast.

As I motored in, I pictured the tall amber colored men of a time long passed who lived off the land gathering shellfish from the surrounding waters and growing strong on the natural resources surrounding the point and the nearby pass.

Dan had lived here all his life and inherited the property from his father. He would often rise before the dawn as his father had to watch the sun break the horizon.

On the trip over, the bay was choppy and the boat traffic had increased as the weather and the season had become more favorable for the weekend warriors from up state. As I approached Dan's dock, I killed the engine and trimmed the motor all the way up.

Trigger was on his perch at the bow of the skiff and I grabbed the push pole and mounted the tower, poling the skiff through the grass beds to the beach. The dock was old and decrepit and stretched out past the grass beds where the water changes to the proper depths for a normal draft boat. Dan never used the dock, and over the years, it had fallen into its current state.

I beached the skiff and Trigger was off the bow, nose to the sand on the trail of some shore dwelling creature.

Unlike the dock, the stairs up the bluff Dan had kept up, and the contrast of the old stairs and patchwork of treated lumber and posts showed the wear of the harsh conditions of the coast. The stairs wound up along the bluff and let out onto the back patio and porch of Dan's home.

Huge live oaks whose branches reached upward framed the home and arched back down toward the ground, only to turn back up towards the canopy. I shuffled through the blanket of leaves as I made my way to the back porch where Dan was sitting in his rocking chair. His old redbone hound Walker was sitting by his side, the gray snout showing his age. It was cool and a light wind blew from the northwest around the house and rattled the waxy leaves of the oaks.

Dan smiled, and I returned it as I shook his hand.

"It's good to see you," he said as he stood to hug me.

I smiled and replied, "Same, you look good."

He laughed. "Ahh, it's an act." He paused for a moment and sat back down. He focused on a faraway point on the horizon of the bay. Finally, he spoke. "A lot has happened since I saw you last."

His gaze shifted to me as he smiled.

I filled him in on everything that had happened since our last meeting. He didn't act surprised.

He said, "Well, you've got to understand that this means you are doing something right. I would be concerned if there was no one that disagreed with what you're doing."

"I know you understand the risks when you speak out against a project where there's so much at stake. You will have your opposition, but I know you also have a community that is behind you in this crusade."

I said, "I can agree with that, and I have support, but their voices aren't as loud as mine. It's become apparent that many of the people who I thought would support me do, but are content to take a backseat to the action and the public part of it only providing encouragement and not speaking out against it."

He returned a knowing smile. "You mean like me?"

I shook my head. "No, this is different. You provide the outlet in the media and also give advice when it's needed. I know you were in this seat in years past, so now is my time to take this on and be that voice." I caught a brief smile, and he said, "I'm glad you recognize that. You know your dad and me. We were right there in your seat when we were younger."

"I know," I replied.

We sat in silence for a moment and I wondered what my father would think if he were still here with us.

I shifted in my chair and kicked my leg up on a cypress stump table.

"I've found that so many people who move here think what I do is blow the whistle on them for things that they see as their right, somehow missing the fact that when they do these things, they trash the environment where they live. Most times, this is the reason they moved here. They are killing the best part of why this place is what it is. One day, they will understand; when the place is unrecognizable, then they'll get it."

Dan's smile gave me some comfort, as I knew he had been here before. It was the same story from years ago as the population grew in the area.

He had watched as his childhood was bulldozed, filled, and paved. Now it was something new. New demons. The trafficking had only recently come to the surface, but was now something that I had stumbled into. Despite the circumstances, I was in it now. I had killed one of theirs and the main local operator had gotten away and headed for Mexico to meet up with the big boss. She knew everything about me and their thugs could be back at any time.

Dan looked up at the trees and again at the bay.

"The best I can tell you is to keep at it. This one may be dead for now, but there are others we don't know about. There's also this smuggling ring you helped to break up. People and antiques, or whatever it was. That sounds pretty heavy. You've handled yourself pretty well so far, but get some real training since you've made some serious enemies. You should take that trip you've been talking about. Clear your mind, get some of that old fashion religion out there on that boat and come back with a clear head and some direction, not only for this whole thing but for your life. I'm sure all of this has given you some unique perspective on your future. It's funny how a brush with death will do that for you."

He smiled, and Walker rolled over as Dan scratched his belly.

The bushes rustled by the bluffs and out came Trigger covered in sand, a huge grin on his sand-covered jowls. Walker assumed the ready position and he and Trigger went to rolling on the ground, an enormous ball of fur, ears and teeth.

Dan laughed and said, "If you need me, you know where I am. Keep me informed on your trip and when you plan to leave. Maybe you can send me your next piece before you head out on your walkabout? I should be able to get it into the next issue."

I nodded. "I've been working on it, but I still need to put some time in and tighten it up." Dan's silence told me he was pondering my situation as well. I knew in my mind I would write about the whole thing and put the trafficking ring out there in the open, free of any influence from the mainstream media.

Dan was silent for a while, then finally spoke. "You understand there is no real winner in all this? You win nothing, you prolong what will come to pass here. The developers never win. They claim a victory for the battle. There will always be another, and they will continue to champion these projects. They don't need the money. That went out the door long ago."

"Sure, they can clear several million on one of these projects, but for most of these guys, they're already set. They do it out of obligation. They see all the people these projects put to work, people that they have been working with over the years and what they stand to gain. There are more families succeeding and growing. It's not that they can't see the destruction, they see it in a different light. One that, to them, translates to people they care about. It's something that so many of us who rail against these projects miss."

"We see the loss up front and the long-term cumulative repercussions of this and we miss the actual people too, realtors, construction workers, service industry workers, and everyone else attached to the end product and what it took to get there. We get the tunnel vision like they do."

I got the feeling he was trying to give me some perspective on all of this. He continued,

"Now this trafficking ring has come to light and we don't know how this will affect what you're doing. Especially now that you're directly involved."

I said, "That's fair. It doesn't make the struggle any different or easier, but it helps me to move forward."

I sat and considered what he had said, letting it sink in.

Then I stood and gave Dan a hug. "Thanks for taking the time and I will keep you up to date on my departure. I'll try to get the piece to you before I head out."

Trigger and I spent the rest of the day poling the skiff in the inlets and bayous across Lost Bay. The oaks and palms rustled in the north wind and a fresh cool air permeated the bay. The sun, shrouded behind me by the trees, cast spangled shadows over the beach and the seagrass beds and mingled with the haze of the day over the bay. Trigger and I motored towards the marina, and he assumed his position as the bow lookout, a trail of sand behind him.

As we approached the marina dock, I killed the motor, and we rode the outgoing tide into the lagoon. The canopy of live oaks and pines framed the last pale light in the west. Overhead, a waxing crescent moon and star hung in the sky. It was the time of day when everything in the western sky was an indiscernible silhouette with no definitive features, only the contrast of the waning day against the sharpness of the black horizon.

That night, I woke hunched over the chart table, my face flattened and numb from the contortion I had been in for at least the last couple of hours. Once back at the Origin, I had been determined to finish the next piece for the paper. It had developed into a story about the human trafficking that so often occurs in the area but seldom makes the news. I failed in that effort and grabbed the remnants of my rum drink on the table, kicked it back and crawled into the bed.

As I drifted into another world, I fell into a half-dream state where reality was seldom concrete and the world I was in felt finite and hazy. I drifted to some other place and time, yet I was still here in this world.

I dreamed I was living in this same place, but it may have been a hundred years ago. There were similar fixtures, boats, water, brass ship instruments, and time moved slowly.

I was on a working vessel, a large shrimp boat, or trawler. We were in the lagoon here, but with little landmarks to calculate my position in that state. I wasn't sure, but I knew I was in a familiar place.

The crew of the ship was hard at work. I could not see their faces, only their salty ropy weathered arms and shoulders working, hauling in the catch.

The rest of the world indiscernible, covered in a windy haze. They were working, and in moments, they hauled in the catch. It was a massive net catch of shrimp and fish. They all pulled it in and went to work, separating the catch and sorting each to where it was to go on the boat.

I was a spectator, and they did not know I was there. It occurred to me I was witnessing what this place I lived in was like

100 years prior before man had fished out the stocks, altered the environment, molding the waterways into what we see today.

I directed my attention over the bow of the ship. I could see no development, and at the location of the canal there was but a small manmade flume; men were working at sluicing logs and tacking them together to move into the port from Lost Bay. Towards the north, I could see the silhouette of the lighthouse at the Navy Base.

My attention then focused back on the catch on the ship and the sheer magnitude of what they took in one pass of the nets. The crew, still shrouded in haze, set out to clean the nets and prepare for another pass as the trawler came about, heading back to the east and over the grass beds. The water was clear and shone a glimmering haze as well, but the individual blades of seagrass were apparent at depth.

A breeze picked up from the south and my gaze shifted to the barrier island and the patchwork of pines, oaks and sea oats, all hunched and wind worn as if a continuation of the sand dunes themselves. I could see the area I believed to be the Towers site and what it must have been a century ago.

Beyond the dunes, the Gulf shone an intense bright green in the near shore break while off the far sandbar blue water had crept in or was always there in those days. A condition rarely observed at present.

As my gaze came back to the boat, I knew I was in the boat's wheelhouse and there was a captain running the controls, glancing back as they made the next pass. I could see his face and I felt a familiarity with him, but I could not place him. He did not waste time as he maneuvered the ship through the grass beds and out towards the center of the lagoon. I was stationary in the boat's cab and he brought the nets in after the pass through the beds. As he shouted orders at the crew, he shifted his gaze and settled on me, his eyes the gray blue of an angry sea focused on me.

I froze in place and he settled on me with no words or orders at all. He was breathing heavily, one hand resting on the helm squared up to me as if to speak, but it never came. At that moment in my dream, the rock of the Origin awakened me as the weight of a person transferred from the dock to the boat.

CHAPTER TWENTY-TWO

I am a light sleeper and any movement of the boat from passing traffic on the canal wakes me. There is a distinction between that and the weight of a person stepping onto the deck of the Origin.

I looked to the stern through the salon but couldn't make out anything through the darkness. I hesitated, then rolled out of the berth, Trigger a furry heap on the deck of the salon. On the way through the cabin, I grabbed a short gaff hanging from the rack by the door, unsure of what I might run into.

There was only a slight orange glow from the dock lights down the marina. I reached the door and cracked it. As I did, a darkened arm reached in, grabbed my shoulder, and pulled me out of the salon. The man wore a hooded sweatshirt, jeans, black vinyl gloves and tactical boots. In his hand, a small caliber pistol glowed in the orange light, an oversized oil can fixed on the end that read FRAM. The pistol wore a small black bag on the side, presumably to catch the brass as it ejected the pistol.

He jammed it in my ribs and said, "shut up. Don't say a word, just listen."

Immediately, Trigger was at the door, violently barking. My captor closed the door and cut him off. He said, "this is all about to be over, but I need you to hear why before I kill you."

I paused. There was an accent there, and the voice was familiar, but I wasn't sure who it was. He lifted his head. I got a shot at his face through the shadows. I searched my mind; the face was familiar, but it had been a while. He spoke again and this time the accent came through thicker, Mexican, no Cuban. It was El Halcon, the man who threatened to testify against me and Seamus in Key West for a murder we didn't commit. His face was much older now, the lines forming around his eyes as he spoke. His dark amber eyes were still the same, lit from behind and sharp. I could smell smoke and cheap aftershave on him as he leaned in. But what was he doing here, and how did he get involved? Was it possible that the man standing here in front of me was the same man that Hen had mentioned as the ringleader in Mexico? We had known him as El Halcon, the captain of the Falcon in Key West. The name hadn't even registered when Hen brought it up, but now it had come full circle. I was on the deck now; the door shut behind me as Trigger continued to bark, spraying dog slobber across the glass door. The gaff hung by my side, hidden in the darkness. He squared up on me and put his finger in my chest. "You need to know you brought all this on yourself. If you would have kept to your own business and stayed out of this, we wouldn't be standing here right now. I have a lot of money tied up in this project. Too much to let some gringo like you screw it up."

He must have seen my face because he hit me in the shoulder. "Look at me!" He grunted. His eyes glowed with a fire and I knew I had to come up with something quick. "You've been a thorn in my side for too long. I wasn't even sure it was you until now." He paused for a moment and stared into my eyes, "but I remember your gringo face and your Irish pal too. I should have cut you down back on stock rock and dropped you out in the Gulf Stream. Nobody would have ever found you." I couldn't respond. I was still trying to fathom how this man and I had crossed paths again and reopened a chapter of my life I thought was long closed.

He reached in his pocket and pulled out a handful of pistachio shells, rattling as he tossed them on the deck. "Wonder where this came from, huh? It helps to know habits of your soldiers." He tossed a few more on the dock.

"You've been planning this for a while, huh?" I asked.

"No, it came to me after you killed one of my best men. I knew I had to come take care of things myself. It solves some problems, and that's what I do."

I shook my head. "Unbelievable," I said.

"I still don't understand how you got involved."

He smiled again, but kept the pistol aimed right at my gut.

"I've been in Mexico since I left my operation between Cuba and Florida. You and your friend put an end to that for me. I had to leave town when the police started asking questions. But you knew that already. Of course, I moved one of my men into that spot to continue in my place. The money was too good." His accent made a snakelike hiss as he spoke.

"After I got to Mexico, I worked the Cancun scene for a while, snatching tourists and selling them off, but the real money was at the border. I had to work for it, of course, but I took over some minor operations and then began moving people through the border and on to the east coast. It was too easy. I came here to take you out of the equation when Liona couldn't handle it. Once you exposed her operation here, things got too hot for her. There was no way she could stay here any longer."

I was struggling to believe all this he was telling me. "Wait, so you run this big operation and you came here to do this yourself?"

He smiled. "Sometimes I take on special cases I may have a personal interest in. Since you and I had some history, I thought it would be nice to look into your eyes as I kill you. Besides, it keeps me young." A darkened smile formed on this face.

"Now we're going to go inside and you're going to have a seat on the couch. The first thing I'm going to do is put a bullet in that dog."

I hesitated a moment, and he motioned with the pistol and said, "get moving." I stepped to the left, out of the direct line of the pistol, and reached for the door handle. In one motion, I brought the gaff up from behind me and hooked his gun hand up and away from me. I drove in with my left hand and put my fist right in his throat.

I followed through and slipped in behind him, then slammed him down on the deck. Dazed for a moment, he tried to put one hand under him to get up. I stomped the side of his head one good time, instantly swelling the side of his face as the gun slid on the deck among the pistachio shells.

There was a sound of wheezing from his throat as he tried to reach both hands up to his face. His left hand was at his throat but his right raised up with a gaff hooked through the meat of his hand. As he struggled to breathe, I kicked the gun to the other side of the deck. Trigger was still at the door to the salon, barking his head off. I cracked it and let him out and he went right to guard position beside the man, still struggling to breathe. I felt no obligation to help him. He would be fine but might have some permanent damage to his windpipe, and possibly the hand. I called the number for sheriff's dispatch once again and explained the situation. Within a few minutes, I saw blue lights crossing the bridge overhead, the ambulance not far behind.

Hutch arrived with another deputy and his sergeant. I ran his sergeant through the scene and they brought the EMTs in to see to the injured assailant, now examining the gaff dangling from his hand. He was breathing now, but it was still a struggle to get deep breaths, and he had yet to speak.

The EMTs loaded him on to the stretcher and carted him away. The sergeant followed them and I yelled, "Hey, I want that gaff back!"

Hutch came from the direction of the parking lot with the crime scene following behind. "Hey man, you good? You can't seem to get any rest, huh?"

"This guy is nuts. He had it all planned out. He had some crazy gun with him. What was that about?"

He laughed, "Ah, it's an old trick using an oil can as a suppressor. It muffles the sound. The net was to catch the brass, so it looks like a professional job. The pros always pick up their brass. No question this guy had a plan," he said, "but we'll let a judge and jury make that call. You're good though, no injuries?" He asked.

I shook my head in disbelief, and I ran Hutch through the history of Mr. Mendez or El Halcon as I knew him. Crime scene went to work as we stood there talking. I recognized one as La Roche from the floater scene. She gave me a nod and a smile as she boarded the Origin. Trigger was behind the door in the salon, watching it all go down and showing his teeth when he felt necessary. Larry the pelican rose from his perch and landed on the bow, expecting an easy meal from these newcomers.

Hutch laughed. "Your pet?" he asked.

"Nah, another local." I said.

About an hour later they had finished up when LaRoche stopped me and asked, "Hey, are you hanging out with Analee from the M.E.'s office?"

"Yeah, we've been seeing each other recently. Why?"

"You better treat her right man, with all this shit you've been in lately," she hesitated. "What I'm saying is don't drag her into it. She's good people, and she's been through enough."

"You have my word," I said and reached out my hand, but she didn't take it. After they had finished their investigation and I made my statement, they left and Hutch followed behind. He was on his cell phone and gave me a wave as he rounded the dock by the Marina store.

Over the next week, I prepared for the trip. I had several options for gear and cruising preparations, but had most of everything I needed aboard the Origin already. I made sure that I had all the ancillary spare parts in the event a failure occurred and made a requisite stock of oil and treatment for the engine, as usual, of these longer excursions into remote places. Stocking and storing dry goods was standard, and I expected a couple of weeks out of port, so it wasn't an island stranding situation I was preparing for.

I was working at Lost the night before I planned to leave when Marco, the rep from the training facility in Orange Beach, sat down at the bar. He gave me a familiar nod, and I set the water in front of him.

"You're Ace right?"

I smiled and said, "yes", reaching out for a handshake.

He obliged and said, "my name is Marco. I came by the other day to invite you over to our facility in Orange Beach."

"Yes, I remember."

"Your friend Dan filled us in on the trafficking ring you helped to crack."

Puzzled, I said, "I never thought of it that way but I guess so, it wasn't even part of the initial push to stop the development it came out later and I'd say that's a benefit if it's stopped or at least slowed in the area. Until recently, I didn't even know that was a problem around here."

He nodded. "It doesn't get much media coverage, you know what I mean? We only like to get the word out when we make a large recovery and we sometimes try to place the victims in the local area depending on their history and circumstances. Keeping things low-key is best. I'm here because I wanted to invite you over to train with us at our facility. We train our operatives in Krav Maga and Brazilian Jiu Jitsu at our gym; it's specialized training working in scenario situations where we try to prepare for what we might encounter in our operations. We'd really like to have you with us. As you get into the program, we can talk more about you joining us in some of our operations here stateside and in regional operations, if you're interested?"

"Wow, man, that sounds pretty serious," I said.

He smiled and said, " at worst, you get some real training so you can handle yourself better in the future. There's no obligation to do anything with our operations. We're offering this up as a thank you since we ended up making some recoveries with local law enforcement. We pulled over sixty people out of the operations here along the Gulf Coast, and it was because of you."

He paused. "Think about that for a minute."

It was hard for me to fathom at first, but the weight of it sunk in after a moment.

"I appreciate you letting me know all this. I really didn't grasp it until now," I said.

He stopped and said, "you were in a unique situation and this was a sidebar to your initial effort. You helped people without knowing it, and now all we're doing is attempting to repay you for some of your efforts."

"The word we're hearing is that you may have been successful in stopping the development. Now the land is being considered for one of the state conservation programs."

I raised an eyebrow; how did he know all this? "What? Where did you get that information?" I asked.

"Well, your friend Dan is how we got your info, and he let us in on the entire story. Your effort paid off tenfold."

I got a hip check from Britt and knew I had to cut this conversation and focus on the bar crowd. "I appreciate you coming by here and talking with me, but I need to get back to work."

"I get it. Call me and we'll get you set up. I'll see you soon."

EPILOGUE

The next day, I pulled away from the dock at the marina and left Analee standing there. We discussed our future, but there was not a promise from either of us. There was a feeling that neither of us was ready for what we knew would be the outcome. There was an unspoken understanding that when we committed, it would be all the way. It was the weight of both our past lives bearing down on us that became what we could not overcome at that moment. I felt a pull towards her and when I looked into her eyes; I knew she felt it, too. It was a matter of time. I let her know I would continue to keep in touch and I would keep her updated on my progress during the next couple of weeks.

My trip gave me the deserved time away from the rest of the world, but also proved to be in vain. The locals did not welcome me as an outsider and pushed me out after I arrived. They ran me out of town within two days and the trip back was a slow one. I had returned a couple of days early after a brief detour up the Choctawhatchee for some fishing on Black Creek.

Later that night, I sat on the Origin with Trigger. It was a clear night and the heat of the day had burned off and replaced by a humid damp night and a salty south wind. Jasmine rode in off the breeze and an oak and rosemary musk fought with it. The thump of a lone car over the bridge broke the calm and to the east I could hear a bird call over the drone of another coal barge pushing across the bay.

The lighthouse made its flash on the dot every few seconds and out on the lagoon it was dark and still. For some time, I thought about the events that had occurred over the past few weeks. My life had changed in so many ways and I felt as if I was another person. What began as me trying to bring awareness about another massive development had turned into a fight for my life, finding someone I cared more about than myself, and, in some indirect way, saving people from forced servitude. The serendipity did not elude me now. It always does as it is happening.

I made some decisions that night. I would continue to be a voice for the Lost Republic and also continue to expose the dealings that so often happen in the shadows.

I had met a woman, one who I was interested in, and this had not happened in quite a long while. We both had been reserved in the beginning and let our guards down as we became more comfortable with one another. In the end, I believed that the wounds we both sustained in those past relationships were healing; however, the memories of those experiences would be with us forever in familiar whispers of a touch from a loved one, or the mutterings of an affectionate statement from one another. I was hopeful for our future in whatever form that took as we continued this dance together.

The latest development came as a surprise and felt that I was now under some unknown obligation to do more to further this effort to save people. I would educate myself more on the matter and go meet the members of this specialized training team. This was a way for me to become better. To push harder to keep these things from happening in the Lost Republic and expose the underground to the public. I had a tall order in front of me, but not one that deterred me, more so it inclined me to do more. I'll take dangerous freedom over peaceful slavery.

And so I sit here under this night sky on the flybridge of my boat, on the edge of this lagoon in this place I call The Lost Republic, and I am reminded of why I call this place such.

There is a Lost Republic everywhere for each of us. It may be an old farm that was sold off for a convenience store or subdivision. A favorite hillside from your childhood that is now gone in favor of a coal mine. Or a once clear landscape that is now dotted with high-rises and cell phone towers.

It could be the same settings you have been familiar with, but the underbelly of such was never exposed. Much like The Lost Republic was for me until recently. These things we can all relate to. It's a matter of timing and position in this world. We all hold steady as best we can. It is only when we stop moving we realize the world around us.

W. J. Speed is the author of The Lost Republic. He is a coastal ecologist by profession and moonlights as a bartender. He currently lives in the heart of The Lost Republic with his wife, children and brown dog.

www.ingramcontent.com/pod-product-compliance
Lightning Source LLC
Chambersburg PA
CBHW020129120726
47903CB00007B/2179